M.A. Nichols

Books by M.A. Nichols

Generations of Love Series

The Kingsleys

Flame and Ember

Hearts Entwined

A Stolen Kiss

The Ashbrooks

A True Gentleman

The Shameless Flirt

A Twist of Fate

The Honorable Choice

The Finches

The Jack of All Trades

Tempest and Sunshine

The Christmas Wish

The Leighs

An Accidental Courtship

Love in Disguise

His Mystery Lady

A Debt of Honor

Christmas Courtships

A Holiday Engagement
Beneath the Mistletoe

Standalone Romances

Honor and Redemption
A Tender Soul
A Passing Fancy
To Have and to Hold

Fantasy Novels

The Villainy Consultant Series

Geoffrey P. Ward's Guide to Villainy
Geoffrey P. Ward's Guide to Questing
Magic Slippers: A Novella

The Shadow Army Trilogy

Smoke and Shadow
Blood Magic
A Dark Destiny

Table of Contents

W ilhelmina Ashbrook leaned her head against the al-
cove wall, stared out the window, and wished she
weren't so wicked. Not that happiness itself was in-
herently evil, but finding any modicum of joy in the death of her
beloved papa certainly earned her the title of wicked.

Her breath fogged the glass. Through the haze, Mina
watched the horses trot past the townhouse. The clopping of
their hooves and the clatter of carriages rang through the air.
London had its enticements; Mina loved the many musicales,
theatres, and other diverse entertainments, but the hustle and
bustle of the city stifled her soul. She longed for a breath of
clean air, a horseback ride across fields, and a chance to avoid
the unpleasantness that came with London society. The country
called out to her, begging Mina to escape the noisy confines of
Town. Her papa had never understood that sentiment, though
she had tried to explain it to him on various occasions.

Now he was gone, and it was difficult not to hope that her
long-standing wish would finally come to fruition. Mina would
give anything to have her dear papa alive and healthy, but she

was unable to change the past nor stop the desire in her heart that saw the possibility of something good coming from this bleak affair. Mina glanced at her drawings lying on her lap, detailing all the improvements she could soon afford for Rosewood Cottage.

No matter that her family thought cottage 'cramped' and 'pokey'. To Mina, it was a haven. With blooming honeysuckle climbing the grey stone walls and shutters painted the perfect green to accent their foliage, Rosewood Cottage was the picture of picturesque. Having been her grandmother's favorite retreat, she had willed it to the one person in the family who loved it with equal fervor, and Mina dreamt of living there.

If only her grandmother had willed her the funds to maintain the property. Or if only her father had been willing to give his daughter a modest increase in her pin money. However, between the Ashbrook's immaculate London townhouse and vast estate in Lincolnshire, her father saw no need for his daughter to abandon civilization to reside alone in the wilds of Herefordshire. Now, his refusal to give Mina the necessary financial freedom was a moot point.

Mina truly was a wicked, wicked woman. For even though the majority of her heart and soul mourned the loss of her beloved papa, lingering in the quiet recesses was the realization that with the reading of her father's will she would finally have the funds to fulfill her dream. Rosewood Cottage. Sadness still clung to her, but the thrill of that possibility chased away some of the melancholy, giving her a light among the dark despair.

Finally, Mina would be able to quit her father's home and set up one of her own. No loving husband and sweet children would fill it, but it would be a home nonetheless. One that she would be free to do with as she pleased. One that allowed her to escape the madness of society when she wished. One that she could decorate and arrange to her delight. Not a borrowed thing she occupied in the interim between childhood and marriage. It would be utterly and completely hers.

The library door opened, and Mina's brother entered. He

was more than capable of stepping into their father's shoes, but Mina sensed the responsibility hung heavy on him.

"Hello, Nicholas," she greeted, pushing the sketches aside, uncurling her legs, and brushing off her black skirts as she stood. "You just missed tea. I can have Cook prepare a tray if you wish." She went to call a footman, but Nicholas stopped her.

"I'm fine, Mina. Truly."

She studied his face and knew his words were untrue but sensed it was best to move on.

"And you, Mina? How are you?" asked Nicholas, scrutinizing her with an intensity she found unnerving on her younger brother's face.

Mina blushed, and a sick feeling filled her stomach. It wouldn't do to admit aloud the thoughts in her head. At least, not in its entirety.

"I was thinking of Father, but that is nothing new," she said.

Nicholas nodded, ushering her to the sofa before sitting beside her.

"I take comfort in knowing he is with Mother now," he said. "I believe it is something he has wanted for a long time."

Mina could only nod. As the oldest child and daughter, she had tried to step into her mother's shoes, but she was no proper substitute. Especially for their father.

"But there is something I need to speak to you about," Nicholas said, sitting even taller. It was a relatively new habit of his, squaring his shoulders and straightening his spine. In some ways it was funny to see him playing the part of 'lord of the manor' but heartwarming at the same time. He was no wet behind the ears lad and had been without purpose for far too long. Having the weight of their father's role on his shoulders would do Nicholas good.

"I've come from the solicitor," he said. His rigidity faded a moment as he flexed his fingers. Mina didn't know what to expect, but Nicholas fidgeting was never a good sign. "I have some rather difficult news about Father's will."

"The finances?" Mina paled. As far as she was aware, they

were robust. She'd managed the household accounts since her mother's passing fifteen years ago, but her father had seldom discussed the details of the estate finances with Mina. Graham would be fine. His naval career would sustain him. But Nicholas and Ambrose would be left to flounder. Mina would have a home with Aunt Matilda, though the thought of it soured her stomach. Mina had barely survived the woman when she'd served as chaperone during Mina's many unsuccessful Seasons. The thought of spending the rest of her life with that horrid woman was enough to make Mina contemplate going into service.

"Calm yourself, Mina," said Nicholas. "All the family holdings are flourishing."

"So, you, Graham, and Ambrose..."

"Will be fine, I assure you."

Mina sighed and touched a hand to her temple. "Perhaps you should have begun with that. For a hard moment, I feared the worse for you boys."

Nicholas grinned. "Always the mother hen, Mina?"

She returned his smile. "Some habits are hard to break. But please, get to the point," she said as he looked no more ready to broach the topic than he had been moments before.

"It isn't *our* inheritance that is of concern. It is *yours*," he said. "Father has provided handsomely for all of us boys, as he assured me he would, and he left strict instructions about how you are to be cared for."

"Cared for?" The words made Mina sound like Cousin Beatrice's pampered terrier.

"Not that I would ever shirk my duty on that account," Nicholas insisted, seeming a touch angry at the thought. "You are my sister, and I will always provide for you. No matter what."

"Of course, Nicholas, I never doubted it, but I have to admit I have no idea what you are trying to say."

Nicholas clenched his jaw, tapping his fingers along his knee. "He left you nothing."

"Nothing?"

"Your dowry is still intact for when you marry."

"When I marry?" scoffed Mina. "At what point am I supposed to marry? No suitors appeared when I was eighteen. Why should one do so when I am a decade older?"

"Mina, there is still time for you." Nicholas's voice took on the exasperated tone Mina often heard whenever the topic of her marriage (or lack thereof) was broached.

"It's the 'still' that make me uncomfortable," said Mina. "It implies that it's improbable, but if the stars align, one day a miraculous husband may appear, so I must keep sitting around waiting for it to happen."

Spinsterhood was not such a sorry state for her family to force 'still' on her every chance they could. It was said with such a pitying tone, as if the best Mina could hope for was to spend her life pining for something she did not have. Mina had grown accustomed to the idea of spinsterhood. It was not her preferred state, but life often differed from a person's dreams, and Mina refused to waste away while waiting for 'still' to find her.

"But there is still time for you to find a husband. You are not terribly old," he said.

Mina sighed at that unintended insult. The poor man hadn't meant it to sound so utterly horrific, so it was best to ignore the slight and move on.

"Nicholas, that is beside the point," said Mina, pulling them away from that verbal quagmire. "Why would Father do that to me?"

Nicholas sighed and glanced at Mina's drawings of Rosewood Cottage. "Because he does not wish you to give up on life and lock yourself away in the country."

Mina had no reply. Her father may not have supported her plan, but to reach beyond the grave and snatch away her dreams was unthinkable. Every time Mina had begged to live at Rosewood, her father had insisted the family houses were hers. Perhaps they had been, but not in their entirety. Though she had been acting the part for years, Mina was not mistress of the Ashbrook estate; it was only acting. A temporary thing. Mina stood in for her mama while her papa lived, and in place of Nicholas's future wife, whoever the lady may be. Mina was desperate for her own home. Her own life.

"He left instructions that Rosewood Cottage should be maintained, and you are allowed to visit from time to time, but he wants you to live with me," said Nicholas.

Mina had no words. Every last one of them escaped her at the realization of what her father had done to her. He'd purposefully left her dependent on her brother. Left her without anything but her allowance. Her future at Rosewood Cottage faded from her mind, replaced with black, stifling thoughts as Nicholas rattled off the various provisions dictating her father's continued control over her life.

Mina wanted to rail and shout against the injustice of it all, but the fight seeped from her. Shouting at Nicholas would do no good. She had never resented her life. She loved it, in fact. She had been blessed with an adoring family and comfortable means. Mina knew many ladies who scrimped for every penny like beggars living off the scraps society left them, unable to earn their bread or marry into a more comfortable situation. Mina was blessed.

She just wished she felt it.

"I know you crave a home of your very own, but you are still mistress here, Mina," said Nicholas, patting her hand. "That's not changing. This is still your household to run."

"It is yours, Nicholas. Not mine. I am only keeping watch over it until you marry," said Mina, her spirits falling with each word. "That's why I wanted Rosewood Cottage."

"Mina, you are being a goose," said Nicholas. "This is your home. You need no other."

Her brother's words echoed her father's with near perfect exactness. Mina's head fell, her shoulders slumping.

Nicholas held her hand. "We can reassess the situation in the future, if need be, but there's no reason for you to leave.

More than that, I need you to stay. I need help taking care of the household side of things, and you are an expert at it. I have no intention nor inclination to marry any time soon. I am afraid, dear sister, you are stuck with your bachelor brother for a long time."

...

"It is good to see you, Mr. Kingsley," said Miss Susannah Weston with a properly demure curtsey. Simon barely contained the heart beating in his chest at the sight of her. The sun filtering through the sitting room window gleamed off her golden hair, as if she were cast in a *tableau vivant* as a heraldic angel. She was perfection personified, and in some mad twist of fate, she had been placed in Simon's life, though he knew he would never be worthy of such a prize.

"Thank you for granting me an audience," said Simon, bowing low over her hand, his lips grazing her knuckles. It was one of the only times he had ever felt her bare fingers, and he yearned for more; every gentlemanly instinct in him forced such urges aside.

Miss Weston smiled, and the next words fled from Simon's mind. She laughed, playfully tapping his arm, and he realized she had spoken though he had not heard the words. Sitting, Miss Weston gestured to the chair beside her.

"I asked if you wished for refreshment," she repeated.

Simon shook his head, mumbling some nicety that came from years of etiquette training and with little thought.

He had never felt so nervous in his entire life, and that was no insignificant thing as he had been in a near constant state of anxiety ever since the first moment he had seen her. Such indescribable feelings had overwhelmed him, making it impossible to even approach her that first Season. Simon had spent it watching her like a lovesick puppy from afar until it was too late to make her proper introduction. He'd had plenty of months to ponder about and curse over his monumental stupidity while he'd awaited the beginning of the next Season. This time, he would not allow such cowardice to stand in his way. Even if he still felt like a quaking, callow youth whenever she was near. Life had taught him not to dream of a loving marriage, but Simon had still hoped for one. Years of scouring had nearly extinguished that desire, but that blessed night two years ago, standing in some nondescript ballroom among a crowd of nondescript people, Miss Susannah Weston had appeared, and Simon knew they were meant to be together.

He needed to get the words right. He did not doubt Susannah's feelings for him. Always walking the line of propriety, she had never been so bold as to say it aloud, but Simon felt keenly that her heart belonged to him as much as his belonged to her. Thinking through the mountain of evidence, Simon felt his anxiety lessen, though he still struggled to speak.

"Miss Weston," said Simon, "I know I should be more prudent and begin with some discussion about the weather or the health of your family, but I cannot. We know each other well enough to dispense with such inanities."

Susannah's smile brightened. "Yes, indeed, Mr. Kingsley."

Simon slid from his seat to kneel on the floor before her, taking her hands in his. He could hardly think with the feel of her fingers entwined with his. "I know I should have spoken with your father, but you are of age, and I wish to speak with you first."

Her hands squeezed his, and Simon forged on. "I love you. My heart burns for you, and it is all I can do to contain it." With that, Simon took a moment to fight back the feelings driving him to sweep her into his embrace and ravish her lips. "Experience has taught me to be wary of love, but you have shown me the glory of it. I know there is no other woman in the world whom I could love as deeply and completely as I love you, and I hope I am that man for you. Please, my dearest, will you marry me?"

Tears caught in her lashes. Susannah's hands held fast to

his, but the look in her crystal blue eyes held a touch of sorrow. "I do care deeply about you, Mr. Kingsley, but I cannot marry you. I'm engaged to Mr. Richard Banfield. He and Papa settled it all yesterday."

Simon's shoulders felt heavy, and he couldn't keep them upright. The whole thing was absurd. She had met the man only a couple of weeks ago. It was not possible. "You are engaged?"

"Oh, Mr. Kingsley," she said, her voice filled with remorse. She reached forward to brush Simon's cheek, giving him a thrill of joy and shock of pain all at once. "I am so sorry. I do wish things were different."

Rebellious hope sprang up, beating back his sense, telling him that his Susannah could free herself from her engagement now that she knew in no uncertain terms how he felt. But Simon's honor would not allow him to voice such thoughts. He despised the idea of encouraging her to go back on her word and hurt another, but that savage part of him allowed those desperate desires to run free.

And then Susannah continued to speak.

"If circumstances were different, I would love to marry you, but Richard is the grandson of a baron. You must understand that I cannot turn down such an offer. My parents would never forgive me. He may be too far down the succession to ever hope for the title itself, but the distinction of marrying into such a family is too great."

With each word, Simon felt the glow of his soul dwindling. His eyes could not focus on the beautiful face before him spouting off the earnest excuses for crushing his heart. Everything of which he had dreamed was gone. For so many years, finding a lady like Susannah had seemed impossible and in that moment, he felt every pain in his life amplified, confirming what he'd always known.

Love may exist, but it was not meant for Simon Kingsley.

Chapter 1

London
Two Years Later

Mina tugged at the tops of her gloves, straightening them for the twelfth time before running her hands down the front of her gown for the seventeenth. And then she straightened the edges of her cloak for the twenty-third. She was a gudgeon. Regardless of how often she told herself her girlish glee was pointless, Mina couldn't snuff out that last little spark of hope that tonight would be different.

The carriage swayed, and Mina daydreamed.

Dressed in her most gorgeous gown, Mina was sure this ball would be amazing. She would never be termed beautiful, but she felt she achieved 'pretty', at the very least. The diaphanous fabric swirled about her, tucked and pinned in all the right places to show her figure to its best advantage. Granted, Mina's figure didn't have a good advantage, but the dress came close to finding one. And it was such a pretty shade of amethyst, which complimented her complexion to perfection.

It was a daring and brash dress, but Mina desperately wanted to embrace something more than the lifeless pastels she was normally forced to wear in Town. Her father would have never approved of such a color for a maiden, but Mina was beyond his influence, and society had long ago rejected her as a debutante.

This was the dress in which a gentleman would notice her. He would see her from across the Hartleys' ballroom and be so enchanted that he would arrange an immediate introduction before sweeping her off into a dance. That thought made Mina laugh at herself. A grown woman making up fairy tales as unlikely as the ones her nursemaid had told her at bedtime.

But that was neither here nor there. Regardless of whether anyone else ever admired her dress, Mina loved it and felt wonderful wearing it. That was enough for her. Even if she dreamt that something more would come of such a beautiful gown on such a beautiful evening.

And that was why Mina needed to leave London.

It was impossible to ignore those niggling desires when surrounded by the swirl and romance of the Season. Young men strutting for the ladies they admired. The tittering heartbeats as the couple captured each other's attention. Even if Mina had not experienced it herself, that traitorous little spark wouldn't let her stop hoping that it would happen for her. Out in the country, it disappeared, but every time she stepped into Town, it resurfaced.

Tired of her pointless daydreaming, Mina shoved all other thoughts aside. Spark or not, gudgeon or not, Mina knew tonight would be wonderful.

"You do look lovely!" said Louisa-Margaretta, leaning across the carriage to place her hand on Mina's. "That is such a bold color, the likes of which you don't see often, but it is so slimming. It looks perfect on you."

Mina sucked in her lips, nibbling on them to keep words from slipping out that were best left unsaid, as she often did whenever her sister-in-law was near. The girl didn't mean her comments to sound the way they did, but Mina felt a touch deflated all the same.

"You both look marvelous," said Nicholas, reaching over to

kiss his wife's hand.

Mina turned her eyes to the passing street, trying to block out the sight and sound of the newlyweds. Forcing her mind to focus, she thought of the ball, dreaming how it would look and what it would be like. Regardless of how much her family believed her to be a veritable hermit, Mina loved a ball and a party; the problem was that they did not like her in return.

But this time she would be no wallflower.

In her gorgeous gown, with her hair styled to perfection, Mina would not be relegated to the corner. She would dance. She would socialize. She would be noticed. How Mina wished Thea was there with her. It had been so much easier wading through society's murky waters with her bosom friend on hand, but Thea was back in Lincolnshire tending her growing brood. Mina would hate Frederick Voss for stealing her dear friend away if not for the fact that he made Thea so blissfully happy.

The carriage drew to a halt, and the door was scarcely open before Louisa-Margaretta (who always insisted people use both names to their full extent, no matter how large a mouthful they were) bounded out with the energy of a girl nearer the nursery than adulthood. Nicholas took both ladies' arms, leading them into the Hartleys' townhouse as Louisa-Margaretta prattled on about everything and nothing.

"Now, stay close, Mina," said Louisa-Margaretta.

Once again, Mina nibbled on her lips and reminded herself of her sister-in-law's good intentions. Obtuse she may be, but a well-meaning obtuse. Louisa-Margaretta simply had no idea how condescending and insulting it was to have a girl eleven years Mina's junior elevated to the position of chaperone. Anyone with sense considered Mina far too spinsterly to need such protection, but that did not matter to the rest of the Ashbrook clan. Much to Mina's chagrin.

As they stepped in through the grand ballroom, Louisa-Margaretta swung into full socializing mode. Nicholas escaped from the hurry and scurry, disappearing within moments of their arrival, and it took all of Mina's charity to not hate him for abandoning her. Louisa-Margaretta's taste in friends left much to be desired. Mina had nothing in common with the giggling girls, and they had no interest in her. Awash in the excitement of their first Season as married ladies, the girls had little more to talk about than the general highs and lows of married life, which left Mina firmly out of the conversation. Not that a single one of them stopped talking long enough to allow Mina to speak.

"Mrs. Ashbrook," said Mr. Fairview with a bow, "might I engage you for the first set?"

"Oh, you dear thing," said Louisa-Margaretta with a smile. "I've already secured a partner, though I would love to see my sweet sister-in-law stand up with you."

Mina hoped her face was not as fiery red as it felt. Her oft-repeated maxim filled her mind, reminding her that Louisa-Margaretta meant well, regardless of how awkwardly she went about things.

Mr. Fairview glanced at Mina and smiled, forcing Mina to chide her treacherous heart for skittering at the sight. She didn't particularly care if she danced with this particular gentleman, but the idea of standing up with anyone was enough to give her palpitations.

"That does sound delightful," he said, making Mina blush even further, "but I promised Mr. George Orbrook I'd join him in the card room if you were unavailable."

Louisa-Margaretta tapped him on the arm with her fan. "You goose. I'm sure he would not mind..." But her sentence fell away when a gentleman arrived to claim his dance, effectively pulling Louisa-Margaretta's attention away from securing Mina a partner.

Within moments, each member of the group was claimed for the dance and Mr. Fairview made his retreat, leaving Mina uncomfortably alone. Not that she felt more comfortable among those girls, but the obvious gap in the crowd around her felt like a clear signal to all in attendance that she was utterly undesirable.

Mina watched the dancers, trying for an air of nonchalance. She was far too old to be carrying on like such a ninny. She should not care if everyone in the ballroom took note of her solitary state. It should not matter. It truly shouldn't. But it did. Mina felt like she should wear a sign around her neck warning of her unsuitability. Though judging by her lack of suitors and friends, it was unnecessary

No matter how much Mina wanted to slip away to an unobtrusive place, it would only guarantee she would not be asked to dance. Her overabundant figure appeared to best advantage standing; sitting only made her look heavier and frumpier than she was. Besides, hiding in a corner would make it more difficult to catch a gentleman's eye. So, Mina stood alone, using every bit of energy to pretend it did not bother her.

As the minutes wore on and the dancers moved through their steps, Mina felt her pride slipping. Before long, she did not care if pity was the only enticement for a partner. She wanted to dance. She wanted someone to see her. Too often, it felt like she had been enchanted by some evil faerie and cursed to be forever invisible. It wasn't even a blatant snub. That would require someone noticing her first, and she was too insignificant to warrant even a passing glance.

The first set turned into the second, and Louisa-Margaretta was claimed for yet another while Mina stood like a valiant soldier, guarding the dance. When an hour passed without Mina speaking a single word, she cried surrender to her aching feet and found herself a seat.

...

Simon Kingsley was turning into his father. Standing alone at the edge of the Hartleys' ballroom, a single word kept popping into his head—insufferable. Insufferable noise. Insufferable people. Insufferable dancing. It had been an absolute favorite word of his father to mutter at varying intervals throughout evenings such as these. Simon understood why.

With only two years into his third decade, Simon should be too young to be so cantankerous, but not when it came to events such as these. Insufferable London and its insufferable Season. He had things of far greater importance to do than preening like all the other insufferable peacocks.

Seeing Susannah—Mrs. Banfield—dancing across the ballroom did not help matters. Simon had thought she'd still be safely ensconced in the country, recuperating. He'd been able to avoid her last Season and most of this one due to her rapidly growing family, but she had reappeared to torment him with thoughts he should not think and regrets he could not fix. His eyes watched her, his heart gliding along beside her.

Her clear eyes met his, and Simon felt that yearning he'd been fighting to free himself of since the moment she had dashed his dreams. All his efforts were gone in a flash at the hint of longing in her eyes. It did not matter that it had been her choice to marry elsewhere; Simon was ensnared.

He should not have come. He should have stayed in the country where he was needed. Another letter from his steward had arrived just that afternoon detailing more issues requiring his attention. But such grumblings were pointless. Simon needed to be here to settle this once and for all. He was tired of handling the household duties. His housekeeper kept things afloat, but she needed a mistress to oversee things. Not to mention the various obligations the Kingsley family owed to the neighborhood and community, most of which the mistress of Avebury Park would manage.

Heaven, help him. Simon needed a wife. The woman he wanted was not a possibility, but he would not go home empty handed. Not again.

Chapter 2

Mina's hands twisted in her lap while her eyes followed the dancers. The lady beside her had not proven the best of conversationalists, but Mina would not be deterred. Miss Brooke was not her preferred companion, but Mina would make do with what she had.

"Miss Brooke," said Mina, grasping at any possible conversation starter, "do you ride?"

To say the woman looked dour would be an affront to dourness. Mina was unsure if Miss Brooke possessed the ability to smile, but Mina would not give up so easily. Miss Brooke was the only unattached person in that corner of the ballroom with whom Mina had not attempted a conversation, and she was determined to have one.

"I don't care for riding," said the lady, her lips puckering.

"Gardening, perhaps? My grandmother kept a cottage with the most enchanting garden," said Mina. But as Miss Brooke looked no more interested in gardening than horses, she let the topic drift and turned her attention back to the dancers.

It was no use. Miss Brooke had no more desire to converse with Mina than Mina had for Miss Brooke, but being relegated to Spinster's Row left Mina with few companions. And now

Mina remembered why she avoided her fellow spinsters. They were a dreadfully difficult lot. Seeking asylum here had not been the best idea.

Mina desperately wished Thea were by her side. Attending such affairs were always so much easier with her dear friend at her side. It was impossible to feel awkward or unlikable with Thea around.

"My dear Mina, here you are!" said Louisa-Margaretta.

Being dragged off by her sister-in-law was slightly less appealing than remaining with Miss Brooke, but Mina managed a smile and stood to greet her.

"Mr. Smith begged to be introduced to you!" gushed Louisa-Margaretta in a hurried whisper before turning to make the introductions. "Mina, may I introduce Mr. Leopold Smith and his mother, Mrs. Eliza Smith."

Mina smiled and curtsied, though the man looked decidedly uncomfortable. She wondered if Louisa-Margaretta was being overly generous when she claimed the man 'begged' to be introduced since he seemed disinclined to say a word.

"Do you live in London or are you here for the Season?" asked Mina. A rather boring question but better than staring silently at Mr. Smith.

"Just the Season," he said. "Mother and I are staying with friends of our family." He cleared his throat then said no more.

"They are up from Plymouth," added Louisa-Margaretta, her smile far too ecstatic for the inanity of the conversation.

"I do enjoy Plymouth," said Mina, trying to coax the gentleman into a conversation. "I was fortunate enough to visit a few years back. Beautiful countryside."

Mr. Smith nodded, and his mother watched the exchange (if it could be called that) without blinking.

The music of the dance ended, and the people rearranged themselves with their new partners. Louisa-Margaretta's smile grew wider, and Mina feared what would come next; subtlety was not among Louisa-Margaretta's talents.

"I believe the next is the *King and Queen*. Mina adores that dance, and she is so graceful," she said, tapping her fan towards Mr. Smith.

Mina had no idea where Louisa-Margaretta would have ever gotten that impression. With the exception of standing up with her brothers—none of whom danced willingly—Mina was never asked to dance. With flushed cheeks, Mina looked at Mr. Smith and he looked at her while his mother looked at the both of them.

"I am pleased to have made your acquaintance, Miss Ashbrook," he said with a quick bow. "I hope I will have the pleasure again soon."

Without another word, he gathered his mother and strode away, leaving Mina at a complete loss to understand what had just occurred.

"Well," said Louisa-Margaretta with a sigh, "that did not go as well as I had hoped but a success nonetheless."

Mina stared at her sister-in-law, wondering if they had been party to the same conversation. "Mr. Smith walked off after speaking no more than two sentences."

"But he asked for an introduction," she said with a smile. "That is something."

"Did he ask for it or did his mother force it on him?"

"That is not important," said Louisa-Margaretta. "What matters is that he asked to be introduced. I am certain that is a good sign. Come, we must find out more about your suitor, the mysterious Mr. Smith."

"Louisa-Margaretta!" Mina's face burned scarlet, and she cast a furtive look around. "Please do not say such things. He asked for an introduction. That is all. I know nothing about the man, and he showed no signs of wishing a closer acquaintance."

Her sister-in-law waved away Mina's words and became intent on finding out anything and everything about Mr. Smith that instant. Searching for some excuse to avoid the ensuing embarrassment, Mina glanced around the ballroom.

"I am in desperate need of some punch," said Mina. "I will meet up with you in a few minutes."

So singularly focused on the task at hand, Louisa-Margaretta hardly noticed Mina slip away towards the refreshments. Once out of sight of her sister-in-law, Mina hid among the edges of the ballroom. This evening could not end soon enough.

...

This was a waste of time. Among all the maidens gathered in the ballroom, Simon could not find a single prospect. He had danced a few sets, but no one caught his fancy. Love may no longer be on the table, but surely, he could find an enjoyable woman with whom he could spend his life. Someone he could talk to. Have a friendship, if nothing else. But not one of the tittering debutantes held his attention for more than half a dance.

"Simon, you look positively thunderous," his friend said with a laugh, clapping a hand on Simon's shoulder. "One would think you'd been forced here at the end of a pistol."

"Not a pistol, Finch," muttered Simon. "Just desperation."

"Don't tell me you are moving ahead with this fool plan of yours."

"Matrimony is not a fool plan," said Simon. Just thinking of everything that needed to be done at his estate was enough to make his head ache, but the thought of having to face two sets of duties for another year wasn't something Simon was willing to do. "I have enough on my plate as is. Having a wife to help carry the burdens would be a blessing."

"The look on your face begs to differ."

There was no refuting that. Being married was a good idea, but getting married wasn't for the faint hearted.

"I am not saying that marriage is a terrible idea," said Finch, "but the way you are going about finding a spouse is. Clearly, you are still preoccupied with a certain someone."

Simon shot Finch a dark look, which the man had the gall

to smile at. Looking away from Finch, Simon could not stop his eyes from finding that very woman among the throng of dancers.

"She did not deserve you then, and she still doesn't," muttered Finch, crossing his arms.

"She simply chose someone else."

Finch said nothing, but the look on his face said clearly that he was unwilling to accept such nonsense.

"It doesn't matter," said Simon. "The die is cast. Not everyone is destined for some great romance. Some marry for practicality."

"But—" he began, though Simon interrupted.

"Finch, it is what it is. Miss Weston is the only woman I have ever loved, and she chose another. It took me years to find her, and I do not have the time to wait for another such lady. If one even exists. And even if I found another, she may not choose me. Love may not be an option, but there's no reason I can't find a helpmate and companion."

"So, you're going to grab some random chit among the fresh debs?"

Simon shuddered at that thought and shook his head. "They keep getting younger and younger."

"It's us who are getting older," muttered Finch.

"That is not a happy thought."

Finch grunted, a smile tickling his lips.

"Leg-shackling myself to an empty-headed young thing is not particularly appealing," said Simon.

"You're underestimating how pretty some of those empty-headed young things are."

"A pretty young thing," grumbled Simon. "My mother was a pretty young thing and that didn't fare well for my parents."

A marriage of speculation and rumor where everyone whispered about the 'what ifs' and 'did you knows' was not for Simon Kingsley. His mother's infidelities were bandied about in countless social circles. Simon had never voiced his doubts aloud, but he often wondered whether his youngest sister, Priscilla, was a full-blooded sibling. And Simon had heard more than a few rumors about his father's indiscretions among the maids and village girls. His father may have been more discreet, but he wasn't any more faithful to his marriage vows.

Simon sighed. "I want a lady who will help me run my estate and cares about seeing it succeed. Someone who could love it as I do."

Finch snorted. "And you think the former Miss Susannah Weston would have fit the bill?"

In reality, that had not crossed Simon's mind. Susannah's suitability as mistress of Avebury Park was never a question. She was a gently bred lady with all the proper knowledge and ability to run such a household. But whether she would have found joy in it was a mystery. Perhaps she was too tied to the glitter of London society to find much happiness in the country.

But that would not have mattered. Their love would have made up for any differences in opinion and character. Having her as his wife would have been enough to ensure their lasting marital bliss.

Finch's question hung in the air, but Simon had no interest in answering it, and his friend eventually moved on.

"So, you're not looking for love or beauty. It sounds like you are looking for a workhorse." Finch chuckled. "Fool plan, indeed."

Put in such harsh light, it did sound foolish.

"I tried to find the perfect wife and failed miserably," said Simon. "Now is the time to settle for someone who I merely enjoy. Someone who will help me with the endless list of things needing to be done on my estate. Someone who will aid me without adding to my burdens."

"If that's all you desire, you are looking in the wrong direction," said Finch, nodding at the fresh-faced debutantes flirting with the young bucks. Motioning to the edges of the ballroom, Finch drew Simon's attention to the spinsters, wallflowers, and the other leftover scraps of society. "Cast your eyes that way."

Simon glanced back at his friend, who met his gaze with a

shrug.

"Don't discount it," said Finch. "Take Miss Mina Ashbrook." He nodded to a lady who sat apart from the others, her slipper tapping in time with the music.

The lady in question was younger than the middle-aged spinsters around her, but she had not been a debutante in several Seasons. She was rather nondescript. Hair that was neither dark nor light. Eyes that were a muddy shade of brown. If Simon had to be honest with himself, her most distinguishable characteristic was her size. People likely called her plump out of kindness, but she was more than a few steps beyond that. Not large enough to make their hostess worry about the structural integrity of the chair, but hefty enough that it was bound to be the first and only thing people notice about her.

However, the manner in which the lady presented herself made Simon the slightest bit curious. While other spinsters in the company clung to their maidenly pastels as if desperate to stave off the encroaching years or draped themselves in severe black as though mourning the loss of their opportunities, this lady's gown was a brilliant purple. The shade likely had some fancy name Simon did not care to learn, but there was a daringness to the color that seemed at odds with her lonely spot at the fringes of the gathering.

"Ashbrook?" asked Simon.

"Nicholas Ashbrook's elder sister," said Finch. "She comes from a good family and has spent most of her life running her family's estate after her mother passed several years ago. So, she has ample qualifications to step in as mistress of Avebury Park. Not to mention she is too mousy to cause you much bother, too unattractive to have a wandering eye, and so firmly on the shelf that she'd likely accept any offer she got."

Simon watched as Miss Ashbrook's cheeks grew redder with each word, her eyes casting down to her hands now gripped tightly in her lap. Simon had not thought her close enough to overhear them, but he got the most uncomfortable feeling she had.

It amazed Mina how three people could all attend the same event, yet have such vastly differing experiences during it. The carriage rocked along the cobblestones while Louisa-Margaretta detailed to Nicholas just how much of a triumph the evening had been.

Truthfully, Mina did not hear a word her sister-in-law spoke. Mr. Finch's words plagued her mind. Mousy and unattractive. Both were apt descriptors and ones she had used herself many times, but hearing him say them was a far cry from her own self-deprecating thoughts. A mousy, unattractive woman for a man who wanted nothing more than a workhorse for a wife.

Truth be told, Mr. Kingsley's words leading up to that awful moment had given Mina an uncomfortable flutter of anticipation, hoping that he might notice her. There was something about him that had long attracted her attention, though he seemed oblivious to her. Though not the type of handsome that drew the ladies in, Mina had found herself dreaming of him on more than one occasion over the years. Dark haired and broad shouldered, Mina's eyes often sought out his, even if he had never met hers directly.

Her secret feelings had never bordered on serious, but it was hard not to admire such a good man. A gentleman to his core. More than that, he was industrious, kind to his tenants, and fair in his business dealings. He had even rescued Nicholas on one occasion during a scuffle at school. Jaded opinions about love aside, the man had much to recommend himself, and a part of Mina had wanted to catch his eye.

And then his friend spoke, and all illusions shattered, shredding Mina's heart.

Nicholas nodded off, and Louisa-Margaretta whacked his arm with her fan. The girl could be brutal with that article. He grumbled, and she poked him again, but he snatched it from her hand, yanking her to him. Mina averted her eyes when his arms came around his wife and Louisa-Margaretta giggled. She actually giggled.

"Mina had quite the triumph tonight," said Louisa-Margaretta, causing Mina's gaze to snap to them. There was not a single thing about the evening that could be counted as a triumph. "Mr. Leopold Smith positively twisted my arm to get an introduction."

"Leopold Smith?" asked Nicholas, glancing at Mina. "I've never heard of the man."

"He's a widower who came to London to look for a new wife," said Louisa-Margaretta. "And he was very interested in our Mina."

"He hardly spoke," said Mina, "and then ran away at the first possible moment. I hardly think that qualifies as being 'very interested'."

"Don't be so dismal, Mina." Louisa-Margaretta tittered. "It's a good start. Besides, his mother asked us to attend the opera with them next week. As we have a box, I invited them to join us."

"His mother," said Mina.

"Don't go looking for reasons to reject him before you get to know him, Mina," said Nicholas, though he had admitted just moments before that he did not know the man so could have no idea if Mr. Leopold Smith was the sort of gentleman worth pursuing.

Neither Nicholas nor Louisa-Margaretta said another word on the matter, but Mina could feel the unspoken words hanging in the air around them. Mr. Smith was a widower, and Mina was a spinster, and no self-respecting spinster would dare turn away an unattached gentleman of any sort.

Chapter 3

S imon preferred a bruising gallop, but in London it was difficult to achieve a sedate canter, so he contented himself with stretching his legs. He needed time to formulate his next plan of attack. The last few social functions yielded no wifely candidates, and Simon could not fritter away the Season.

Winding his way through the park, Simon's mind pulled apart the possibilities. He did not think himself a demanding sort of man, yet it seemed impossible to find a woman who fit his needs. Someone capable. Kind. Hard working. And even if he did not require some otherworldly romantic connection with the lady, he hoped they could be friends. He did not relish the idea of tying himself to someone with whom he could not hold a conversation.

A friend and companion. It should not be that difficult to find someone who could fill that role. Finch may mock him for his matrimonial goal, but Simon was determined. This would be the Season in which Simon Kingsley wed.

Just ahead of him, Simon saw Miss Ashbrook walking along the path with her maid, and his chest tightened for all the wrong reasons. Thoughts of Finch's words at the Hartleys' ball made Simon's stomach churn. His friend had claimed it impossible for Miss Ashbrook to have overheard their words, but Simon knew she had and it shamed him to the core. Truth or not, a gentleman did not speak like that about a lady. Anyone for that matter, but especially not a lady and especially not where she could hear. Unfortunately, Miss Ashbrook had left before Simon could apologize.

Simon glanced around, searching for someone to give him an introduction, but he didn't recognize a single person in the park. Perhaps it was for the best. Simon had no idea how to broach the topic without doing further harm. Simon told himself an apology was unnecessary, even though he knew it was a lie.

The basket in Miss Ashbrook's hands shifted, and a bundle tumbled to the ground, unseen. With a few quick steps, Simon retrieved it but couldn't think how to get it to her without a proper introduction. Decorum fought with decency, and Simon drew close enough to catch Miss Ashbrook's eye. When she saw him, she stopped, a blush filling her face.

Giving a quick bow, Simon lifted the bundle towards her. "I don't mean to intrude, Miss Ashbrook, but you dropped this."

Miss Ashbrook glanced at his hand and then down at her basket. "Thank you, Mr. Kingsley. I appreciate it. I cannot believe I was so foolish as to do that. The children would never forgive me if I lost some of their treats."

Taking the bundle from Simon, Miss Ashbrook tucked it firmly into the basket.

"I'm glad to be of service and hope you will forgive my impertinence."

Miss Ashbrook looked at him, her brows drawing together. "Impertinence?"

"To approach you without a formal introduction," he clarified.

Miss Ashbrook looked down at her basket, her hand shifting on the handle. Her eyes wandered back to his face, and Simon could tell he had said something wrong, though he had no idea what it was. Simon did not enjoy feeling like a cad. Especially for some unknown reason.

"We have been introduced before," she said, the words coming out so quietly that Simon almost missed them. Her eyes dropped to her basket. "Four times, actually."

Simon cleared his throat and fought back a wince. "Four?"

Miss Ashbrook nodded, and she looked at him again. Simon knew she would see his discomfort, and he did not attempt to hide it. He deserved his shame, and Miss Ashbrook deserved to see it.

"When you were introduced to my cousins, the Miss Mowbrays. At least, they were the Miss Mowbrays at the time. Beatrice, Judith, Lydia, and Evangeline."

Simon pictured each one of those ladies, but for the life of him, he could not remember having met Miss Ashbrook at the same time. If Finch hadn't mentioned it at the Hartleys' ball, Simon would not have known Miss Ashbrook's name.

The lady watched his face, her own growing sad. With a quick curtsy, she turned to leave, but Simon could not let things stand as such. In the last week he had hurt the poor lady severely multiple times, and it would not do to let that continue.

"Miss Ashbrook, please," said Simon.

She stopped and turned back to him, her face betraying a hint of apprehension that hurt more than he cared to admit. Finch may have been the first to bruise her feelings, but Simon knew he had done his fair share to earn her caution.

"I truly regret the pain I've caused you," said Simon, tripping over his words to find the right ones. "It's obvious that I have, and it appalls me to know that I have hurt you—both today and last week at the ball. I wanted to say something then but did not have the opportunity. I wish I could say that my friend was suffering from some unimaginable illness that causes thoughtless outbursts, but I shan't excuse his behavior, what he said, or my part in the matter."

Miss Ashbrook's eyes never once left his as he spoke each faltering word. Embarrassment, shock, gratitude; each filled her face in the slight movements of her features. Most ladies he knew would not allow such displays, but Miss Ashbrook's came through clearly enough for him to catch every emotion she felt.

Mina stared at the man while each stuttering word tumbled out. She would never have thought Mr. Kingsley capable of becoming flustered, but she saw and heard the evidence of his discomfort as he forced himself to speak. His struggle to apologize without offending while simultaneously offending again (which brought more apologies) was humorous enough to make it difficult for Mina to hold onto her pain.

Between Mr. Finch's words and Mr. Kingsley's inability to remember even one of their many introductions, Mina's pride had been quite wounded. Yet here Mr. Kingsley was trying to make it right. It may only be a few words, but Mina saw the sincerity behind it, and it touched her. Not many people care about the feelings of an inconsequential spinster.

"It's fine, Mr. Kingsley," said Mina, surprising herself. Though it surprised her even more that she felt like smiling at the relief he showed.

"Thank you, Miss Ashbrook, but I'm afraid it may be a while before I believe it," he said with a rueful smile.

"You think me that petty?"

"Definitely not. I simply mean it may be a while before *I* feel it is fine."

At that, Mina did smile. Ducking her head to hide the faint blush, she tried to keep her feelings at bay. She knew she must be the biggest ninny in all of England to go from being affronted to affected, but it was hard not to feel a thrill of pleasure at the thought that he cared. Mina held no delusions that his words had anything to do with her specifically, for any true gentleman would feel the same, but she had so little experience with gentlemanly behavior that Mina's heart had no protection against such niceties.

Snuffing that silly spark of feeling, Mina met Mr. Kingsley's eyes again, firm in the belief that she needed to keep herself from running away with nonsensical ideas. She knew better than to throw her heart after a man simply because he had been kind to her. She should know better. Unfortunately, her heart rarely listened to reason.

"Thank you for your kind words and for your help with my bundle, Mr. Kingsley, but I should go." Mina shifted the basket, letting it remind her of her responsibilities and the importance of not losing herself during a short conversation.

"Might I be of assistance?" he asked, gesturing to the basket. "It looks as if you and your maid have your hands quite full."

Mina glanced back at Jenny, who stood a respectful distance away. Mina had forgotten all about her lady's maid standing there and hoped she hadn't behaved embarrassingly. The last thing Mina needed or wanted was the servants gossiping about her making eyes at a man in the park.

"I don't wish to inconvenience you, Mr. Kingsley. We are quite capable, though I'm afraid we must be going, or we will be late."

"I insist," said Mr. Kingsley, pulling the basket from Mina's hands. "I've no more business to attend to today, and find myself with time on my hands. The least I could do is escort you to your destination."

"It's a fair distance," warned Mina. "It was so lovely today that I couldn't bring myself to take a coach."

"I came out expressly for a walk, so it is no bother," said Mr. Kingsley, smiling.

It was dangerous to see him smile. It did terrible things to Mina's heart. She needed to focus on the path ahead instead. Turning, she led him through the park with Jenny trailing behind them.

"With the sun shining, it's as if summer has come early," said Mina. "In June, this weather would feel too crisp, but in the middle of March, it feels perfectly warm."

The weather. Such an inane topic, but it was a safe place to start.

"Yes, I'd thought of going for a ride," said Mr. Kingsley, "but I do not care for riding in London."

"It's far too crowded for a decent gallop," agreed Mina.

"You ride?" Mr. Kingsley glanced at her, but Mina kept her eyes on the path.

"Though I spend a lot of time in London, I fear I prefer the country. I spent most of my youth there, and every proper country girl knows how to ride," she said with a smile. "It's the best way to see the countryside."

"I completely agree. I long to get back to country."

Mina smiled, her mind turning back to her home. "The city has some wonderful things to offer, and I miss the theatre and museums when I am away, but for the most part, my heart belongs among the rolling hills and fields. There are so many things I love about it, and no matter how much I enjoy the trappings of Town, I find myself counting down the days until I can return home."

"I feel the same, though my reasons aren't entirely sentimental," said Mr. Kingsley. "I have a hard time leaving my estate. There are so many things that need doing that it is hard to stay here."

"I imagine so," said Mina. "Where is your estate?"

"Essex," he replied.

Mina sighed. "That is beautiful country."

Mr. Kingsley gave her an even more handsome smile, and Mina tripped over her own feet. Having spent nearly three decades walking, it should not have been so difficult, but her limbs would not cooperate. A steadying hand came to her elbow, and Mina's cheeks heated at the feel of Mr. Kingsley's touch. Though she wished she had hid her ungraceful gait, Mina was not unhappy with the brief touch.

"Have you spent much time in Essex?" he asked.

From there, the conversation continued with a steady, easy flow. If pressed, Mina would not have been able to give a full recounting of the varied subjects they discussed during that walk. They went from Essex to favorite foods, then somehow landed on plays and circled around to Mr. Kingsley's estate, along with a dozen other tangential topics along the way. There was nothing remarkable about the conversation to relay except that it happened; Mina could count on one hand the number of times she had spoken so intimately with a gentleman, and none of the other times had felt so natural.

The more they spoke, the more Mina felt at ease with Mr. Kingsley, and she could not remember the last time she had felt so comfortable around another person—other than her beloved friend, Thea—and Mina was uncertain why. Normally, she would spend a conversation worrying over the things she said and if they might be construed as offensive, forward, or awkward, but none of those feelings bothered her while speaking with Mr. Kingsley.

Talking with him felt natural. Easy. As though they had a longstanding relationship and not a brief meeting in a park. It was wonderful, and Mina was saddened to know her destination was drawing closer.

"Might I ask where we are headed?" asked Mr. Kingsley, glancing around. "When you said it was a fair distance, I didn't think we'd be leaving the city."

Nerves nipped at her, and Mina feared he was frustrated. Having been so at ease until that moment, she found herself even more agitated at the prospect. She knew it was his fault for insisting on coming, but she hated to think she was causing problems for him.

"I did warn you, Mr. Kingsley," said Mina. "The home is not much farther."

Mr. Kingsley caught her eye with a faint smile. "I was only teasing, Miss Ashbrook."

And now she did feel like an utter fool, her cheeks blazing. "We're visiting a foundling home."

"A foundling home?" asked Mr. Kingsley.

"They are often in desperate need of clothing and food, so I bring baskets of supplies and goodies," she said, indicating the basket Mr. Kingsley held for her. "I do it for the needy at home, and I carry on the tradition while in Town."

Mr. Kingsley peeked at Mina from the corner of his eye. "Most ladies are home receiving visitors or making social calls themselves, yet you are taking food to the poor."

"I have few people to visit and fewer that visit me, so social calls do not take much of my time, but more than that, I like being useful. My sister-in-law performs the duties of hostess, and I am not needed at home," said Mina. She was unsure why the words came out, but she said them nonetheless.

Mr. Kingsley nodded and looked as though he understood, and for once, Mina felt like someone truly did.

"Life is dull when there's nothing to do," he said.

"Precisely," she said with a grin. "These children need help, and it gives me something to do. That's all."

"I'm certain there's more to it than that," said Mr. Kingsley.

And Mina was certain that the unveiled approval in his eye would linger in her mind for many days.

Chapter 4

Louisa-Margaretta meant well. Generally, Mina needed to remind herself of that at various intervals throughout the day, but tonight she was having to do so every other minute, which left Mina feeling very unkind. Her sister-in-law had good intentions, but sitting in the theatre box with Louisa-Margaretta all but proposing marriage to Mr. Smith on Mina's behalf made it exceptionally difficult to lay hold upon any semblance of benevolence. Her sister-in-law's overzealousness came from a genuine wish to help, but the fact that Louisa-Margaretta refused to acknowledge Mr. Smith's unsuitability made Mina want to scream. A very unladylike, ceiling shaking scream.

Mina had held her tongue through the hours of preparation she'd suffered at Louisa-Margaretta's hands. The tightening to get her figure into a dress not designed for such an ample size. The poking to tame her uncooperative hair into the latest fashion. The pinching to get the perfect rosy glow in her cheeks. From the tips of her squished toes to the top of her throbbing scalp, Mina ached.

If it were not for the fact that she was the most uncomfortable she had ever been in her entire life, Mina would admit this was the loveliest she had ever been. However, the ends did not justify the means. Especially when the ends involved catching the eye of a man who hadn't spoken more than ten words to Mina throughout the evening. Louisa-Margaretta glowed as she watched Mina sitting beside Mr. Smith, and still Mina held her tongue, no matter how much she wanted to storm out of their box and quit this infernal evening.

At least the music was beautiful. Though the crowds milling around the theatre hardly noticed the performance, Mina was enraptured. *The Magic Flute* wasn't her favorite opera, but the music more than made up for the story's shortcomings. Others may be there 'to see and be seen', as they say, but Mina did not understand how they could care about Mr. and Mrs. So-and-So when there was such enthralling music to be heard.

When the curtain dropped for intermission Mr. Smith leaned over. "You seem to be enjoying yourself."

"Yes," said Mina with a smile. "It's hard not to. Are you enjoying it, Mr. Smith?"

"It is tolerable." And then the man said no more.

"And you, Mrs. Smith?" asked Mina, turning to his mother.

"I do not care for the opera," she said, staring at Mr. and Mrs. So-and-So through her opera glasses.

Mina had no response to that, and Mr. Smith seemed no more inclined to speak, but as Nicholas and Louisa-Margaretta were ensconced in their own private conversation, Mina searched for any topic to draw the reticent Mr. Smith out of his self-imposed silence.

"I understand you have children, Mr. Smith," said Mina.

"Yes."

"Are they enjoying London?"

Mr. Smith frowned. "They are in the country."

"Staying with my daughter," added Mrs. Smith.

"And how many children do you have?" asked Mina.

"Seven," said Mr. Smith. "The oldest is eight and the youngest is three months."

Mina's delectable dinner sat heavy in her stomach. She had

known he was a recent widower, but with his youngest child only three months old, it was far shorter than Mina had supposed. There were too many implications that came with that realization, which made Mina exceptionally uncomfortable with the man. Practicality said he needed help raising his children, but the idea that he could abandon them so close to their mother's death to cavort around London chilled her. She tried to recall how long he'd been in Town, and though she couldn't remember exactly, Mina was sure it had been a month at the very least.

Giving him a wary glance, Mina found herself picturing those seven forlorn children and wondered what sort of father could do such a thing. To say nothing of the fact that such a man was obviously looking for nothing more than a replacement mother. Someone to act as his children's permanent nanny.

"Is there anything else you need, my love?" asked Nicholas, standing and placing a kiss on Louisa-Margaretta's hand.

Mina saw Mrs. Smith elbow Mr. Smith in a manner that was likely meant to be discreet.

"Miss Ashbrook," said Mr. Smith, "would you care for some refreshment?"

"Yes, thank you." At that moment, Mina would have said just about anything to get the man away from her.

He gave a curt nod and followed Nicholas out of the box. Louisa-Margaretta turned and smiled. Luckily, the girl remained quiet, but she tapped her fan on Mina's knee with a look that was far too pleased for Mina's peace of mind. Louisa-Margaretta meant well. Mina repeated that again and again in her mind.

...

"You seem preoccupied," said Finch with a nudge.

Simon tried to ignore his friend, but he was as successful as

he had been at ignoring Miss Ashbrook during the performance. He had come to the theatre with every intention of using
the evening as an opportunity to further his matrimonial en-
deavors but had spent most of the evening thinking about that
unusual lady. In truth, the conversation they'd shared a few
short days before was often on his mind.

Though Miss Ashbrook had little outward attraction, she
was an exceedingly pleasant person. Knowledgeable, too. She
had more understanding of running an estate than any lady Simon had met. His own mother had never shown much interest
in the household outside of throwing parties and spending her
pin money. In truth, Miss Ashbrook knew more about it than
most gentlemen of Simon's acquaintance.

The lady was a strange combination of engaging and reserved. Anyone looking at her would know she was shy, but
once in a conversation, she proved chatty, well spoken, and sur-
prisingly witty but not in the biting way common to society.

"The Season is quickly ticking away, and I've yet to find a
suitable wife," said Simon. "Of course I'm preoccupied."

"Preoccupied with Miss Ashbrook?" Finch chuckled.

Simon stared at his friend.

"Do you deny it? You've been watching her all night. You
cannot be serious about pursuing her. From what I hear, she's
a good enough sort of lady, but do you want to spend your life
shackled to someone so unattractive?"

"Better someone unattractive than boring or silly or inept,"
argued Simon. "Besides, I am not interested in Miss Ashbrook."

"Good, because I hear Mr. Leopold Smith is looking to
make her the new Mrs. Smith." Finch pointed to the man beside
Miss Ashbrook.

Simon had spoken truthfully. He hadn't considered Miss
Ashbrook a potential candidate before that moment, but a
twinge of regret struck him at Finch's pronouncement. He liked
Miss Ashbrook; perhaps not in the way a suitor should like a
lady, but he admired her. She would make Mr. Smith a fine wife,
and Simon wouldn't stand in the way of the possibility of her

being courted by a proper suitor.

"I need a drink," said Simon, standing abruptly.

"And a chance to bother Miss Ashbrook?" asked Finch.

Ignoring the smirk on his friend's face, Simon walked out of the box.

...

What was he doing?

Simon stood outside the Ashbrook's box, wondering why he was lurking outside, wishing for some valid reason to enter. As intended, he had retrieved his refreshment, but when he'd passed their family box on the way back to Finch, he'd been unable to go any farther. Simon kept wondering what Miss Ashbrook thought of the performance. She had admitted to liking opera, and from what Simon had witnessed, she appeared to be enjoying it tonight.

He almost walked away, but Simon's treacherous feet pulled him inside instead.

"I do not understand why they insist on singing in German," said a lady. "It's not as if we are in Germany. There is no reason they cannot simply translate it into clear, comprehensible English."

Simon saw Miss Ashbrook, her sister-in-law, and another lady sitting inside, who he knew to be Mr. Smith's mother, though Simon wondered what sort of gentleman brought his mother along while courting.

"Good evening, ladies," he said with a bow.

"Mr. Kingsley," said Mrs. Ashbrook. "How wonderful to see you tonight. If you came looking for Mr. Ashbrook, he stepped out for some refreshment."

"No, I came to ask if you and Miss Ashbrook were enjoying the music."

A slight flash of surprise crossed Mrs. Ashbrook's face, but the girl was quickly learning to be a proper society matron and covered it with a demure smile. "It's perfectly lovely."

"We were discussing how they ought to be singing in English," said Mrs. Smith. "German is a most unattractive language. Though I do not know which is worse, the opera or Mrs. Wilson-Upton's turban. Terribly gauche thing." The lady raised her opera glasses and proceeded to stare at the offending headdress. "But I see Mr. Templeton is here tonight, and the lady on his arm is most certainly not Mrs. Templeton. I hear he claims she's a distant cousin or some such nonsense, but he's standing awfully close to her, don't you think?"

"And you, Miss Ashbrook," said Simon, interrupting the lady's jabbering. "Have you enjoyed the performance?"

A smile stretched across her face. "Yes, Mr. Kingsley. And though I do not speak German," she said with a mischievous twinkle in her eye, "I know the story well enough. Besides, it's the music that's delightful. Herr Mozart had such a way of layering the various parts of music together. It's entrancing."

"Since the theatre is your favorite part of London, I am happy you find the music so enjoyable."

Mrs. Smith tried to interject a comment, but Mrs. Ashbrook said something that pulled the lady's attention away, and the two began discussing the frippery of some lady's gown.

"Were you able to settle the problem with Mr. and Mrs. Larker?" asked Miss Ashbrook.

Simon blinked, taken aback that she remembered the trivial dispute he was facing with one of his tenants. "It's too early to tell, but your advice on the matter helped."

Miss Ashbrook blushed. "I'm sure you would have figured it out on your own, Mr. Kingsley."

"Miss Ashbrook," said a man at the box entrance.

Simon turned to see Mr. Smith and Mr. Ashbrook holding glasses of lemonade for the ladies. Mr. Smith stepped around Simon, handing the drink to Miss Ashbrook.

"Thank you, Mr. Smith," said Miss Ashbrook, and Simon liked to think that she appeared less enthused by the gentleman's presence than she had been with Simon, though he had no idea why he should feel that prick of jealousy.

"It's good to see you, but I should return to my seat," said Simon with a quick bow before leaving.

...

Mina picked up a paintbrush resting on her dressing table. Louisa-Margaretta had insisted they begin the evening preparations far earlier than Mina had intended, and she'd had not time to put away her painting supplies. Mina ran her fingers over the bristles, loving the soft feel of them while her thoughts were preoccupied with Mr. Simon Kingsley. Speaking with him the other day was one thing, but Mina could not account for why he would go out of his way to stop by their box tonight.

Of course, there were plenty of reasons her fickle heart wished to believe. After that first conversation in the park, Mina had been fighting hard to keep her feelings under control. She liked him. Mina would be a fool to deny it, but she'd be a greater one if she believed his present behavior meant anything romantic in nature.

Her mind replayed his conversation with Mr. Finch at the Hartleys' ball. Mr. Kingsley was looking for a helpmate. Not love. Though Mina wanted so much more of a hypothetical husband, part of her hoped that this marked attention meant he was looking for her to fill that role in his life. Not a romantic one, to be sure, but that could change. Having watched many couples fall in love, Mina knew that few felt that spark of love the moment they met. More often than not, romance came after friendship.

A knock at Mina's chamber door pulled her from her musings, and she called to the person. The door opened, and Louisa-Margaretta hurried into the bedchamber, flinging herself onto Mina's bed.

"What a splendid evening, Mina!" she said, grabbing the end of her braid and twisting it around her fingers. "I think he is quite interested in you."

Mina stilled and stared at her sister-in-law while her heartbeat quickened. If others were noticing Mr. Kingsley's attention, it couldn't be all in her head. "I wouldn't say that."

"Oh, definitely," she gushed, staring up at the canopy. "I swear I saw him watching you most of the evening."

Mina's face flushed, and she placed the brush down on the dressing table. She hoped her face was suitably calm when she turned and joined her sister-in-law on the bed.

"Do you truly believe so?" asked Mina, terrified to say the words aloud. Speaking them made them so much more real.

"It's simply perfect, Mina. Just perfect. I am so happy that you might finally have a husband of your own." Louisa-Margaretta smiled, her whole face lighting up, and Mina felt guilty for every uncharitable thing she'd ever thought about the girl. They may have little in common, but Mina knew that for all of Louisa-Margaretta's faults, she was a good person who loved Nicholas.

Mina didn't know how to reply. It was still too hard to give voice to her hopes, and for all her warm feelings in the moment, she didn't have the relationship with Louisa-Margaretta that made her comfortable speaking so freely. Mina ached to see Thea and have a proper *tête-à-tête* with her dear friend. Thea would never laugh at Mina's hopes and dreams. No matter how fanciful.

"To think, you'd be a mother," said Louisa-Margaretta. "Those little children need one, and you would be perfect for them. I cannot imagine a better situation for you!"

Mina's heart wilted under the heat of her shame. Of course, Louisa-Margaretta meant Mr. Smith. Anyone looking at her would know that Mr. Smith was the suitor pursuing her. Not Mr. Kingsley. Even though he had never visited them in public or private before, no one would think that his dropping by could be a mark of interest in Mina. It was Mr. Smith with his humorless personality, parcel of children, and shrewish mother that everyone viewed as being a good match for the spinster, Mina

Ashbrook.

"Louisa-Margaretta, I appreciate that you feel Mr. Smith would make a decent husband, but I don't feel he is right for me," said Mina.

"Whatever are you talking about?" Louisa-Margaretta gaped. "It's perfect. At your age, you shan't be able to have a lot of children, and with Mr. Smith, you would step right into the role of mother. What more could you want?"

"Of course, motherhood is wonderful, and I wish to have children," said Mina, choosing her words carefully, "but I helped raise three brothers and I know it's difficult enough that I would rather have a husband who would share the burden and not add to it. I have no desire for a husband who wants me to be a glorified nursemaid so that he can walk away from his responsibility and never think on his children again. Motherhood is wonderful thing but too difficult to romanticize and not worth taking on a terrible marriage."

"You don't know that it would be terrible," she insisted. "Mr. Smith obviously likes you."

"He likes a wife with a hefty dowry."

"Most men like that."

"He is a wastrel, Louisa-Margaretta. He burned through his first wife's dowry and has pawned his children off on relatives so he can be free to pursue a wealthier wife than he would find in the country. He lives off his relations."

Louisa-Margaretta smiled and sighed, as if that were the silliest concern to have. "Even if he is a wastrel, it wouldn't matter. Nicholas and I would support you. Your family shan't starve."

Mina felt sick at the thought. She may accept that a chance at romance was near impossible for her, but the idea of marrying someone she could not respect was horrifying. She had no need for a wealthy husband, but she did want someone industrious. Not a man who had wasted his money and lived off charity. Mina may not know the whole story, but she knew enough to fully believe Mr. Smith's negligence had brought about his family's reduced state, and she could not admire such a man.

"Hold off judgment until you know him better," said Louisa-Margaretta. "Of course, you shouldn't marry a dislikeable cad, but you shouldn't dismiss a suitor without giving him a chance first."

Listening to her sister-in-law's words, Mina wondered if her brother and his wife would be so eager to say such things if she were a young woman in her first or second Season. Likely, Mr. Smith would never have been given an introduction when Mina was twenty. At thirty, it appeared her family's expectations of suitability in a suitor had lowered considerably.

That realization twisted her heart. Mina knew her options were few. No one knew more about that than she. It was she who had spent years sitting on the edges of ballrooms and dinners, hoping to find a good man. It was she who'd faced years of rejection. Her brothers often complained about how difficult it was for gentlemen to approach ladies. They would turn to Mina looking for confirmation that they bore the harder lot in the courting life as they were the ones who had to do all the pursuing, but she felt no sympathy for their plight. A gentleman may face rejection when he approached a lady but only when she made it expressly known. That lady faced rejection from every gentleman who did not approach.

Having suffered countless rejections, Mina intimately knew how limited her options were. But having them thrown in her face in such a blatant fashion was like being kicked by a horse. Like her heart stopped beating altogether.

"You just need a chance to get to know him better," said Louisa-Margaretta. "I will invite him to the dinner party Nicholas and I are throwing in a few weeks."

"Dinner party?" Mina hadn't known there was to be one, but that was Louisa-Margaretta's right; she was mistress here and did not need to ask permission.

Mina forced herself not to cry under the soul-crushing weight of so many disappointments. If she did so, her sister-in-law would wish to know why, and Mina would never admit how much it hurt that she was no longer mistress of the Ashbrook household. It had been Mina who had thrown the dinner parties for her father. She had stepped into her mother's shoes, but now she had no role.

A person without a purpose.

Chapter 5

Mina stared at the library shelves but didn't have the energy to pick a book. She'd been in the same predicament just minutes before while staring at the piano, trying to decide what to play. Or her easel. Or any number of other diversions Mina had attempted since she woke that morning.

She hated feeling like this. Having the desire to do something but no interest in the activities at her disposal. They were all so pointless. Mina enjoyed learning new skills and honing those she had acquired, but she missed having something of value to do. Something that mattered. Her own pursuits were fine and well, but they held none of the satisfaction she felt at running the household, caring for the tenants, or any of the other numerous duties the mistress was required to undertake. Louisa-Margaretta had stolen it all away the moment she married Nicholas.

Her muscles felt weak, but Mina didn't have any tears in her. She had shed enough of them over the years, and this was not a moment for such displays. Tears required energy and passion. Mina lacked both, and she allowed the weight of her sadness to pull her down onto a chair.

None of her charities needed her today. None of her hobbies were diverting. She had no function, no responsibilities. Nothing. She was unnecessary here. Louisa-Margaretta and Nicholas loved her but did not need her. Mina wanted to slip back into her bedchamber, close the curtains, and climb into bed. Perhaps she could sleep her melancholia away. Tomorrow had to be better.

But Mina still had to face the dreaded dinner party in a few short days.

A sliver of anger pierced through the numb cloak enveloping Mina's heart. She was a grown woman with no life and unable to even set her own schedule anymore. Living under her brother's roof, she was left to the mercy of Louisa-Margaretta's whims and social calendar. When Mina had been mistress of the house, she'd had some freedom. Nicholas and her father rarely argued about her social life—the little that it was—as long as the house was in running order and she acted within society's dictates.

And now Mina was under the thumb of a girl not even in her twentieth year. Mina didn't know how much more she could handle. She was superfluous in this household and lacked the basic freedom to decide whether she wanted to go to the Richmonds' for dinner tonight or if she'd rather stay home. Mina had a home of her own in which she desperately wished to live but didn't have the funds to do so.

Perhaps if she'd spent her childhood as other girls, Mina might not have noticed the walls of her gilded cage tightening around her, but having tasted the joy of being one's own mistress made the bleakness of her life starker. And it didn't need to be so. She had Rosewood Cottage. Mina would be happier there. Though it wouldn't require the level of work to run as their London townhome or country estate, it would be hers and Mina would be her own woman.

All the thoughts swirling in Mina's mind built up a sense of righteous indignation. She loved her father and Nicholas, but the idea that she was being dictated to from beyond the grave was too infuriating. Not to mention living with the constant matrimonial pressure. Mina had learned to accept the unchangeability of her situation, but her family refused to. Mina wondered if they ever would or if Nicholas would simply keep her prisoner in his home for the rest of her life while he and his wife threw desperate bachelors and widowers at Mina.

She was doomed to be the pitiable spinster sister.

Standing, Mina decided she needed to say something. Nicholas had said they could revisit her future at Rosewood Cottage. From Mina's perspective, there wasn't a single reason he needed her here now that Louisa-Margaretta was well established as mistress of the household. And with a further two years proving how nonexistent Mina's matrimonial prospects were, Nicholas would be unable to argue that she needed to keep trying.

Walking down the hallway, Mina's mind strung together a series of arguments, picturing how she should broach the topic, how Nicholas would react, and how she would defend her position. Nerves plagued her. Not that she feared her brother, but Mina knew how staunchly he was against her moving to Rosewood Cottage.

Reaching the study door, Mina knocked without a concrete plan but knowing she needed to do this; she needed her own home. After Nicholas called to her, she entered while forcing herself to remember that she was the elder sister. She was practically a second mother to Nicholas. That had to count for something, even if he held all the power in this situation.

"Mina," said Nicholas, gesturing for her to sit in the chair before his desk, "how are you today?"

"I need to speak with you."

"I assumed so, but you look awfully serious. Should I be worried?" he teased.

Mina shook her head. "I thought it was time for us to discuss Rosewood Cottage."

Nicholas cocked his head, his brows drawing together. "The

cottage is fine. I received word a week or two ago from the care-taker about some minor repairs needed, but nothing outside the ordinary."

"No," said Mina, forcing her hands not to twist in her lap. "About my moving to Rosewood."

Nicholas dropped his quill to the desk and crossed his arms. "I thought we had discussed this."

"Two years ago, and you said we could reassess the situation."

"I cannot have my sister move out to the country alone."

"I wouldn't be alone, Nicholas," said Mina with a frustrated huff. "Of course, I would hire a companion. Heaven knows there are plenty of genteel but penniless ladies who could serve that purpose. And there would be staff—"

"It is unnecessary," he insisted. "I cannot see why you think you need to leave. Louisa-Margaretta and I love having you here. This is your home."

Mina sighed. Touching a hand to her head, she tried to think of how to explain it without hurting Nicholas's feelings. "That is the problem. You love me, but you do not need me. Your wife has things well under control. She doesn't need my help running the household. And as much as you want this to be my home, it isn't. Not anymore. It is yours."

Nicholas's face grew stern, and Mina knew she'd mis-stepped, though there was no other way to explain it.

"Do you truly not think of this as your home?" he asked, a frown tugging down his mouth. "Do you feel uncomfortable around us?"

"That has nothing to do with it!" Mina fought for compo-sure, but she felt overwhelmed as the conversation pulled away from her control. She took a breath, willing herself to calm. "I love you both so much, but I miss the country. I love my cot-tage."

Mina stopped, blinking back the tears while giving her thoughts time to coalesce. Her shoulders hunched, and her cheeks burned, but she forged forward. "I feel useless here,

Nicholas."

He opened his mouth, but she cut him off. "You and Louisa-Margaretta are wonderful and make me feel more than welcome, but I went from having all the work of a household to nothing. My days were filled with things that needed my attention, and I was happy knowing that my actions helped make my family's life better. Because of my efforts, the house ran smoothly, our employees and tenants were cared for, and I had purpose.

"And now..." Mina hated that the tears pushed harder for release. She did not want to cry, but all the months of frustration and powerlessness swarmed her, bringing out every hidden heartache and every unresolved emotion. "Now, I am just the spinster sister."

Mina closed her eyes, allowing the tears to fall. It was pointless to fight them; better to let them out and move past it. She gave herself a few moments before regaining enough composure to look at her brother. Pity filled Nicholas's eyes. The last thing Mina wanted was to be viewed as some pitiful creature. She wanted him to understand.

"I am sorry you feel that way, Mina," said Nicholas. "I hope you know Louisa-Margaretta and I do not think of you like that."

"I know," Mina said, her eyes drifting down to the rug on the floor. "So much of my life has not gone as I had wished. When I was a child, I wanted this type of life. I wanted no responsibilities. I wanted to be a child and not a substitute mother and mistress of the household. But now that I have lost it, my life feels so empty. All the work that filled my days is gone, and I am left with nothing but time on my hands."

"Don't say that." Nichols stood and came around to sit in the chair beside Mina. "You have so much you do. You paint and play the piano. You volunteer with a number of charities. You read and write endless letters to Thea and our brothers, not to mention the balls, musicales, and theatre events."

"True, but with the exception of the charity work, none of

them give me the same satisfaction. There were times when you children drove me to distraction," Mina said with a faint smile, quick flashes of memories warming her heart. "There were times that I hated that responsibility, but living a life of amusement is unfulfilling. Attending parties and dances where no one cares whether or not I am there is agonizing, and I love my hobbies, but I need something more. It may sound silly, but I miss feeling as though I make a difference. That my work matters. Painting an entire museum's worth of artwork is entertaining but does not give me that same joy."

Nicholas's head bobbed in agreement. "I understand, Mina. Frittering time away on frivolity isn't something our family has ever cared for, but I do not understand why you want to leave London while things are going so well with Mr. Smith."

Mina forced herself not to groan, though her face showed her feelings well enough. "Things are not going well with Mr. Smith."

"Louisa-Margaretta said—"

"Louisa-Margaretta is desperate to believe he is a good match for me, but he is not. I shan't marry that man."

"But you'd have everything you want," argued Nicholas while patting her hand. "A home to take care of, and a family that needs you."

"I've no doubt I would be needed, but I'd be married to a man I neither like nor esteem. Being a mother is a difficult job. I would love to be one, but being an instantaneous mother to seven children would be grueling and to do so without having the mutual love or respect of my husband would be madness."

"I don't think you've given it enough time to see if you two rub along."

"Rub along?" Mina wanted to laugh at that. Spending time with Mr. Smith was as enjoyable as hugging a porcupine. Probably less. "Nicholas, the man and I have nothing in common. I've spent hours forced into his company, and as far as I can see his only interest in me is my mothering skills and dowry. His mother shows more interest in courting me than he."

Nicholas leaned back in his chair, taking on his 'lord of the manor' expression. "Louisa-Margaretta told me of your concerns, and I think you should be more open to the possibility."

Mina took a fortifying breath, glancing down at her hands. Biting on her lip, she glanced at Nicholas once more. She did not want to see the truth in his eyes but needed it all the same. "Would you say that if I were in my first Season? If I were eighteen, would you want Mr. Smith courting me?"

Nicholas kept his expression neutral, but Mina knew him too well to be blind to the truth lurking behind his body language. He thought her too old to be picky.

But what Nicholas couldn't understand was that as much as she longed for a family of her own, Mina wanted happiness more, and marrying for the sake of marrying would never ensure that. As much as she hated the prospect of her life continuing on in the same fashion as it had, Mina hated the idea of a miserable marriage far more. Mina had witnessed enough of married life to know that being unhappily unattached was far better than unhappily married: the latter was a far more difficult lot to change.

"Dealing with hypotheticals isn't helpful," said Nicholas. "The past is not what I am worried about, it is the future. As much as you may disagree, I don't believe you will find happiness alone in the country. Here you have a home and family, and here is where you should stay."

Nicholas tried to say more, but Mina stood, forcing the gentleman to his feet. Before he could make himself feel better by spouting senseless platitudes about the rightness of his decision, Mina left, shutting the study door behind her. She may not be able to choose where she lived, but she did not have to listen to her jailor's justifications.

Chapter 6

Simon laid down the letter from his steward. Thorne was more than capable of handling business, but Simon hated leaving him alone for so long. There was enough to do on the estate to keep several stewards busy, but Simon enjoyed doing the work himself. He had tried his hand at other gentlemanly pursuits, but none gave him the same satisfaction. He needed to get home. London was pointless. It had its moments of entertainment, to be sure, but most of the social inanities simply reminded Simon why so many gentlemen of his acquaintance became lazy and self-absorbed, bent more on seeking the next bit of fun than doing anything of value.

Months in London, and he'd yet to find a lady to replace Susannah. Simon knew it was pointless to keep searching, but some part of him dreaded giving up. He could never bring himself to admit it aloud, but Simon longed for a family. A proper family. Filled with love and joy. No rough and tumble gentleman would dare voice such desires, but that was what Simon had been waiting for all these years, and why he kept torturing himself by returning to London. With Susannah, that dream had been within reach, and now, there was no hope to claim it.

He was tired of waiting and could not endure another year

of shouldering the work of both master and mistress. Simon did not care for handling the household staff or linens or menus. He needed someone who would oversee the many aspects of running a household. His housekeeper, Mrs. Richards, handled the day-to-day housework decently, but Simon suspected that the house was not quite so well run without a mistress to oversee it. Not to mention the long list of community duties a mistress handled; Simon couldn't go a week without someone petitioning him for the Kingsley family's aid with some charity or village function.

Looking down at the desk with the papers stacked neatly in their appropriate piles, Simon knew he would never love another as he loved Susannah. It was pointless to keep searching; it was time to find a lady with whom he could share a life. A companion. Someone to help him with the work to be done. Someone to fill his empty house.

As it had many times before, Simon's mind turned to Miss Ashbrook. Finch's jokes aside, Simon found she truly was the perfect candidate. She was intelligent and capable, and spending time with her wasn't a burden. In all honesty, it was a joy. There was an ease of conversation between them that made him feel like he had known her far longer than a month and a half. She did not prattle away about dresses and frippery or seem liable to be shrewish and domineering like his sisters, Priscilla and Emmeline respectively.

Simon could have sworn he and Miss Ashbrook did not travel in the same social circles, but having grabbed his attention, Simon noticed they were thrown together quite frequently. Since their first conversation, no more than a couple days would pass before he would see her. Balls, the theatre, dinner parties, Miss Ashbrook was always there, quietly in the background, and each time Simon found his way to her side. Finch may think him bound for Bedlam, but there was no denying it, Simon enjoyed her company. Admired her, even.

Twisting a quill in his hand, Simon pictured a life with Miss

Ashbrook. The corner of his mouth pulled upwards while he imagined a future together. He hated to admit—even to himself—but Finch's assertions of Miss Ashbrook's inability to break their marital vows gave him an extra boost of contentment. Simon knew Miss Ashbrook was not the type to do so, but his father had likely believed the same of his wife when they'd married. Knowing Miss Ashbrook possessed little to attract a paramour gave Simon peace of mind. He could not abide the thought of his marriage copying his parents'.

And it was not as though Miss Ashbrook were entertaining other suitors. Though Mr. Smith continued to pay his addresses, it was clear that Miss Ashbrook did not care for him, which was another testament to the lady's good sense. From what he had learned about the man, Simon doubted marriage to Mr. Smith would be a happy affair. Frankly, Mr. Smith didn't seem very keen about Miss Ashbrook, either, which made Simon question the man's taste. She may not be an obvious marriage candidate, but she was by far the best Simon had come across.

Susannah's face came back into his thoughts, and Simon turned away from it. There was no hope for love now, but Simon found himself content to settle for a lawfully bound friendship with Miss Ashbrook.

...

"Dear Mina," said Louisa-Margaretta, lowering the teacup to rest on its dish, "I do think music is wonderful entertainment, but cards are so much more engaging, don't you agree?"

Mina did not agree. Not when it meant being forced into hours of awkward conversation with Mr. Smith. She had nothing against cards, but a musicale would provide a polite way to avoid dealing with drawn out pauses between occasional discussions about the weather; there were only so many ways to describe the state of the roads. And Mina shuddered to think of watching Mrs. Smith constantly inflicting her son with that domineering elbow of hers; the poor man must be suffering internal injuries from Mrs. Smith's constant prodding.

But Mina's feelings on the issue did not matter. Louisa-Margaretta was determined, as was her right. It was her dinner party to plan in any way she wished, even if Mina's well-meaning brother insisted on including Mina in the undertaking.

Though neither Nicholas nor his wife had said anything, neither of them were well versed in subterfuge; when Louisa-Margaretta had arrived in Mina's room begging for help planning the dinner party a mere half hour after Mina's disastrous conversation with Nicholas concerning Rosewood Cottage, Mina knew what had transpired between the spouses. After all the words Mina had spoken with the utmost convictions of her heart, Nicholas had decided giving his sister a minor task would solve her doldrums. There would be no need of moving to Rosewood Cottage if there were a card game to arrange.

Mina watched Louisa-Margaretta outlining the various virtues of her plan and felt sorry for the girl. Louisa-Margaretta wanted to throw a party of her own choosing and was stuck having to cater to her sister-in-law's mood. Mina fought to keep the despair from showing on her face. Rather than feeling needed, this whole situation made Mina feel like even more of a burden.

"I agree," said Mina. "Cards will be wonderful."

Louisa-Margaretta smiled, placing the cup and saucer on the table and grasping Mina's hands. "Do you truly think so? I am so nervous and desperate for it to be a success. But I know it will be brilliant if you are there to help me."

The party was already planned. Louisa-Margaretta had arranged it all with more efficiency and skill than Mina would have expected from one so young and inexperienced. Any help Mina offered was only the honorary kind.

"Mr. Smith and his mother are sure to accept soon," said Louisa-Margaretta with a coy smile.

It was pointless to argue. Mina had done so enough times

before to recognize a lost cause. Nicholas and Louisa-Margaretta would never push her to marry Mr. Smith if she truly did not wish to, but this courtship (if it could be called that) was beyond Mina's control. She would not be rid of Mr. Smith until he lost interest or she rejected his express offer of marriage.

Louisa-Margaretta's gaze turned to the clock on the mantle, and she shot to her feet. "Is that the time? Dear me, I'm late for my shopping excursion with Beatrice. Are you sure you wish to stay here, Mina?"

"Yes, thank you," she replied with a natural and entirely unforced smile; Louisa-Margaretta's unbridled optimism was difficult to fight. "I've some things that need doing."

Louisa-Margaretta accepted the lie without hesitation, and in a whirl of petticoats and silk, she swept out of the room, leaving Mina alone. Leaning forward with her head on her palm, Mina hoped the headache pricking at the back of her head would leave, though she suspected it would remain until the Season was over and the family retired to Lincolnshire.

But then Mina remembered that they would not be heading home. Nicholas had been invited for a house party at some friend's estate in Scotland. As a courtesy, the invitation was extended to Mina, and she wanted to weep and wail at the thought. That was what her life had been reduced to. A courtesy. She would live on the social courtesy of her brother and sister-in-law, whose much wider circles did not include a single person with whom Mina counted as a friend.

Mina massaged her temples and tried once more to think of an escape. She felt wicked for feeling that way. Nicholas and Louisa-Margaretta were unfailingly kind and loving towards her. They wanted her to be happy and actively tried to help her attain it. Unfortunately, their definition of happy differed greatly from Mina's.

A throat cleared, and Mina looked up to see Andrews waiting with a properly deferential look on his face. The butler extended a silver tray, and Mina was dumbfounded to find a calling card resting on it.

"Mrs. Ashbrook has left for the afternoon," said Mina.

"It is for you, miss," he said, extending the tray once more.

"For me?" Mina blinked at the card.

Picking it up, she saw *Mr. Simon Kingsley* written across it; her thumbs brushed the paper, and Mina felt a blush rising in her cheeks. Looking at Andrews, Mina nodded and called a maid to clear away the remnants of their tea. Standing, she ran her hands down her skirts and tried to ignore the fluttering in her heart. Then the man in question entered with a bow.

"Are you well, Miss Ashbrook?" asked Mr. Kingsley while they took their seats on the sofas opposite each other.

Mina fought back another blush. She'd hoped to look better than that. "Just a touch of a headache, I'm afraid."

"Is there something I might get you?" His eyebrows were raised, and he looked ready to stand.

"No, Mr. Kingsley, but thank you for your concern." It was so rare for anyone to notice her discomfort that Mina had to control the wild imaginations in her head. The man had asked to help her, not declared his undying love, and it was silly to dream as if he had. "I apologize that my sister-in-law and brother are not here to receive you as well. They are both busy this afternoon."

"I was hoping that was the case. I came to speak with you."

Mina's brows rose. "Me?"

Simon had anticipated his nerves, though that fore-knowledge had not helped. Marriage was an irrevocable decision. Sweat gathered on his palms, and he flattened them against his lap. The jumble of thoughts crashing about his head refused to be corralled. Like a herd of high-spirited horses, they bucked and ran, turning every which way.

"Are *you* well, Mr. Kingsley?" asked Miss Ashbrook with the same mix of curiosity and concern that had been showing on his face when he had asked that question.

"You look out of sorts," she added. Her brows drew together, and she leaned towards him. "Did the weather turn foul at Avebury Park?"

Simon hadn't expected that question. His heart slowed, and he found himself able to swallow again, something he hadn't realized was so important until he'd been unable to manage it. Seeing her obvious concern about something he had mentioned only in passing at least a fortnight before made his anxiety evaporate.

Calm washed away his trepidation, easing his mind. Simon knew this was the right decision, and the more he entertained the thought, the more certain he felt. In many ways Simon counted her a friend, though their relationship was still young. He may not love her, but Miss Ashbrook was a good woman and would make him a good wife, and Simon looked forward to spending more time with her.

"The weather is fine," he said.

"Then your tenants' farms are safe?" She leaned forward, as if anxious for an affirmative.

"Yes. Old Joe's leg may have been predicting a tempest, but it turned out to be no more than a drizzle."

"Wonderful news," she said, her shoulders relaxing. "I've been worried about it."

And that was why Simon knew that of all the unattached ladies he had met, Miss Ashbrook was the most likely to be the right match for him. Her honest concern strengthened Simon's belief that if nothing else, Miss Ashbrook would be a good and kind mistress for his estate. There was no more room for fear in his heart. She was the one.

"Miss Ashbrook," said Simon, "as you know, I've been wanting to settle."

She shifted, clasping her hands. "Yes, I recall your conversation with Mr. Finch about the matter."

Simon sought for another apology, the words stuttering and faltering with each failed attempt, but Miss Ashbrook held up a hand. "That wasn't a condemnation, Mr. Kingsley. Simply a comment. There's no need to apologize when you have already done so."

Not an auspicious beginning, but Simon forged ahead. "Yes, well, I know this may seem abrupt, and I know that we do not share any feelings of love, but I think we are well suited and enjoy our time together."

Miss Ashbrook stared at him, her spine rigid and her fingers frozen in place.

"I know I am making a muddle of this," he continued, "but I was hoping you would consent to become my wife."

Chapter 7

"Wife?" The word stunned Mina. Partway through his speech, she had guessed where his words were headed, but it hadn't given her enough of an opportunity to prepare.

"I'd hoped to have more time, but my estate is in desperate need of its master and in even more desperate need of a mistress. I am afraid I cannot linger in London much longer. I need to return and wish to do so with you by my side."

Mina had no words to give Mr. Kingsley. If Mr. Smith had said such things, it would've been easy to answer. Mina never aspired to a marriage of convenience nor thought herself willing to tolerate such a thing, but it was different with Mr. Kingsley. He may not have feelings of love, but those feelings resided in Mina's heart.

Mr. Kingsley had his faults, like all people do, but Mina admired him fiercely. Where most of his class frittered away their funds and lived a life of idleness, Mr. Kingsley strived to improve his estate and the lives of those beneath him. It was hard not to admire him when he spoke so passionately about the welfare of his tenants and community.

And Mr. Kingsley was right. They did get along well. She'd

never felt so comfortable around another living soul, outside her family or Thea. And in some ways, she felt more comfortable around Mr. Kingsley than her own relatives.

But to marry without his love felt like a betrayal of her dreams. Mr. Kingsley had been honest with her, and for that she was grateful, but picturing an affirmative coming from her lips made her stomach tie itself in knots. He wanted a housekeeper with whom he got along. That may be enough for him, but not for her.

Mina wanted a true home. A family. And that was built on more than mutual tolerance.

"Mr. Kingsley, might I ask you a question before I answer?"

The corner of Mr. Kingsley's mouth twitched. "With what I just asked you, I'd be surprised if you didn't ask at least one."

Mina's gaze dropped to her lap, her fingers tugging at her skirts. "Why do you wish to marry?"

Mr. Kingsley leaned back, his eyebrows arching. "I believe I already explained why in that conversation with Mr. Finch."

"No," said Mina, while staring at her hands. She couldn't bring herself to look him in the eye in that moment. For the first time since that meeting in the park, Mina was decidedly uncomfortable around Mr. Kingsley. "You described why you should hire more help, but there is a vast difference between a paid employee and a woman with whom you are bound to for life."

"Ah." Mr. Kingsley shifted in his seat.

It wasn't an unreasonable thing to ask, but a part of him had expected Miss Ashbrook to just accept. Of course, being a woman of sound mind meant she would not jump into marriage without thought, but digging into his motives dredged up feelings and memories Simon preferred to keep buried.

"I do wish for help," said Simon. "That is all too true. There are many things that a mistress does for the estate that I have neither time nor inclination to do. However, you are right. That is something that can be remedied in other manners."

Simon took a moment to gather his thoughts before continuing.

"I have a flourishing estate, but I find that I long for more." Simon swallowed past the lump in his throat. His cravat felt far too tight, but it was too late to back out at this juncture. "I want it to be more than just a place I live and a source of income. I want it to be a home."

The silence that followed that statement made Simon wish to escape the room, but he held firm. There was more to say, and if Miss Ashbrook was to be his wife, Simon knew he needed to be open. Even if that meant admitting something he had never said aloud.

"My family life was not a happy one," he said, while wanting to tug at his cravat, "and I have long wished for one. For something to come home to other than an empty house and the never-ending work to be done. My estate means everything to me, but I know there is something more to be had, and I believe that includes a family that can fill my house with laughter and joy."

"You think I can give that to you?" asked Miss Ashbrook, her eyes locked on her hands. He wished she would look at him and give him some hint at her feelings.

"More so than any other woman of my acquaintance," said Simon, unwilling to tell the absolute truth—that it was more so than any other *unattached* woman. But it did no good to dwell on things he could not change and would only hurt Miss Ashbrook.

"Why?" she asked. Miss Ashbrook met his gaze once more, but her eyes held a slight challenging glint to them. "The only reasons you've given is that we are well suited and you enjoy my company, but I cannot believe there are no other ladies who fit that description. There must be plenty with whom you could make that home you desire."

Simon paused again. He didn't entirely comprehend it himself, but he would try to explain it. "We have known each other a short time, but it is clear that you are a woman of sense and compassion." With each word, Simon thoughts coalesced, bringing with it a deeper understanding of his own heart. "But more than that, the more I get to know you, the more I esteem and admire you, which is not a common occurrence for me with many of our class. I've never felt so at ease with a lady before. Nor have I sought out a lady's advice and valued it as I do with you."

Miss Ashbrook ducked her face, her cheeks flushing, and Simon found himself smiling at her. She had asked him to elaborate and then found herself uncomfortable with the results.

"And what of love?" Her voice came out softly, her face still turned downward.

Simon paused, unsure how to proceed. He knew what she wanted him to say. He knew what many other gentlemen would likely spout in that situation—declarations of undying affection to sugarcoat the speedy decision they were making.

"I don't know much about love," said Simon. "In my experience, it's generally not worth pursuing."

At that Miss Ashbrook looked up at him. He wished he could decipher the inscrutable look on her face. Normally, her thoughts and feelings were so clearly stamped in her features that Simon had no idea how to read this stoic Miss Ashbrook.

"You do not believe in marrying for love?" she asked.

"I had hoped for it," he said, pulling the words from that hidden part of his soul, "but I fear it's not for me. I do know that I count you a friend, which is the first time I can say that about a lady. More than that, I would consider you one of my closest friends. That alone would put us on far better footing that most married couples of my acquaintance."

Miss Ashbrook studied him, and more words came from his mouth.

"I may not be able to give love, but I do promise to be faithful and honor our vows," he said, allowing the earnestness to seep into his voice, making it feel like a private vow between the two of them. "I swear you will have no need to fear on that account."

A smile tickled the corner of Miss Ashbrook's mouth. "I believe in your honor, Mr. Kingsley, but I should like—"

At that moment, a woman swept into the room with all the energy of an agitated lapdog yipping at a passing sparrow.

"Mina, you'll never believe what I just witnessed!"

Simon came to his feet, but between her movement and the wide-brimmed bonnet on her head, it took a few seconds before Simon was able to see the woman's face well enough to recognize Miss Ashbrook's sister-in-law.

"I was not two minutes from our door when Mr. Smith paraded by with Miss Fanny Osgood on his arm. That vile man and his even viler mother didn't even have the decency to look ashamed." she said, throwing her bonnet onto the chair. "After he made it clear he was courting you, he has the audacity to chase after a woman with more money than sense—"

Mrs. Ashbrook halted mid-sentence the moment she saw Simon standing opposite Miss Ashbrook. Her eyes widened and her face paled, displaying all the improper shock and dismay of a young girl caught in an uncomfortable situation. She froze for a full five seconds before the mantle of dignified society matron smoothed her expression into polite decorum, though Simon could see the curiosity blazing in her eyes.

"Mr. Kingsley," she said with a demure smile, "how lovely to see you. May I offer you some tea or refreshment?"

She sat beside her sister-in-law, and Simon took his seat again. This was not going the way he had planned and was becoming more difficult with each passing moment. "No, thank you, Mrs. Ashbrook. I stopped by to call on Miss Ashbrook."

"I do apologize if I interrupted," she said. Mrs. Ashbrook held her posture, but her eyes flicked between the pair of them. It did not help matters that Miss Ashbrook's cheeks were the color of a ripe strawberry.

Mina could not decide which was worse. Having Louisa-Margaretta walk in on this scene or the manner in which she had done it. It was no secret that Mr. Smith was courting her, but to have it bandied about in such a fashion in front of Mr. Simon Kingsley after what had just passed between them was more than Mina could bear.

Or so she thought.

"This is perfectly serendipitous," said Louisa-Margaretta, reaching over to pat Mina's knee. "As it happens, we are holding a dinner party in two days and Mr. Smith is unable to attend, which will positively ruin our numbers. I know it is last minute, but would you be interested in joining us? I would have invited you sooner, but I had no idea you and our dear Mina were so close. It would be wonderful for her to have an acquaintance there."

Mina wondered if it were possible to burst into flames. Her face felt warm enough for it, and it would be preferable to sitting through this agonizing scene. It was hard enough to hear Louisa-Margaretta invite Mr. Kingsley because she felt Mina needed a friend, but to have done so while making it clear that he was a last-minute substitute was too much. The only thing that saved Mina from complete and utter devastation was the flicker of humor in Mr. Kingsley's eyes as he accepted.

Within moments Mr. Kingsley gave polite farewells, though Mina couldn't recall a single word that was spoken. Once the door was closed behind the gentleman, Louisa-Margaretta pounced on Mina, desperate to winkle out all the details of the interlude she had interrupted, but Mina made her own escape. Hurrying to her bedchamber, she locked the doors and collapsed onto her bed.

In all her life, she could never have imagined this day happening. A proposal for a marriage of convenience. Mina never thought such a man as Mr. Kingsley would propose to her for any reason. If it were Mr. Smith, there'd be no hesitation and no question as to how she'd answer, but with Mr. Kingsley, the situation was far more complicated. His speech about wanting a home filled her heart, twisting her resolve every which way. It had given her a glimpse into Mr. Kingsley's soul, and it was everything she'd hoped for in a husband.

Except love.

Clutching her pillow, Mina stared out at her bedchamber, her eyes unfocused while her mind churned. She had plenty to think about and only two days to decide her answer.

Chapter 8

Mina had been dreading the upcoming dinner party, but this new complication Mr. Kingsley had dropped in Mina's lap made the whole situation infinitely worse. For the last two days, she had thought of little else but his proposal, and Mina was no closer to an answer.

Scattered among the guests in the formal sitting room, Mina found her heart heaving when each was announced, both anticipating and dreading Mr. Kingsley's arrival. The others ignored her, which suited Mina as she shared little in common with her brother and sister-in-law's peers. Besides, it allowed Mina time to further agonize over the impending answer she must give Mr. Kingsley.

Of course, at this point, there was little more for her to consider. Mina had dissected every minute detail of Mr. Kingsley's personality and proposal more thoroughly than any naturalist could ever do in a year's study of a newly discovered beetle.

A marriage of convenience. The thought made Mina shudder. Marriage was too daunting a task to be taken so lightly. Done well, it enlightened the lives of both parties. Done poorly, it destroyed far more than just the man and woman involved, and a marriage of convenience was far more likely to fall into the second category.

But Mina admired Mr. Kingsley greatly. Besides feeling the same admiration and respect for him as he expressed for her, Mr. Kingsley's description of what he wanted in life mirrored perfectly Mina's own desires. A home. The way he spoke of it called to Mina's heart. She did not know much of his history or his family, but there was something inside him crying out for a better life. It was a feeling Mina understood.

That was not to say that she did not love her brothers but having a home of her own—a haven, a special place that was hers—was something Mina longed for. Knowing Mr. Kingsley sought that self-same thing made his offer even more appealing.

And if she refused him, it would force an irrevocable break between them. Mr. Kingsley had become such a fixture in her life that the thought of being parted from him hurt. Every bit of London society was made that much brighter when Mr. Kingsley appeared among the throng. If they separated now, Mina knew that would be the end of it. Mr. Kingsley would find someone else, and she would lose him forever.

"Dear Mr. Kingsley," said Louisa-Margaretta, swooping in from across the room to greet the gentleman. Lost in her thoughts, Mina had missed his entrance.

"It is so good of you to come," she said, taking his arm and leading him straight to Mina.

The directness in which Louisa-Margaretta presented him made Mina want to run back to her room and lock the door again. Mina knew her face must be a vibrant shade of crimson.

"As you see, Mina is well," said Louisa-Margaretta. Mina may not have breathed a word about Mr. Kingsley's proposal, but her sister-in-law sensed something afoot and was keen to capitalize on it.

"Yes," he replied, a hint of a humor in his voice. "Thank you, Mrs. Ashbrook, for the invitation."

Mina was saved from any more of Louisa-Margaretta's less than subtle machinations when another guest arrived, pulling the hostess's attention elsewhere. Mr. Kingsley took the seat beside Mina on the divan.

"I apologize, Mr. Kingsley," said Mina. "I love my dear sister-in-law, but she is an unstoppable dervish."

Mr. Kingsley smiled, and Mina's heart thumped loud enough she was sure he heard it.

"I'm grateful to play knight in shining armor and save you from an evening alone among such lively people," he said, glancing at the others around them. There was nothing particularly wrong with her brother and sister-in-law's set, just that they made Mina excessively tired just being near them. From Mr. Kingsley's tone, she guessed he felt the same way.

"Louisa-Margaretta painted me to be quite a charity project, didn't she?"

Mr. Kingsley chuckled. "No, though I am glad to keep you company. It would be exhausting to be here all alone. At the moment, I feel very old."

Mina joined his laughter, understanding precisely what he meant.

"You must be anxious for the Season to end and return to your beloved countryside," he said.

Mina couldn't tell if he were hunting for clues about her answer to his most important question or simply making small talk. As Mina did not have an answer to give, she felt grateful for the crowd that made it difficult to discuss such a delicate topic directly. Thus Mina could avoid it altogether, if she pleased. And she did.

"Yes, but unfortunately that is some months away," she said, her smile fading. Mina tried to hold onto it, but her future was a daunting prospect. "Nicholas has been invited to an estate in Scotland, so we are bound for the north to spend an indefinite amount of time with his friends at a house party."

"More of this?" he asked, nodding to a raucous group caught up in gales of laughter.

"And long discussions about people I neither know nor with whom I wish to be acquainted," said Mina with a smile, "but Nicholas and Louisa-Margaretta set our calendar."

Mina felt a flush creep across her cheek. She should not have said so much. She was grateful for her family and knew her situation could be far worse. She had a good home and loving siblings. That was enough.

"For someone who so obviously loves taking care of others, it must be difficult to have your role usurped and give up being mistress of the Ashbrook estate," said Mr. Kingsley.

Mina's eyes darted to him, astonished to hear him say that. "Usurped is a bit strong."

"But accurate," he replied. "From what I understand, you ran your father's household and your brother's before his marriage. You have been mistress for more than half your life. To give that up and be subject to the whims of another must be trying."

Mina attempted but failed to keep tears from gathering at the corners of her eyes. It was a foolish thing to do, but to hear someone else understand and acknowledge her was a rare thing. The only other person in the entire world who grasped Mina's turmoil was her dear friend, Thea. No one else even tried to understand her position, yet Mr. Kingsley grasped it completely and without Mina having to explain it. Mr. Kingsley offered his handkerchief, and Mina took it, dabbing discreetly at her eyes. Luckily, no one else in the party noticed. Mina hated the thought of making a scene.

Clutching the handkerchief, Mina looked into Mr. Kingsley's eyes and saw so much in their depths. A caring man who dismissed the possibility of finding love in his life. Mina guessed his experiences with it had taught him to be so jaded, but that did not mean that love could not grow. With time, there was no reason that such feelings wouldn't develop in his heart as they had in hers.

Mr. Kingsley did not love her. Mina had no doubt about that, but in so many small things—the way he looked at her, spoke to her, and treated her—she knew he had tender feelings towards her. Given time to blossom, Mina felt certain love would grow in his heart, and for the first time since he had proposed, Mina was confident in what she wanted.

The conversation lulled, and Mina warmed to the thought of being with this good man for the rest of her life. Love or not, Mina knew her best chance for happiness rested with Simon Kingsley. Her present path could not possibly be better than binding her future to him.

"Mr. Kingsley." Her voice came out far softer than she meant it to. Mina saw the understanding in his eyes as the significance of her tone. His gaze grew more intense as she spoke. "I have thought long about our earlier conversation, and I find myself feeling as you do. I value our friendship deeply. It has been one of the few things that has brought me any joy in fair amount of time."

As she spoke, Mina watched hope and eagerness enter Mr. Kingsley's face. It was so touching to think that this gentleman so clearly wanted her affirmation. Seeing the emotion, Mina knew his proposal was not born out of convenience or desperation. Those may have been the elements that forced him to look beyond his normal social circles, but here and now, Mr. Kingsley's proposal came from a desire for her to be his wife. Not just anyone, but Mina Ashbrook.

And Mina felt no shred of fear or doubt when she said, "In answer to your question, yes."

Chapter 9

Mina breathed in the scent of lilacs coming from her bouquet. Lilies were her favorite flowers, but lilacs reminded her so much of her mama, that it seemed only proper to honor her by using them. Running a thumb along the ribbon that had been used in her mother's bridal bouquet, Mina wondered what she would think about her daughter's impending marriage.

Playing her reasons over in her head, Mina reminded herself why this was a good idea. Her confidence came and went with such frequency that she felt ready for Bedlam. They were just wedding nerves. That was all. Every person standing at the marriage threshold was taking a risk, and it was natural to feel nervous about it.

Mina wanted the whole thing over. Better to be done and move on than waste away in a sea of doubts.

The door to the sitting room opened, and Thea walked in, her face as somber as Mina's own.

"You look lovely, dearest," she said, walking over and placing a kiss on Mina's cheek.

"I am so glad you could come," said Mina, tears gathering in her eyes. "I could not imagine going through this without you by my side."

"I'm just sorry that I was unable to arrive before last night. Frederick and the children were very unhappy to be left behind." Thea gave Mina a sad smile. "But I should think having your dashing fiancé at your side should be enough."

Mina mentally pleaded with Thea to not broach that topic again. Though Thea had been bone tired when she'd arrived, they'd spent most of the evening discussing Mina's marriage in great detail. There was little more to say on the subject.

Thea took one of Mina's hands, squeezing it with a hint of tears in her eyes. "I hate to do this, but I must ask one last time. Are you certain you are making the right decision?"

Mina drew in as much of a breath as her corset allowed. In her enthusiasm for this momentous occasion, Louisa-Margaretta had insisted on it being cinched far tighter than Mina generally wore it; she also never wore a long corset as it seemed unnecessary when high-waisted gowns hid her midsection, but her sister-in-law had been quite determined. Pressing a hand to her stomach, Mina gathered her strength about her.

"Yes, Thea," said Mina, "I wish I had a love like yours, but I have hope that Simon will come to feel for me the way Frederick feels for you. Love or not, the best marriages are based on respect and friendship, and we have that. Attraction and love can grow from that, I know it can. And I am happier around Simon than I ever am with Nicholas and Louisa-Margaretta. Even a bad day with Simon is better than what I have living on my brother's charity."

With each word, the fervor of her words grew. It spread through her, calming her nerves and solidifying her resolve.

"You always have a place in my home," said Thea, though they both knew her dear little house could not fit another living soul.

"And spend my days sharing Penny's bed with her freezing feet and twitching limbs," said Mina with a laugh.

"There is room on the floor," Thea replied with a genuine smile.

Mina reached for her friend's hand, squeezing it tight. "It is not desperation that drives me to do this. My situation has pushed me to consider something I never would have before, but I'd never marry simply to be married. You know that. I truly think Simon and I can have a happy future together. He is such a wonderful man, and I greatly admire him."

Thea gave a knowing look, and Mina amended her comment. "I more than admire him. I care so much for him, and I know he does not feel the same now, but I feel it in my soul that he will. From friendship will come love."

Thea's own eyes misted. "Of course, dearest," she said, pulling Mina into an embrace. "I wish you nothing but happiness."

The door swung open, and Louisa-Margaretta bustled inside with the same excitement she'd had since the engagement was announced, dragging Simon behind her. "What a perfect day!"

Simon's eyes caught Mina's, and she saw the same patient resignation she felt whenever her sister-in-law was running at full tilt, though with a good-humored sparkle in his eye. Freeing himself of her, he walked to Mina and bowed over her hand before leaning over to whisper, "Is she always like this?"

Mina held back a very unladylike snort. "Only when awake."

She heard Simon chuckle, and he tucked her hand in his arm. "Are you ready?"

Just like that, Mina found herself escorted by her husband-to-be from her former home to the church to stand before the handful of family, well-wishers, and the rector. Mina had attended a few weddings over the course of her life and had heard the ceremony enough times to be familiar with it, but in that moment, the rector could have been speaking Latin for all that Mina understood it.

The ceremony flew by with surprising speed, and before Mina could blink, the vows were exchanged, the wedding register signed, and the newly wedded couple were swept into a carriage bound for their new life together. Side by side, they sat silent and solitary. Mina was unsure of what to say. In a short space of time, their relationship had fundamentally altered, and in some ways, it felt as though she were a stranger in her own life.

"Remember to breathe, Mina," said Simon, and Mina found herself shaken loose of the spell, her body relaxing.

Glancing over at her husband, Mina smiled. "I would, if Louisa-Margaretta hadn't insisted on lacing my dress so tight." She shifted, attempting to find a comfortable position.

"I hope you are not too disappointed about missing out on a wedding breakfast," he said, reaching for a carriage blanket resting on the seat opposite.

"I am as anxious as you are to return home," she said as he laid the blanket across their laps. "Perhaps more."

Simon's face broke into a broad smile, and Mina's heart quickened. Sitting so close to him, Mina was keenly aware of the fact that this was only the second time they had truly been alone. With the engagement lasting just long enough to make the necessary wedding arrangements, it had been a flurry of activity; even when they had found a moment to spend together, someone inevitably interrupted with some direly important ceremony detail that required their attention. But now, here they were. Together. Alone.

Mina looked into Simon's eyes, feeling such contentedness and saw it mirrored in his face. Something intangible hung between them, and Mina had never felt so connected to another person. Her husband. Mina gazed into his eyes, and she wondered if he would close the distance between them and press his lips to hers. Their first kiss. How Mina hoped for it, sending out a silent litany that he would do so. In her mind, she pictured him leaning towards her and wondered what it would feel like.

"I received a letter last night from Mr. Thorne," he said. "I'm glad we left early so we can arrive tonight rather drawing this out into a two-day journey."

Mina's corset kept her from drooping as her spirit deflated. Whatever she had felt, Simon appeared oblivious to it, which was not a comforting thought. But he began speaking of the future of Avebury Park, and Mina quickly found herself distracted from her disappointment as they planned and plotted their life together.

...

The sun had long since set when they arrived, but the moon was high and full, filling the night with white light. The carriage pulled along the drive, and Mina slid closer to the window to get a view of her new home. The trees lining the pathway cleared, giving her a beautiful vista of Avebury Park. Though roughly the size of her family's estate, it was far statelier with its neoclassical architecture and pale stone facade that reminded her greatly of the buildings in Bath.

As they approached, Simon pointed out various aspects of the house and property, giving her more information than her exhausted mind could absorb, but she loved that he did so, all the same. A few servants moved about the entrance, making ready for their approach, and when the carriage stopped, Simon helped her out.

Mina's heart felt like it was ready to burst. They were home.

It wasn't until they approached the estate that Simon realized how nervous he was about bringing Mina home. His throat tightened as he pointed out various landmarks and gave some of its history. Avebury Park mattered deeply to him, and its new mistress needed to love it as much as he. Mina certainly had the skills to be a proficient caretaker, but that was not the same as caring about the estate.

Escorting her from the carriage, Simon watched the pleasure shining on Mina's face. With each step towards the main entrance, he felt her excitement growing. Mina did not seem bored with the barrage of information he sent her but asked questions and appeared to find utter joy in it all. It was not the behavior of someone being polite. Mina already loved Avebury Park. Seeing it made Simon more certain that he'd made the right decision that morning.

"Welcome home, sir," said Jennings with a bow.

"It's good to be home," replied Simon, "and even better to introduce the new Mrs. Kingsley."

It was true. The weight of the marriage search had been lifted. Just giving the introduction made Simon realize just how much of a relief it was to have the whole situation settled. Come tomorrow, Simon could turn the running of the household to Mina, leaving him free to concentrate on the estate as a whole. No more worries about the maids, the silver, the pantry, the ordering of coals, the dinner menus. Not that he'd done much of that, having allowed Mrs. Richards to decide the bulk of it, but with Mina by his side, he'd never have to be bothered with any of those details again.

Placing a hand on Mina's back and guiding her through the introductions to the staff, Simon realized there was more to his contentedness than just having a partner to help shoulder the burden; it was having Mina. Simon never thought he could have a companion that was so easy and engaging to talk to.

And watching her as she greeted the servants further strengthened Simon's happiness. Though shy at times, Mina was gracious and kind. She was exhausted from their trip and no doubt famished, yet she took the time to meet every servant from the butler and housekeeper down to the lowly scullery maid and hall boy and did so with quiet dignity and grace. Simon was grateful that Finch had so thoroughly and uncomfortably brought Mina to his attention at the Hartleys' ball. Without it, Simon knew he may never have noticed her and would still be moping and miserable.

As much as Simon wanted to show her every last bit of the house right that minute, Simon knew his wife needed to rest. It may not have been that far a journey from London, but it was enough to make him long for his bedchamber. Calling to Mrs.

Richards, Simon asked the housekeeper to show his wife to her chambers.

...

Mina sat on her bed, a candle burning on the nightstand beside her. She wanted to curl up in the soft sheets, but the uncertainty of what was to come kept her from getting comfortable. She was out of sorts and had felt so the moment she'd crossed the threshold of Avebury Park. There was no denying that the building was beautiful, and a part of her was instantly bound to it. Being swept up in Simon's enthusiasm and their plans for the future, Mina had been aglow with excitement, but something shifted the moment she'd stepped inside.

Avebury Park was a lovely estate, but the atmosphere inside it was cold. Lifeless. It reminded her of what Simon had said when he proposed. He wanted a home. The brick and mortar were all in place, but something inside it felt dismal. It was too early to identify the source, but Mina was determined to sort it out.

Her current agitation was not helped by the fact that she found herself alone in her private bedchamber, leaving her with a tangle of questions about Simon's expectations for their marriage. Mina was not so naive to be unaware that many couples had separate chambers, but those of her acquaintance eschewed that practice. With Simon's desire for a family, Mina had anticipated a different arrangement.

Perhaps he would join her. Perhaps not. Mina wished she had a little more certainty.

Her eyelids were heavy, and Mina wanted to sleep, but nerves kept her from lying down. A sound came from the next room, and Mina stood, staring at the door adjoining their chambers and waiting to see what Simon would do.

Simon paced his bedchamber. He knew what he should do—what was expected—but he could not force himself to turn the doorknob that would bring him into Mina's bedchamber. He saw the flicker of candlelight through a crack in the door frame and knew Mina was still awake, but he could not do it. The thought of being with her in that way made his stomach twist in knots.

Every time he approached the door, Simon saw Susannah smiling at him, holding his hand, dancing with him. It was silly and stupid, but he felt unfaithful to her and their love. It was one thing to take on a partner and companion; it was another to share that part of himself Simon had thought would only be for Susannah.

Simon dropped onto the bed, his heart heavy with regret.

She was married. He was married. There was no changing those facts. When still on the hunt for a wife, Simon had expected to move forward with his hypothetical marriage in every aspect, but faced with the reality of the moment, Simon could not do it. It was agonizing to cross this threshold with someone other than Susannah.

And then there was Mina herself. In all the thoughts of planning the wedding to her, he'd not thought about the wedding night with her. He did not think of Mina in that manner. She was a friend. A chum. Not a lover. Even without Susannah there in his heart, Simon struggled to think about intimacy with Mina. His wife. Likely, Mina had not thought about it any more than he had; their marriage was not based on romance, after all. He was making a fuss about nothing.

Exhaustion pulled at him, his body begging him to slip into bed. It was so much easier than dealing with the problem at hand. Face the issue another day. Blowing out the candle, Simon slid between the covers and slipped off into sleep without a second thought.

Mina watched the mantle clock. With only a single candle

in the room it was too dark to see the numbers accurately, but she saw a fair amount of time pass since the last sound had come from Simon's room. When the final flicker of hope faded, Mina blew out the candle and climbed into bed.

She was a grown woman who had faced more than her fair share of rejection, but tonight's snub was more wretched than the rest. It was one thing to be overlooked in a ballroom; it was another to be cast aside by your husband. For all the lectures Mina had heard about the animalistic natures of men, the one she had married would not even kissed her.

Chapter 10

A blank piece of paper should not be intimidating, but as Mina stared at the sheet sitting on her desk, she felt as though she were facing a monument feat. She dipped the quill in the ink, knocking off the excess, and pressed the nib to the page, still unsure what to write. Mina had no idea how to describe the whirlwind that was her life without worrying her brother. Graham would excuse her postponing this letter until the wedding was over, but two weeks had passed since that day, and Mina could not put it off any longer. Silence would worry him just as much.

Dearest Graham,

Please forgive me for not writing sooner. Things came together in such a hurried state that I'm at a loss to describe it all. I am married. No doubt Louisa-Margaretta has already apprised you of the various details concerning the flowers and lace, so I will be brief. The wedding was uneventful, undistinguished, and unremarked by society as they could not be bothered to remember who the bride was, except for a general sense of disbelief that the Ashbrook spinster was marrying at last. If it weren't for the announcement in the papers, everyone would have believed it to be nothing more than a farce.

That was an easy beginning. Biting and satirical enough to get a good laugh.

With Simon eager to return to the Kingsley estate, the wedding breakfast and trip were postponed, but I was pleased with that decision as I was just as eager to see my new home. Avebury Park is a lovely place, and I am anxious for you to visit, not only to view it but to aid me in taming the wild beast that has taken residence in the Park.

The housekeeper is a terrifying creature. She roams the halls feasting on poor hapless maids who dare cross her path. I am certain she would prefer it if the house were run more like one of your ships. She would march about with a cat o' nine tails at the ready to keep her staff in line. On top of that all, she is not keen on turning over her role as head of household and has been stirring up a quiet mutiny. I believe the stalwart butler, Jennings, is positively afraid of the creature, and Simon and his steward are ignorant of the issue. I will be forced to face down the demon, but my list of allies grows thin. I am in desperate need of my dear brother to come to my aid the next time he is ashore.

Mina smiled at the image of Graham striding through the entrance, bellowing orders like a proper naval commander. Placing the quill down, she leaned her chin on her palm and stared out her sitting room window at the garden below. Joking aside, she knew she needed to do something about the woman.

As much as Mina wished to avoid a confrontation, the house was not run as efficiently as it could be, to say nothing of the general air of melancholy that clung to the servants. It pained her to see them scuttle about the house like frightened children. Within one day of arriving at Avebury Park it was made perfectly clear why Simon had been so desperate for a wife to help shoulder the burdens.

Simon. Just the thought of the man brought a flutter of feelings, and not all of them were pleasant. Confusion stood in the forefront and was becoming Mina's closest companion.

Her busy schedule had been a justifiable excuse to avoid writing Graham, but Mina knew it wasn't the true reason she dreaded writing this letter. Since their arrival as man and wife, Mina had spent much of her time acquainting herself with the household while Simon was busy with the work that had accumulated during his absence. With the exception of mealtimes, they scarcely spent more than a few minutes in each other's company. Not exactly the marriage Mina had expected. Though she was unsure why she had expected more from a marriage of convenience.

It would not be so disheartening if the moments they did share had more substance to them, but there was some discomfort lingering between the two of them. Nothing that worried Mina for their long-term happiness, but it was as though the shift in their relationship brought with it a hitherto nonexistent awkwardness. Mina supposed that was to be expected when one went from a burgeoning friendship to matrimony in the space of a few short weeks.

None of which Mina wished to share with her brother

Mina shook her head at her own fickleness. Sitting here bemoaning that life was imperfect. Things may not be what she'd hoped for, but her life was far more enjoyable than it'd been before Simon. There was so much work to be done and so many things that needed her attention that Mina had no desire to go back to being Louisa-Margaretta's shadow.

Brushing away her silly thoughts, Mina picked up her quill

and realized the nib had grown dull. Pulling through her desk drawers, she hunted for her sharpener, but it was nowhere to be found.

Standing, Mina left her sitting room and made her way through the halls to Simon's study. It was the one place in the house guaranteed to have one. Knocking on the door, Mina inched it open and found the room empty. No doubt, Simon was out inspecting some part of the estate, so Mina wandered to the desk and pulled open a drawer.

Atop all the normal things one would expect to find in a gentleman's desk sat a lady's glove. It was dainty and of fine quality, the type a lovely young lady would wear. With slow movements, Mina picked it up, laying the leather against her larger hand.

For all of Simon's jaded opinions on love, here sat a monument to the truth of the matter. Simon Kingsley was brokenhearted.

The finely stitched initials made it clear whose glove this was. SW. Susannah Weston. Even without it, Mina would have guessed it was hers. There had been rumors of Simon's attachment before Miss Weston had become Mrs. Banfield. At that moment, a memory slid back into Mina's mind, one of Simon and the lady dancing together. Mina no longer remembered where or when it had occurred, but gentlemen do not dance with a lady for two sets without there being a significant reason.

Seeing the love token sheltered in Simon's drawer deflated Mina's spirit. It was one thing for her husband to have emotional scars, but it was another for him to pine for someone else; and there was no other way to categorize the glove's placement of honor. Mina had accepted Simon was not ready for a romantic relationship. It did hurt to know he found her unattractive, but Mina was determined to not let it draw her into the dark depths of despair. Love and attraction can grow. She'd seen it so many times in so many other couples and knew it was possible for her and her husband. Though some formed an instant connection, more often than not, Mina believed it was a gradual thing.

Setting the glove back where she had found it, Mina closed the drawer. There was nothing to be done about that now. She was Mrs. Simon Kingsley, not Susannah. Simon's heart may be fractured, but Mina would not give up on it. On him. Time and patience was all she needed. Their current awkwardness aside, Mina felt something grand and magnificent was possible between them.

Without warning, Mrs. Richards strode into the room. "What are you doing in Mr. Kingsley's study? This is his private sanctuary."

Mina refused to feel like a child caught sneaking cakes from the pantry and narrowed her eyes at the housekeeper. If the woman held her nose any higher in the air, she'd be staring at the ceiling.

"I am looking for a sharpener," said Mina. "My quill is dull, and I've misplaced mine."

"Mr. Kingsley doesn't like people in his study."

"I understand that, but I wish to finish my letter to my brother before I dress for dinner," said Mina. She didn't know why she insisted on explaining herself. This was her home, after all, but Mina didn't know how to go about dealing with this difficult woman. Mina had managed staff in the past, but none had been so rude.

"Dinner isn't until eight," said Mrs. Richards. "You have plenty of time to wait for Mr. Kingsley's return before you go poking about his things."

"But I ordered for dinner to be at six," said Mina. "Eight is far too late."

Mrs. Richards' lips pursed, her nose inching higher into the air. "In London, all posh households know dinner is at eight."

Mina wanted to shout. Mina wanted to kick something. Mina wanted to do some very unladylike things. This woman did not need to make every little thing a battle, but from the moment Mina had arrived at Avebury Park, Mrs. Richards had been intractable.

"We are not in London," said Mina, "and I specifically instructed that dinner be at six."

"At Avebury Park, we eat at eight. My mistress was always very particular about the proper way of doing things. She was so fancy and fashionable, my mistress," she replied. "Besides, Mr. Kingsley prefers a later dinner."

Mina had no reply to either statement. From what little she'd gleaned from their conversations about his family, Simon's mother hadn't taken an active role as mistress at Avebury Park in years, yet Mrs. Richards spoke as though Mina had supplanted the lady. As to the housekeeper's claim about Simon's preference, Mina didn't know her husband well enough to say for certain if it were true or not.

When Mina did not speak, Mrs. Richards' lips curved into a triumphant smile, and she turned around with her nose poking precariously high and left without waiting for Mina's dismissal.

With a sigh, Mina collapsed onto Simon's chair. Rubbing her fingers along her temple, she tried to stave off the headache threatening to strike. Jests aside, Mina needed Graham's help. She was failing and didn't know how to gain control of the situation.

What Mina needed was to dismiss the beast of Avebury Park. There was no conceivable future where Mrs. Richards would bring the spirit and feeling into the household that Mina desired. Mrs. Richards didn't suit Mina, nor did Mina think that likely to change, but she was unsure of how to go about such a task. In her experience, most conflicts in the staff only needed patience and communication to resolve themselves; Mina had never needed to forcibly remove a member of staff from their position.

"Oh, Mina, there you are." Simon's voice startled Mina, making her shoot up from the chair. Her face flamed as she felt, once again, like a child caught doing something naughty.

"I'm sorry for intruding into your personal space," she said, tripping over her words. "I was looking for a quill sharpener and—"

"This is your home," he interjected. "You are welcome to it. Check the upper left-hand drawer."

Simon dropped a few letters on his desk and sat down in the chair opposite Mina. She pulled the drawer open, snatching up a sharpener, and sat back down. The two of them sat for a quiet moment that wasn't entirely comfortable, but Mina couldn't let this stand between them. They needed to reclaim the friendship they had, so she grasped onto anything that might spark a conversation.

"What have you been up to today?" she asked.

Simon gave her a smile, and a bit of the tension faded. "It's been a wonderful day. I'm finally caught up on my work, which is a relief," he said before launching into a description of what he'd done. His passion for it captivated Mina's attention. It was hard not to get swept up in his excitement for the good and his frustration at the bad. Simon cared so much for his land, his employees, and his tenants that Mina's heart warmed even more towards him.

Chapter 11

The carriage bobbed, and Mina ran nervous hands across her knees. Her dress and coiffure were as close to perfection as she could manage, and Simon looked as dashing as ever. The evening would be a success. Mina knew it would be.

The thought of attending an assembly full of strangers made Mina queasy, but the promise of dancing with Simon made her forge through the nerves threatening to ruin the evening. With him at her side, Mina knew everything would be perfect. No longer relegated to the sidelines to be politely ignored, Mina would dance with her husband and enjoy herself in the way she'd always wanted to.

Their first outing as husband and wife. The first time she'd be presented in public as Mrs. Simon Kingsley. A chance to meet the neighborhood. Having been in residence for such a short period, it was understandable that no one had come to call on her. Most likely, they all thought the newlyweds had not yet arrived home from their wedding trip. This would be Mina's opportunity to find her place in local society.

"You look ready to faint dead away," said Simon. "On my honor, they shan't devour you."

"Said by a man who has never faced down a pack of unforgiving matrons," said Mina. "Regardless of what you do, they probably pat you on the cheek, call you a 'dear boy', and send you on your way."

Simon smiled and did not disagree.

The carriage pulled to a stop, and Simon helped Mina out, tucking her hand in the crook of his arm.

"It shall be fine," he whispered to her.

Entering the assembly hall, Mina felt a wave of peace. The rooms reminded her so much of those back home that it helped Mina forget that the people inhabiting them were strangers.

"Mr. Baxter, Mrs. Baxter." Simon greeted them with a bow before introducing Mina. "The Assembly looks as lovely as ever."

Simon spoke warmly and seemed oblivious to the coldness coming from the couple. Perhaps it was Mina's imagination, but she got the strong feeling that they were not particularly happy to see either of the Kingsleys, though Mina could not imagine what they found so detestable. As far as small talk went, the conversation was stilted and unremarkable, with the exception of the severe eye Mrs. Baxter gave her every time Mina deigned to speak.

"Mrs. Baxter, would you be willing to introduce Mrs. Kingsley around?" asked Simon, as he caught sight of a gentleman on the other side of the room. "Mr. Drake is begging me to join him in the cards room."

Mina tried to keep the panic from her expression, though from the tightening of Mrs. Baxter's lips, Mina knew the lady had seen it. Anxiety pushed Mina to call after Simon and beg him to return, but she would not give into such an entirely pathetic and desperate impulse. Besides, she refused to coerce her husband to stay at her side.

Mrs. Baxter led Mina to another group of ladies, and Mina sent out a silent prayer that she would get through this. The important thing was that she had a companion beside her. However unlikable Mrs. Baxter appeared to be, it was better to have someone at her side than to go it alone. Mina wished she could muster up more bravery, but approaching strangers was beyond her capability. Mina didn't lack conversation if approached, but to insert herself into unsolicited discussions made her sweat and tremble in a very awkward fashion.

The ladies in the group were all Mrs. Baxter's age, though there were a few interspersed that looked to be daughters in their early twenties. Mina tried to act as though at ease, even if she was too young to fit in with the matrons and too old to fit in with the daughters. Mrs. Baxter performed the necessary introductions, but Mina forgot the names the moment she heard them. Names were not Mina's strong suit.

"So, you are Mrs. Kingsley," said one of the ladies. Mrs. Coombs? Crewe? "I've been most anxious to make your acquaintance."

Mina smiled and hoped it didn't look too tight or pained. "I've been looking forward to mixing with Bristow society."

"Yes," the lady said with a grin that looked far too predatory for Mina's comfort. "Well, I've been so interested in seeing the lady who caught our Mr. Kingsley. As none of our local girls enticed him, I knew you must be a rare breed of woman." The way the lady said 'rare breed' reminded Mina forcibly of the girls she'd known during her Seasons in London; the type that flatters one's face before plunging the metaphorical knife in one's unsuspecting back.

"Oh, yes," added another of the ladies. "I hear you had a whirlwind courtship. It happened so fast that no one in Town appears to have known about it."

"A speedy love match," said Mrs. Baxter, the barest hint of ridicule lacing her words. "Mr. Kingsley must have been excessively entranced by you."

The carefully chosen words. The delicate tone and emphasis. Mina had been in society for too long to be naive to their meaning. They were mocking her. They knew Simon was no more in love with her than his horse. Probably less, for at least he'd spent several years getting to know his steed. Knowing the ladies' intent should have made it easier to deflect the barbs, but they struck too close to Mina's vulnerabilities.

She wished she had some witty rejoinder to send back, but none came to mind. Mina never knew how to deal with the society cats that adored clawing at her. She found it better to avoid them but caught up in Mrs. Baxter's web, Mina was stuck talking with these ladies.

This was going to be a long evening.

...

It had taken Mina well over an hour to separate herself from Mrs. Baxter and her cold-hearted cronies and now found herself in a very familiar spot. True, she'd never been in this assembly hall before, but Mina was well acquainted with the ostracized edges of the ballroom. She'd spent many an hour there and found they were basically the same, regardless of the venue. Sitting in her chair, she watched the dancers, tapping her foot along to the music. If she focused on the lively tunes and the beauty of the room, she may be able to forget the unmitigated disaster this evening had become.

Mina knew she was a fool for expecting her role in society to change. It wasn't that she'd anticipated some magic transformation, but Mina had believed tonight would be different. At a bare minimum, Simon would dance with her and be the friend she'd thought him to be.

Her thoughts were growing too maudlin. The despair of the evening was wearing at her, forcing tears into Mina's eyes. She fought them back, blinking and covertly fanning her face, but there was not a thing to be done about the matter.

From somewhere to the right, a conversation caught Mina's attention. A group of young ladies stood gathered together a short distance away, and though she did not recognize any of them, the leader looked too similar to Mrs. Baxter to be anything other than the lady's accursed progeny. With their heads together and their fans flapping in a perfectly practiced manner, they gossiped in the exact same fashion as their mamas.

Mina sighed. She had just escaped such conversations, but it appeared she was to be subjected to another round of genteel mockery.

"...I must say I am shocked that they would parade around as if nothing were amiss," said the young Miss Baxter.

"After the way Mr. Kingsley treated you, I am surprised he would wish to stay in the neighborhood," added another of the girls.

Their mamas were far more expert at their subtle criticisms and backhanded compliments; these girls needed more practice to be as deadly, but no doubt they were on their way to flourishing careers as backbiting society matrons.

"His finances must be far worse than he lets on," said Miss Baxter. "Why else would he marry such an unattractive thing? I hear she came with a hefty dowry."

"That's not the only thing hefty about her," tittered the third girl.

"Even so, the dowry wasn't grand enough to entice any of the other gentlemen in London. They say she is nearly thirty," said the first cohort with a tone that made thirty sound as though it was akin to a bout of the black plague.

Mina *was* thirty, to be precise, but the girls weren't looking for precision. They were looking to cause pain; speaking with the edge of a hushed tone to make it sound unintentional but with enough volume to carry. It was not the first time Mina had endured such treatment. If only it wasn't so effective. She knew she shouldn't care about the opinion of these shallow people, but as much as Mina wished to dismiss them, their words pierced her heart.

"So, you are the young lady who snapped up Simon Kingsley."

Mina blinked a few times, pushing away the tears before raising her gaze to the elderly woman standing before her with a regality that would put the Royal Family to shame. Mina was not in the mood to deal with another person come to gawk and mock, but as much as she wanted to ignore the lady, Mina's manners wouldn't allow it. Even if the lady's own manners allowed her to approach without an introduction.

"I rather think it was he who snapped me up," replied Mina. It was an accurate reflection of her marital situation, and Mina hadn't meant it to be a clever verbal parry, but the lady chuckled nonetheless.

"I've wanted to meet Bristow's newest resident," the lady said before sitting down beside Mina. "I would've come by Avebury Park for a proper introduction, but I was out visiting my grandchildren and only arrived home yesterday."

Before either Mina or the mystery lady said another word, a pair of Mrs. Baxter's friends approached with a curtsy to the lady beside Mina.

"Lady Lovell, it is so good to see you returned to us," said one of the ladies, followed closely by the other saying, "We hope your travels were enjoyable."

Lady Lovell's eyelids lowered a touch, though she showed no other outward signs of emotion. She also did not speak. Apparently, her manners allowed more leeway than Mina's.

"Mr. Ellis and I were so hoping you would be back in time for our dinner party next Thursday," said the first lady.

"As I have not accepted any of your other invitations, I don't see why I would do so now," said Lady Lovell, placing both her hands atop her cane. The lady's gaze turned so cold, Mina was surprised the others had the fortitude to stay standing, though she noticed Mrs. Ellis tremble.

"Dear," said Lady Lovell to Mrs. Ellis, "I hate to say it, but you must look to your daughter." She nodded her head towards one of Miss Baxter's confidants who was now entertaining a group of laughing young men, flirting flagrantly with each of the gentleman. "With the tear on her flounce, one might get the most audacious ideas about what she has been up to while your attention is so divided."

Mrs. Ellis paled and hurried over to her daughter with the

other lady trailing behind her. Taking the girl by the arm, Mrs. Ellis hurried her daughter into a sitting room to assess the damage, though Mina noticed no issues with the girl's dress.

"Jumped up nincompoops," said Lady Lovell. "It makes them feel important to bow and scrape at my feet, though they'd be shocked and dismayed if they knew they were attempting to win over a merchant's daughter. It's insufferable."

Throughout her speech, Lady Lovell became more animated, even knocking her cane against the floor to punctuate her words. Such a caustic appraisal of society would sound harsh coming from any other person, but Lady Lovell did it with just a hint of self-derision to make her words humorous.

"One must be careful with whom one associates," said Mina. "Being in trade is a serious condition that afflicts most of the population. It would be horrible to catch such a dreaded disease." Mina had heard Thea's husband joking about such matters on more than one occasion, having been inflicted with it for over a decade.

For a brief moment, Mina was unsure if her humor was acceptable to Lady Lovell. Having just met the lady, she couldn't be certain that such teasing would not be offensive. But she got a sense that Lady Lovell was no ordinary society matron, and Mina was rewarded with a deep laugh from the lady in question.

"My dear," said Lady Lovell, "having watched the local harpies sharpen their claws on you, I would not have guessed that you had such pluck. I'm glad to discover I was wrong."

Mina's face heated a touch. "I fear I do not always make the best impressions in settings like this among women like them."

"They are a gruesome bunch."

Mina chuckled at that. "And as my husband has seen fit to abandon me to their clutches, I've found it imperative to cry retreat."

"Never give up ground to ones such as them," said Lady Lovell. "It will cost you dearly."

True words, Mina had to admit. If only she knew how to stand her ground.

Lady Lovell watched Mina with a careful eye, and Mina wondered what the lady saw. A moment later, Lady Lovell tapped her cane against the ground and declared, "I wasn't sure what to expect when I came over, but I just know I'm going to enjoy you immensely. I've decided you and I are going to be good friends, Mrs. Kingsley. No, I am sorry, but that will not do. I refuse to call you anything but Wilhelmina."

"That would be delightful, but I prefer Mina, Lady Lovell," she said with a smile.

"Imogene, please," she replied, "and I'll warn you now that I am extremely interfering and opinionated and must be immediately excused if I ruffle your feathers."

"Then you must excuse me when I choose not to listen to your interfering opinions," Mina teased.

Imogene laughed. "Like I said, I'm going to enjoy you. But as my first act as your dear friend, I'll tell you to not listen to a word those ladies say. They are simply seething with anger that your husband chose you instead of one of the local horse-toothed harpies."

Mina stifled a snort.

"I apologize for being so harsh, but really," said Imogene. "For all their prancing about as though they are the *crème de la crème* of British society, they are far from it. If it were not for their outrageously rude behavior to anyone below their notice, I'd simply ignore them, but when they choose to go out of their way to be cruel I cannot let it stand."

As the two women talked and laughed, Mina thought the evening was not a complete loss. And just as the clock chimed ten o'clock, Mina saw her husband striding towards her. The thrill of seeing him approach flushed away the last remnants of the women's vitriol. He was coming to dance with her, making the evening complete. Simon would approach, offer his hand, and lead her through the next set.

What a tedious evening. Simon didn't understand why anyone enjoyed dances. Unattached lads and lasses endured them for the chance of a romantic encounter, but beyond that, they served no purpose except to torture and annoy the guests. Married women gossiped and vied for social status, and their husbands (who were there under duress) gambled and drank the time away. At least this time, his status as a married man kept him safe from the machinations of the matchmaking mamas and the desperate debutantes. That was a small blessing.

He hoped Mina'd had her fill, and they could escape home.

Scanning the room, Simon found her sitting at the edge of the dance floor, deep in conversation with Lady Lovell. The two ladies looked diverted, and Simon was pleased to see Mina fitting into Bristow society so easily.

As he approached, Mina turned and smiled at him, her face lighting up with unabashed joy; her eyes glowed and her entire face transformed. She may not be a classical beauty in any sense of the word, but that look gave her something different and unique that Simon found striking.

"Good evening, Mr. Kingsley," said Lady Lovell. "I've been acquainting myself with your lovely wife. You certainly had your head on straight when you married her."

Mina's cheeks flushed a violent shade of red, and Simon found himself amused at her artless embarrassment at the compliment.

"I certainly believe so," said Simon with a quick bow before addressing his wife, "but if I may, I was wondering if you were ready to leave."

Mina stiffened, her face freezing in a grimace-like smile. Lady Lovell's right eyebrow drew upwards, and Simon was at a loss to understand what he'd done wrong. That eyebrow was far too accusatory to ignore.

"I'm done in and assumed you would be, too, after a couple hours of dancing, but if you'd rather stay, I am certain I can find another card game," Simon offered rather magnanimously, if he did say so himself. He was ready to leave, but if Mina were desperate to stay, he'd find something to do. Mr. Baxter had been more than happy to win a few quid off Simon, and Simon had been more than willing to part with it as it had warmed Mr. Baxter's attitude towards him considerably.

Mina's eyes looked watery, and Simon couldn't understand why. He was being courteous and obliging. He hadn't demanded anything of her. He simply expressed a desire to leave, and the woman was getting emotional.

"No, we can leave," she said, blinking back the moisture while she stood.

"It was lovely to meet you, my girl, and I'll be sure to come by for a visit tomorrow, if you're willing to entertain an old biddy like me," said Lady Lovell with a smile.

Mina's face regained a degree of the former radiance as she replied, "You are always welcome, Imogene."

Lady Lovell's grin dropped as she turned her eyes to Simon and gave him the clipped farewell, "Mr. Kingsley."

Simon cut a quick bow and escorted Mina away, unsure how he had become the ogre in this scenario. These women must be twisting his words into something sinister or cold hearted, and the thought chaffed. His mood only grew darker as Mina's spirits grew visibly melancholy during the carriage ride home.

Marriage was not supposed to be so complicated or irritating.

Tonight was far worse than any other ball or assembly Mina had suffered through. With the bright exception of Imogene, Mina had been mocked, criticized, and ignored, which was not wholly unlike other balls or dances she'd attended, but Simon's behavior crippled Mina's heart.

"If you wanted to stay, you should have said so," said Simon, nearly growling in his displeasure as he stared out the carriage window at the passing darkness. "I wasn't forcing you to leave."

"It's not that," said Mina, her voice sounding pathetic.

"Then what?"

Mina did not know how to answer in a way that would not make her sound like a miserable child. Or worse, make Simon pity her and her antisocial ways. To admit she wanted to dance would only make him feel obligated to stand up with her, and that was not what she wanted. Not truly. She wanted him to desire to do so of his own volition. She'd seen him do so with plenty of other ladies before, so it was clear he didn't have a passionate distaste for it. If his partner was enticing enough.

For once, Mina had hoped to have a willing partner. Instead, she had a man who hadn't even noticed she'd been a wallflower the entire evening.

There was no way to explain it all, so Mina said, "It's nothing. Truly."

Mina didn't know why she'd bothered speaking as both of them knew it was untrue. Simon scowled at the window and grew more tense and distant with every passing second. When they arrived home, Mina didn't wait for his assistance and hurried out of the carriage and up the front steps, not slowing until she was safely away in her room, the tears coming before she shut the door behind her.

Only a few weeks in, and Mina wondered if Simon regretted their marriage.

Chapter 12

Light came through the dining room windows, casting the space in a brilliant morning glow. The beauty of it was lost on Mina as she stifled a yawn. She wished her exhaustion was because of a night full of dancing and frivolity at the assembly, but there was nothing joyful about the disappointments and worries that had driven her to toss and turn in her bed. After hours of attempting to sleep, Mina had given it up as a lost cause and went to work. Before breakfast had been laid out, Mina had written several letters, organized her art room, taken a stroll through the gardens, read some of the latest issue of *Ackermann's Repository*, and practiced on the pianoforte. She should've met with the housekeeper to discuss menus and household concerns, but Mrs. Richards studiously avoided Mina most mornings.

Smearing blackberry jam on her roll, Mina went through her schedule for the day. The household had no interest in her opinion, but there was still plenty for her to do. She could visit the tenants in the afternoon; one of the first things she had done as Mrs. Kingsley had been to meet each of them, but that had been more social in nature, and it was prudent to go again and see what she might do to help them and the village. If she wasn't mistaken, there was a school, so that did not need to be organized, but there might be improvements to be made.

And there was the yarn she needed to purchase for a baby blanket. Normally, Mina preferred having one ready for the tenants before the babe arrived, but as the Johnsons' youngest had done so just before Mina's own arrival, there was no choice but to make it after the fact.

And she should find out if the vicar and his wife had a charity box for the new additions to the area; if not, she could put one together with all the necessary baby items to help ease the financial burden to the needy families.

Mina bit into the roll and took a sip of her hot chocolate, savoring the flavor. She didn't know what Cook put in it, but there was a special something extra in it that drew out the rich flavors.

In truth, she knew what needed to happen today. The other duties could be attended to later, and dealing with matters of the household was Mina's first priority. No matter how much she dreaded the inevitable difficulties. Mrs. Richards was a formidable woman, and Mina already knew she was not a woman to be crossed. Yet, that was precisely what Mina intended to do.

The dining room door opened, and Simon entered. Both he and Mina froze, and she would bet a pony (as her brothers would say) that he was reliving the awkwardness of the previous night just as she was.

"I didn't expect you up so early," said Simon with a nod before striding to the table. He hesitated only a moment before selecting the chair beside Mina. She didn't know if that action was to be interpreted as a good sign or a bad one. The hesitation was certainly unwelcome.

"I am always up at this time of the day," said Mina. Her morning routine was firmly set, just as Simon's was. They were regular enough that within days of their marriage, both of them were well aware of the other's daily habits.

"In my experience, the morning after an assembly, ball, or party sees little of ladies," said Simon as the footman brought out his usual breakfast.

Mina halted mid-bite and stared at him. She knew there were still a lot of mysteries surrounding their personalities, but Mina was surprised that he expected such behavior from her. At least the man had the sense to look chagrined when he noticed her expression.

"Perhaps my mother and sisters are not the best examples," he said, spreading a napkin across his lap. "You've shown yourself to be quite different than them."

The words sounded right, though his tone held another dose of hesitancy. Mina was uncertain herself where that sentiment came from, though she suspected it could be attributed to last night's interlude. After hours of fitful thoughts, Mina decided Simon had been oblivious about her feelings, and no doubt, he'd made his own inferences about her behavior.

The conversation halted, dying on the vine as the two of them munched, and Mina was at a loss as to how it could be mended, but before she could think of a topic, Simon spoke.

"Are you feeling better?"

Mina felt his unwillingness to ask it. Likely, Simon was terrified she'd be reduced to further hysterics.

"Yes, thank you," she said. It wasn't a lie exactly. She was no longer weeping at random intervals, so Mina thought she was better, but not by much.

"It looks like the weather will be fine today," he said, staring into his teacup.

For the first time in hours, Mina felt like smiling. The weather. The most inane and innocuous topic. Used to divert unpleasant conversations or spark one where there was none, it was a staple of British gentility. To hear him resort to such tactics made her want to laugh.

"Indeed," she said, hiding her smile behind a sip of hot chocolate. "It would be a perfect day to take a ride out on Beau, but Louisa-Margaretta still has not sent him. I miss a good ride in the morning."

"Yes, I remember you said you enjoyed that," said Simon,

looking her in the eyes for the first time. "There are quite a few fine animals in the stables you could use in the meantime."

"Thank you, but I could not possibly allow myself to be unfaithful to my dear Beau. He is too good a friend for me to treat him so poorly."

"He's a temperamental beast?"

"Hardly," she replied, filling her words with a hint of melodrama, "but he does get forlorn when I leave him each Season, and I've found the only remedy is to remain true to him in my absence."

Simon gave Mina a smile, and her heart grew lighter for it. "When are your things to arrive?" he asked.

"Another few weeks at the very least. With the wedding, Louisa-Margaretta and my brother decided to leave London early in order to pack my things. She insisted on overseeing the project herself, so it's likely we might be celebrating our anniversary before it arrives."

Slowly at first, the conversation picked up, and some of the awkwardness melted away. Not in its entirety, but it was a start.

...

This exhausting day was not even halfway through, and Mina felt as though it had stretched on for weeks. She leaned forward on the sofa, rubbing her temple. She'd taken a tisane, but Mina knew from experience that her headache would not dissipate so easily. A byproduct of her sleepless night, the only cure for it was the one thing Mina couldn't get. She'd attempted a nap, but her mind remained too restless for such things.

Examining the drawing room, Mina distracted herself by redecorating it in her mind. It had to be one of her favorite spaces in the house. The windows opened to the garden, filling the room with a floral perfume, and it received the perfect amount of light in the afternoon. All in all, it had the makings of an ideal room for entertaining, even if it was not the ideal room for making grand statements of wealth and pomp. It was smaller than the formal sitting room and was far more simply decorated, making it clear to Mina that the previous mistress of Avebury Park had not put much thought into the space. But with just a few touches here and there, Mina knew it would fit her needs admirably.

The door opened, and a footman entered. "Lady Lovell, ma'am."

Mina nodded and stood.

The woman in question breezed in through the door, thumping her cane all along the way. Without waiting for Mina to invite her, she sat down on the sofa opposite Mina and gave her a long, scrutinizing look.

"You didn't sleep well," she said.

"Would you like some refreshment?" asked Mina.

"None of your polite diversionary tactics," said Imogene, punctuating the statement with a crack of her cane. "Out with it."

"No, I did not sleep well," replied Mina, feeling the first flutters of a smile lightening her spirits.

Imogene sat silent for a moment. "That's it? No deeper explanation? No weeping and wailing? Cursing your husband to the eternal pits of hell? I expected much more entertainment, Mina. I'm disappointed."

At that, Mina laughed. The woman looked so put-out, but in a good natured, comical way and not at all like the poisonous gossipmongers that littered society.

Imogene's face shifted, her eyes growing soft. "Laughter aside, I'm serious, my dear. How are you faring?"

Mina could handle pushing and prodding, but the heartfelt question brought tears to her eyes. Mina felt lost in a sea of uncertainty, and Imogene had just thrown her a rope. There was no one for her to talk to. She wrote Thea daily, but the mother of four (five, if you counted Frederick, which Thea often did) had her hands full with her brood. Even with Mina shouldering the cost of the post, Thea could not afford the time to correspond as often as Mina wished. That aside, it was never as consoling as a proper *tête-à-tête*.

Though she knew she must make a pathetic picture, Mina unraveled the story in its entirety to Imogene. Her life, her disappointments, her marriage, all laid bare before this relative stranger. But Mina couldn't help herself. Once begun, there was no stopping the confusing mess from spilling forth.

As it progressed, Imogene shifted closer until she moved to sit beside Mina and put an arm around her shoulders.

"You dear girl," said Imogene, her voice rough. "After our short conversation last night, I had an inkling that I would adore you, and this just confirms it."

Mina glanced at her.

"Do not give me that look, Wilhelmina Kingsley," said Imogene with a stern yet grandmotherly eye before retrieving a handkerchief from her reticule and placing it Mina's hand. "We are very alike, you and I. Not in all things, but in our hearts, I believe we are kindred spirits. And as I said last night, I am domineering and opinionated, so you must accept my statement as fact."

Mina gave a watery chuckle, dabbing at her eyes with the handkerchief. "You must think I am a gudgeon."

"No, I think you're hopelessly optimistic and kind, though the world has taught you to be otherwise."

Imogene opened her reticule and retrieved a portrait. It was of a young man with a powdered wig, the type Mina had seen in her family's portraits from fifty or sixty years ago.

"This is my husband, Gilbert," said Imogene, her fingers brushing the metal frame. "My dearest love, though it took me several years of marriage to realize it."

Imogene smiled at Mina's look of confusion. "Like many of our age, we had an arranged marriage. Not terribly different than your own, though Gilbert was looking more for a handsome dowry than a helpmate. The first years of our marriage were difficult. There was no love and little kindness.

"Like you, I struggled with society, but it was because of my low birth and perceived pretension at marrying so far above my station. I let my struggles bleed into my marriage, and Gilbert let his frustrations at losing his bachelor lifestyle do the same. But eventually," Imogene paused and repeated that with emphasis, "*eventually*, that changed. First, we had cordiality. Then respect. Then friendship followed. From that grew the greatest love I could've ever imagined."

Imogene laid the portrait down and took Mina's hands in hers. The warmth and kindness in the lady's eyes and the gentle reassurance of her touch brought more tears to Mina's eyes. She was a grown woman who should not need such mothering, but Mina was grateful to receive it all the same.

"Don't give up hope," Imogene said. "From what you say, you and Simon have a stronger foundation than we did, and he is far more mature and sensible than Gilbert was at his age. Be patient. All men have varying degrees of obtuseness written into their makeup. It is in their blood and there's no helping it, but given time, he will see your true value and love you all the more for it."

Mina nodded. It was too early to give up hope of a happy ending.

Imogene patted Mina's knee and gave a firm nod. "Now, tell me all about this cottage of yours. It sounds lovely."

Chapter 13

Mina took a deep breath, forcing her hands to unclench. Wringing them would display weakness, something she couldn't do if she were to win the forthcoming battle. Thinking of the regal ladies of her acquaintance, Mina summoned their spirits to strengthen her own.

The formal sitting room gave an especially austere air to the occasion. As the ladies of the neighborhood continued to boycott her society, Mina hardly spent any time in it, but it was the perfect arena for the skirmish. Sitting on the edge of the sofa with the most perfectly composed posture, Mina waited for the fight to commence.

Having spent a month studying the household and familiarizing herself with its strengths and weaknesses, Mina was as prepared as she could be to face Mrs. Richards. Despite the indomitable housekeeper's best efforts to keep her in the dark, Mina knew every in and out of the household. A grown lady should not be forced to sneak around her own home, but Mina had found herself in that unenviable position and had seen with her own eyes just how deplorable conditions were in Avebury Park, and Mina would not stand for it.

Without bothering to knock, the beast entered, and Mina

readied her weapons.

"You called?" Mrs. Richards asked. With two words, the woman conveyed both annoyance and disdain, and Mina was decidedly sick of it.

"Mrs. Richards, as it was imprudent to make changes the moment I arrived without knowing how this household runs, I waited before addressing things," said Mina. "But the time has arrived to discuss the operation of Avebury Park."

"You disapprove of the way I run the household?" Mrs. Richards' lips pursed, her nose tipping towards the ceiling.

Mina recognized the defensiveness and felt a trembling in her hands. She wanted a rational discussion, not a heated argument.

"You've done an excellent job," said Mina. Normally, she did not approve of lying, but in this instance it was a necessity that fell more into the range of diplomacy than dishonesty; caution was needed when dealing with a woman who had the personality of an annoyed badger. "But I have opinions on some areas that could be improved. A different perspective can be very helpful in discovering new levels of efficiency, don't you agree?"

"If the household is already efficient, why go to the bother of changing it?" she asked.

At that moment, Mina had a shocking revelation. Mrs. Richards reminded her of Jeb Oliver, her family's stable master. He was ornery and stubborn to a fault, but Mina had grown to love the curmudgeon. He had a soft spot for horses and those who shared his fondness for the creatures. It was through that shared passion that Mina had won him over. She just needed to find a common ground with this battle axe of a housekeeper.

"Perhaps efficiency isn't the best word, but I care deeply about the success of this household," said Mina, grabbing onto that hopeful connection they shared. "I have a few ideas that worked in my family's households that could make Avebury Park a better place to live and work. It wouldn't hurt to discuss them."

Mina hated that she sounded as though she were begging to be allowed the chance to fulfill her role as mistress of the house, but her pride was unimportant if she reached an understanding with her irascible servant. Slow and steady handling would work better to sway Mrs. Richards.

Without waiting for Mina's invitation, Mrs. Richards sat on the opposite sofa. Mina could only imagine how her mama would have reacted to such presumption, but in the moment, Mina felt grateful that the housekeeper appeared opened to discussion. Moderately open.

"I desire to see greater economy when it comes to meals," said Mina. "Mr. Kingsley and I do not need such fine and costly dishes every night. I prefer simpler fare—"

"And make us look like paupers?" Mrs. Richards' tone made it sound as though 'pauper' were the worst possible thing a person could be called.

"I am not speaking of dinner parties and social gatherings," said Mina. "I am speaking of the day to day menus."

"The household accounts can handle the expense," said Mrs. Richards with that tell-tale nose creeping upwards.

Mina focused on her hands, attempting to keep them the picture of confidence. "Just because we have the funds does not mean we should waste them. Besides, we could use that excess and invest it in improving the servants' quarters. We have far too frequent changes in the staff, and I believe that happens in part because of the poor quality of their living spaces. I've been to poorhouses that have a more inviting atmosphere. Our servants' quarters have only the barest of bedding, candles, and fires to keep them alive, and their meals are hardly fit to feed the pigs."

"So, you'd have me feed the master inferior food in order to provide the servants with better lives?" Mrs. Richards' nose was higher than Mina had ever seen. This was not going the way she'd wanted.

"You've shown incredible economy," said Mina, trying to keep her voice calm and reasonable, "but there's no reason to allow the servants to be so mistreated. It is important to Mr. Kingsley and me that Avebury Park be efficiently run and an enjoyable place to visit and reside. A massive component of that is our servants. If nothing else, treating them so poorly leads to them giving notice, which cases upheaval. I have seen this in my family's households. A happy staff results in stronger loyalty and long-term benefits that—"

"You'd prefer to allow them free rein to come and go as they please? Why don't we invite them to move into the family wing?" interrupted Mrs. Richards, her voice rising. "I will not allow you to make me a laughingstock when the household comes to ruin with your outlandish ideas. Mr. Kingsley has been very happy with my work all these years, and I don't mean to change."

There was a glint in the woman's eye that chilled Mina's heart. She was well versed in the household's accounts and finances, and there was plenty of money and no need to treat the servants so shabbily. Mina had assumed Mrs. Richards was simply a skinflint, but listening to her talk about the servants in such hostile terms, it was clear that Mrs. Richards had no love for Avebury Park or its residents. She loved only herself and her employer's ostentatious lifestyle that elevated her in the eyes of her peers. She loved the power she held over the lower servants.

Mina was no novice. She knew and understood the cut-throat positioning among the servants. She appreciated Mrs. Richards' pride in her lofty station, and Mina would never wish to hurt the housekeeper's feelings by making her feel as though she'd been downgraded in position. However, Mina saw the truth of the matter. What angered Mrs. Richards was the improvements to the servants' living quarters. It was not economy that drove the woman to treat the staff like chattel; it was cruelty, and Mina could not abide a bully and tormentor.

Before Mina responded, the door opened, and Simon strode inside, leaving Mina caught between relief at having an ally and embarrassment at needing one.

"I heard raised voices," he said at Mina's questioning

glance.

"Mrs. Kingsley is demanding I change things," said Mrs. Richards before Mina had a chance to even greet her husband. Jumping to her feet, the housekeeper turned to Simon. "I've been running this household for twenty years, and I do not want to see all my work pulled apart on a whim."

Mina opened her mouth to reply to that provoking comment, but Mrs. Richards continued. "What she is suggesting will cause disruption and havoc."

"And destroy the very fabric of the estate?" asked Simon, a teasing eyebrow raised at Mrs. Richards.

"Of course not, sir," the woman said with the perfect air of contrition and a fair amount more respect than Mina had seen in Mrs. Richards in the entirety of their acquaintance. "It would take more than that to harm Avebury Park, but I don't see the benefit of overturning the entire system just because the new mistress wants things done differently. It's enough of a struggle to keep the house running without changing things for the sake of change."

That was far cry from what Mina was proposing, but it was clear from the shift in Simon's expression that Mrs. Richards had chosen the right argument to engage her employer's interest. Simon's teasing glint disappeared, and his gaze grew concerned as he looked at Mina. Before she had a chance to defend herself, Simon dismissed Mrs. Richards. Judging by the housekeeper's superior air as she strutted from the sitting room, she knew who had won this argument.

At least Simon had the good sense to wait until the door was firmly closed behind Mrs. Richards before he spoke. Mina rose to her feet, feeling like a young girl awaiting a scolding.

"What is happening, Mina?" he asked. "The last thing we need is more issues among the staff, and I don't want to be forced into mediating between you and them."

His tone was polite, but the words pained Mina. Though said without a hint of anger, Simon's frustration was clearly felt.

"There are issues with the way Mrs. Richards has been running the household," she said, her cheeks burning. It was silly to get so emotional that tears pricked at her eyes, but to have him side with Mrs. Richards without even asking for clarification hurt deeply. "Yes, I want to make changes but only to improve things."

Simon drew closer, his hands settling on Mina's shoulders. It should not feel so comforting to have that bit of contact, but Mina's traitorous heart wouldn't listen to reason.

"I didn't mean to upset you," he said.

His hands fell away, and Mina was disconcerted at how much she felt their loss.

"I am sure you are right, and there are things that need to change," he said. "However, you need to be cautious about upsetting the way things have been. Mrs. Richards has a lot of experience running a household. Things haven't been perfect, and I hope you will improve it, but I would hate to see everything upended just because we do things differently than at your family's estate."

Mina wished she were braver and had the fortitude to speak up at that moment. Simon married her for the purpose of helping out with the household. It was clear that things were not working, and Mina wished to fix them, but however unknowingly, Simon was effectively tying her hands when it came to Mrs. Richards simply because he feared Mina would upset things further. He'd expressed confidence in her abilities when he'd married her, but obviously he did not trust them as much as Mrs. Richards'.

Simon wanted a wife to make things better but without changing the way things were run. Mina wondered if he saw the hypocrisy in his actions, but as most people were blind to their own shortcomings, she doubted it.

"Are you interested in attending the assembly on Friday?" he asked.

Having been so lost in her own thoughts, Mina hadn't noticed the shift in conversation until Simon asked her a second time.

"The assembly?" Mina blinked, struggling to gather her wits. "I'm surprised you would ask. You don't seem to enjoy them."

"I don't," said Simon with a self-derisive smile. "I only attend under duress, but I would gladly accompany you if you desire to go."

Mina's eyebrows raised. "So, you are offering me the opportunity to force you to go?"

"Not my most eloquent of invitations, but you haven't answered my question."

It was not a difficult decision for Mina. Though touched by his offer, Mina had no interest in inflicting an unpleasant evening on either of them.

"Thank you, but no," said Mina. "I find I am not so fond of assemblies."

Mina had never thought of herself as much of an actress, but Simon appeared to believe the lie for he smiled and took his leave. The moment the door was shut behind him, Mina slumped onto the sofa with a heavy sigh.

It wasn't supposed to be this difficult. Mina was just trying to fulfil her role the best she could, and there was no support from the man who had plucked her from her former life and dropped her in the middle of this mess.

Mina yearned for Thea's comfort and good sense. She'd know what to do. Mina could not live like this. It was no better than her life before. At the outset of her marriage, it had seemed like an improvement, but it was now apparent that nothing had changed. She was still subject to an oblivious man while another woman usurped Mina's role as mistress.

This had to be fixed. Things had to change. Mina refused to accept that this was her life. If only she knew what to do. Standing, Mina hurried from the room to fetch her bonnet and a bribe, knowing just the right person to talk to.

Chapter 14

"She did what?" Imogene's voice came out shrill, but her righteous anger on Mina's behalf was comforting. "And he told you to defer to her judgment?" But Imogene needed no confirmation before launching into a tirade about halfwit husbands and upstart servants.

With a displeased huff, Imogene rang the bell sitting on the side table beside her.

"Roger," she said to the footman who entered the sitting room, "please bring us some tea to go with the lemon madeleines Mrs. Kingsley brought me."

"Those were a gift," said Mina. "Advanced payment for listening to my ever-growing list of troubles. You need not share them with me. I know how much you adore them."

Imogene's face softened. "Thank you, my dear, but you cannot expect me to be patient and wait until you've gone to enjoy them, and I cannot do so in front of you, so we must share them. Besides, refreshment is most certainly required to tackle an issue such as this."

"I apologize for foisting my problems on you," said Mina, her shoulders drooping.

Imogene waved off her concerns. "Nonsense, my dear. I'm

honored that you would think to confide in me. I appreciate anyone who simply tells their problems rather than forcing me to winkle it out of them like the interfering biddy I am. It gives us more time to come up with a solution."

"So, it's not hopeless?" asked Mina. She hated that her voice sounded so pathetic. Then again, she hated that she'd come running to Imogene like a lost puppy looking for its mother.

Imogene gave Mina a look that conveyed her deep disdain for such an attitude. "Really, Mina. Don't tell me that you are one of those 'woe is me' misses. I took you for someone made of sterner stuff. It is one thing to be upset and have your moment but giving in to hopelessness is another. Chin up, my dear. You have a difficult road ahead, but it's not insurmountable."

Mina wanted to believe Imogene, but the situation did not seem so hopeful in the moment.

"You are dealing with bad habits on all fronts, I'm afraid," said Imogene. "Mrs. Richards is used to a rudderless ship, and I am guessing you have never dealt with unruly staff before."

Mina did not need to confirm it; the older lady's eyes saw straight through her.

"And it does not help that their previous mistress had such a dislike of domesticity," said Imogene with pursed lips. "Amelia Kingsley never cared about anything other than herself, and you are paying for that, both from the staff and your husband."

The conversation paused for a moment as Imogene's maids brought in the ordered tea. Watching their quick and easy movements, Mina felt quite jealous and homesick for her old household that ran just as efficiently. The servants at Avebury Park were not inept, but Mrs. Richards' strong armed tactics upset the staff, leaving them in no fit state to fulfill their positions to the best of their abilities.

Once the tea and madeleines were served and the maids gone, Mina asked the question she had wanted to since Imogene mentioned the former mistress of Avebury Park.

"What did you mean about Simon's mother?" asked Mina.

"I'm afraid I know little about his family. He rarely speaks of them, and most of my friends are as little acquainted with the ins and outs of society gossip as I am."

Imogene nibbled on a madeleine with a coy smile. "That puts me in a terrible bind, my dear. To tell you the truth would land me in the role of gossiping busybody."

Mina blushed, but before she opened her mouth to apologize, Imogene laughed. "I am jesting, Mina. As you well know, I adore being a busybody. Though only on the side of the righteous, of course. However, I feel in these circumstances, it would be best for you to get the story from your husband. I will say that Amelia and John Kingsley married for love in a time when most marriages were arranged on some level, but what little love they had soured quickly."

That piqued Mina's curiosity, and she desperately wanted to wheedle the rest out of Imogene, but Mina sensed there was a lot to Simon's family history and knew that Imogene was probably right. Until Simon was ready to tell her himself, it was enough to know that the Kingsleys were a damaged family.

Mina sipped her tea, more from an innate response to the cup in her hand than a desire for the drink. Simon was such a mystery, and she wanted nothing more than to run to him and shake every secret free, but to force him to do so would only harm their tenuous relationship. Unfortunately, Mina knew she needed patience. A quality she was running short on at present.

Never mind the underlying fear that lurked in the nether reaches of her heart—that time may not be enough for her and Simon.

"I see a lot of thoughts churning in your mind, my dear," said Imogene between nibbles. "It is best to let them out or you will end up a Bedlamite."

Mina set down the dish and gathered her hands in her lap. Staring down at her fingers, she struggled for the words.

"I..." she began, though she faltered. Thea had expressed these same concerns when Mina had agreed to this insane arrangement, but at the time, Mina had felt far more certain than she did now.

"Mina," Imogene prompted, her voice tinged with kindness. Mina looked up and found Imogene's eyes gazing into hers. Neither of her grandmothers had shown much of a maternal nature towards Mina and her brothers, and seeing it in Imogene's eyes warmed Mina's heart. It had been so long since she'd had a mother figure of any sort in her life that Mina's soul latched onto Imogene. Luckily, the lady seemed equally determined to take on that role.

"What if I was wrong?" asked Mina. Saying the words aloud brought a swift flash of panic. "What if Simon never grows to love me? What if I married into a loveless marriage that is little more than a business arrangement?"

"Oh, dear heart," said Imogene, abandoning her tea and madeleines on the end table. "Answer me this: do you feel as though you have a friendship with Simon?"

If it had been only a few weeks ago, Mina would have said yes. Outside of Thea and Imogene, Mina felt more comfortable and close to Simon than anyone. Even her brothers. She thought back on the conversations they'd shared, their similar goals and ambitions, and knew that they'd had a solid friendship, though at the moment she felt less confident in her answer.

"I will take that as a hesitant yes," said Imogene, scrutinizing Mina's face. "And why do you love Simon?"

The question gave Mina a jolt as she had never admitted her feelings aloud. Not to anyone. She had admitted to caring deeply for Simon, but there was a vast difference between caring and loving. Yet even with his strange behavior of late, Mina could not deny that her feelings ran deeper than admiration.

"Do not get missish on me, Mina," said Imogene. "I can see it plain as day that you do."

Mina's eyes grew wide and panic swept through her. She could not bear the thought that her secret was so clearly written on her face.

"Calm down, my dear," said Imogene. "I doubt that anyone

else has guessed, but I have a sense for such things. Now, tell me why you love him."

Mina sighed. "He has such passion for his life, and he works so hard to improve his estate. Not just for his family, but for his tenants. It is hard not to admire someone who strives to better the lives of others. And he is honorable. And he may not always see past his own nose, but when he does, he is kind and giving."

The words flowed forth, bringing up every heartfelt feeling she had for the man. During it, Imogene's eyes glimmered with joy.

"Sweet Mina," she said when Mina finished. "Don't you dare give up hope. Love is a fickle thing, but it often sprouts when respect and friendship are present, and you certainly have that in spades. Simon has not had great examples of love in his life, and he may be a little slow to understand just what it is. Just show him your sweet heart and devotion, and he will see the truth."

Mina gripped Imogene's free hand and allowed the comfort to drive away her fears.

"But we must do something about your housekeeper," said Imogene, shifting the conversation back to its start. "Luckily, I have a plan."

Chapter 15

Mina sipped her morning hot chocolate and watched her husband. It had been over a fortnight since he had sided with Mrs. Richards, and enough time had passed that she felt no lingering frustration at his behavior. If it had been done maliciously, Mina's anger would still be blazing, but Simon was only guilty of ignorance, and that was far easier to forgive. Besides, with Imogene's plans coming together Mina knew Mrs. Richards would be a moot point before long.

Munching a roll, Simon read the newspaper. Though he would never make the ladies swoon with rapture, Mina loved the cut of his jaw and the bump on the bridge of his nose from when he broke it after being tossed from his horse at age eleven. More than that, she found herself drawn to him. His pigheadedness about Mrs. Richards' aside, Mina adored their time together. Even amicably silent, Mina was contented with her dear husband.

Putting down the cup, Mina pushed such silly schoolgirl thoughts aside. She should not allow herself to get so distracted. She had work to do. The housekeeper may not appreciate Mina's help, but there was much that could be done for the estate that was beyond Mrs. Richards' purview. Tenants to visit.

Charity baskets to organize. Mina focused on those things.

"Mrs. Kingsley," Jennings said upon entering the dining room, "the shipment of your things has arrived. The footmen are bringing in your trunks, and your horse is being taken to the stables."

Mina popped up from her chair, begging Simon's pardon as she rushed from the room. She knew she was being terribly ill-mannered, but Mina did not care in that moment. Her dear Beau was finally here. Not bothering to put on better shoes, she hurried out the front door to the stables, tip-toeing around the dirt and muck.

"There you are!" she cooed, rushing to the fine creature and wrapping her arms around his neck. It was frightfully undigni-fied, but only the grooms were there to witness the scene, and they appreciated her mad display. Beau stomped a hoof and huffed at her hair, and Mina pulled back to rub his nose but got a wet kiss instead.

"Oh," she squeaked, wiping the moisture away. "Have you missed me, Beau? I've missed you."

"He has an interesting coloring."

Simon's voice startled her. Mina spun around and found him standing just behind her. In her rush, she had not realized he'd been following her.

"Do not say a word against him," warned Mina, rubbing Beau's nose.

Simon held up his hands in surrender. "I wouldn't dream of it."

Simon drew closer, inspecting her horse, and Mina's eyes narrowed. She was perhaps a little too sensitive on Beau's be-half, but Mina loved him and would not allow anyone to speak ill of her beloved horse. He was a glorious beast with impeccable breeding. His beautiful, rich coat of brown was so dark that it faded into black; if it weren't for the odd shaped streaks of white marring his perfect coloring, he would've fetched a hefty price at auction.

"He cannot help his birth defects," said Mina, cautiously

waiting to see how Simon reacted. She'd heard enough taunts over the years, but she would not trade Beau for a dozen horses with unblemished coats.

"No, indeed," said Simon, running his hands over Beau's head and shoulders. "All things considered, he is one of the finest horses I have ever seen."

"Except..." prompted Mina.

"That is a trap if ever I heard one," said Simon, turning a laughing eye towards Mina.

"It is something I have heard enough times. 'He is magnificent except...'" Mina allowed the sentence to hang for a moment while she petted Beau, her fingers brushing close to Simon's. "I raised him from a colt. One of my neighbors breeds the best horses in the county, and I was visiting the day Beau was born. They were thrilled to have the new addition until they saw his coat. With such birthmarks, they knew he would never fetch anywhere near the price they desired. I heard them debating about whether or not it was simply easier to be rid of him, so I begged my father to buy him. We got him for a song, and he has been my faithful friend ever since."

Her eyes strayed towards Simon, and she found him watching her. Mina could not interpret the look in his eyes, though it gave her a hint of warmth.

"Would you join me for a ride?" he asked.

"Are you sure you are not too busy?"

"Nonsense," he said. "I haven't taken you on a proper tour of the grounds yet. You have been working hard ever since you arrived here, and it's time you had a bit of fun."

Mina held back a chuckle, and Simon's brow wrinkled.

"What?" he asked.

Mina shook her head with a smile. "You have been even busier than I and have had far less fun, but I will take your offer and slip into my riding habit before you change your mind."

Simon ordered the grooms to ready Beau and his own

horse, Spartan, before going to change. He may have left the stable just moments after Mina, but he returned in his riding gear long before she did. Waiting for her arrival, he was left to ponder the all too uncomfortable feelings nipping at him. The words Mina had said were not meant to be hurtful. She was no society lady who could cut with words more accurately than a soldier with his sabre. But her assessment of him made him feel oddly lacking.

His wife thought him too busy to join her for a ride. A simple ride. Something that would bring them both such pleasure, and Mina assumed he would not make time for it. It made him sound dour. And the way she defended her silly looking horse, as if he would stoop to mocking something she so obviously loved. But it was clear that others had, and it filled Simon with unease.

Brushed to the side and overlooked. That seemed to be Mina's lot in life before their marriage, and she acted as though she expected him to treat her the same. It did not sit right with Simon. It especially did not sit right that he had done so on more than one occasion before their marriage. And continued to do so, apparently.

"My apologies for making you wait," called the lady in question as she jogged from the house. "It was near impossible to find my riding habits among my trunks."

In that moment, Simon felt a deep gratitude that Mina was his wife. Few other ladies of his acquaintance would care about holding him up, and no other would rush to join him. As his mother rarely remembered she had children, Simon's older sister had stepped into the role and spent most of his childhood spouting countless statements concerning the should and should nots of ladies and gentlemen. Undoubtedly, Emmeline would be mortified at such a display of emotion and physicality. For Simon, her enthusiasm and conscientiousness made him smile.

Meeting her partway, Simon relieved Mina of a bundle she clutched to her chest. At his raised eyebrows, she said, "It's for the Johnsons. I thought I would take the opportunity to bring it to them while we were riding out."

"Certainly."

It took a few moments before he and Mina were on their steeds; the majority was spent convincing his wife to allow him charge of the Johnson's bundle. If it had not been for the fact that it was clear Mina was being so stubborn simply because she did not want to be a burden to him, it would have rankled. Instead, it reemphasized what he suspected; Mina was unused to such aid. It made Simon wonder more about her history.

Minutes later, the horses left the stable yard and headed towards the countryside. Simon had heard many a lady claim to be adept at riding, though few ever lived up to expectations. Mina did not fail to impress. Having reached an open patch, she gave Simon a smile and nudged Beau into a gallop. Simon liked to think that holding Mina's package was what kept him from outpacing her, but that would be far from the truth.

Cutting across the countryside, they wound their way towards the Johnsons' cottage. Pulling Beau to a stop, Mina allowed Simon to catch up. Both horses were breathing heavily, and Mina beamed as she rubbed Beau's neck. High color filled her cheeks and her eyes shone, and Simon could not help but feel a similar swell of joy in his own heart.

"I should not have pushed him so hard," said Mina as they walked the horses towards the cottage, "but it's been too long since we've had a bruising ride, and I could not help myself, even if poor Beau is getting on in years."

"Yes, I wanted to take it easy on Spartan, too," said Simon, as though that would explain his performance.

Mina set her laughing eyes on him, a smile tugging at the corner of her lips. "Oh, certainly. You were taking it easy on Spartan, allowing me to trounce you so soundly."

Simon attempted to keep a straight face, but he knew his mirth showed through. "I wouldn't say trounced."

"Routed? Obliterated? Decimated? Are those words more to your liking?" Though said with feigned innocence, Mina spoke each with a tinge of humor, and Simon could not hold back the laugh anymore. It was hard to nurse a wounded pride when rewarded with Mina's cheekiness. For appearing so shy in public, Mina had a saucy side to her that Simon loved to see emerging with more frequency.

As their horses stopped, Mrs. Johnson came to the door while her brood gathered around her. Before Simon had a chance to aid her, Mina slid from her saddle and retrieved the package from his arms.

"Good morning, Mrs. Johnson," Mina greeted her, walking over to the woman while Simon dismounted. "I hope we are not disturbing you so early in the morning."

"Of course not, ma'am," said Mrs. Johnson with a quick curtsy before Mina began asking about the Johnson children, and the two fell into an easy conversation. It was surprising to see how friendly both women were. Simon knew Mina did not sit about whiling away the hours with endless social calls and teas like many ladies, but he had no idea she'd spent so much time getting to know their tenants.

Mrs. Johnson unwrapped the package and pulled out the blanket Simon had seen Mina knitting over the last couple weeks. There were tears in the woman's eyes as she ran her hands over the stitches and thanked Mina profusely, which brought a blush to Mina's cheeks.

"I shan't keep you from your work," said Mina, turning back to her horse. "I am glad you like it. I hope it will keep Baby Mary warm."

Mrs. Johnson gave Mina another curtsy and her heartfelt thanks. Simon watched as the woman gathered her children back into their home. Scooping up the boy clinging to her skirts, the mother drew him close and kissed his cheeks before shutting the door behind her. It was such a simple display, but it entranced Simon. Such affection was so rare in the world, it was hard not to get swept up in it.

Turning away, Simon caught sight of Mina atop a boulder, using it as a makeshift mounting block. Simon hurried to help her, but she climbed up into her saddle before he could.

"You make it difficult to assist you," he said, looking up with a teasing eye.

"Assist?" Mina's own eyes showed nothing but puzzlement. It took a moment before understanding dawned, and she asked, "With mounting?"

"And unmounting. And carrying your packages. Among other things," he said before climbing on Spartan.

A flash of nerves and sadness crossed in her face, and Simon held up a staying hand. "That was not a condemnation, Mina."

Watching the emotions on Mina face never failed to entertain. In some ways she was such a mystery, but in others, she was an open book for anyone willing to read it.

"I'm afraid I did not even think of it," she said with a blush. A different flush of embarrassment chased that, leaving Simon to wonder if it was because she was embarrassed of her embarrassment.

"Did not think of it?" he asked as their horses walked away from the Johnson's cottage.

"I have little experience with gentlemen," she said, turning her face up to the morning sun. "I was busy helping my father run his estate from a young age and rarely socialized with people outside my family.

"Not that my brothers are not gentlemen," Mina added quickly. "Just that they rarely thought of me as a lady."

She paused before adding, "That did not come out right."

Simon chuckled. "I catch your meaning. Sisters are a different kettle of fish. I am afraid that I am as guilty as your brothers when it comes to treating my sisters as ladies, but I wish you would let your husband play the part of gentleman from time to time."

Mina glanced at Simon with a shy smile and gave him a nod.

They rode alongside each other, their horses crossing the hills. The summer sun crept up in the sky, casting its lovely light upon the landscape. The grass was vibrant and glowing, the summer wildflowers adding dashes of yellows and purples. Oaks and poplars ringed the meadow, and the sunlight shimmered on the surface of the pond in the distance. The fields sat on the other side of the water, the wheat growing tall and golden. There was no more beautiful spot in the world, though Simon could not decide if it was better on a brilliant summer day such as this or more magnificent on a winter's night when the moon was full and high in the sky and the snow thick upon the landscape.

Simon glanced at his wife, surprised at the ease with which they traveled together. She did not demand every moment of his attention, yet seemed pleased to chat about any number of topics. The more he came to know her, the more he found himself grateful for the stroke of luck that had brought her into his life—even with some of the hiccups that had accompanied their first couple months of matrimony.

"The new irrigation system is going in there, isn't it?" asked Mina, pointing to the edge of Bryer's pond.

"Yes," he said, raising his eyebrows. The fact that she remembered was surprise enough, but that she actually engaged in the topic that many of his acquaintance found tedious was dumbfounding. "Our steward, Mr. Thorne, is making the necessary plans. Construction will start in the next couple weeks so that it will be completed before winter. I would have liked to start sooner in the season, but there were a few issues that needed to be resolved."

"How exciting," she said without a hint of the polite boredom that many a person used when he discussed such things.

"You find irrigation systems interesting?"

"Perhaps not all the details of the design and construction," she said, giving him a rueful look. "I will admit that the engineering behind it is not particularly engaging, but hearing you speak of it with such passion is."

Simon was unsure why such a simple statement warmed

his heart so, but he found himself fighting to contain the school-boy grin on his face. There was no reason to beam like an idiot at a passing comment.

"And," said Mina, continuing her stream of thought, "I enjoy discussing the good it will do. It will help increase the farm yields and protect them from dry seasons. It is hard not to be interested in something that will do so much for so many of us, both master and tenant alike. You are exceptionally industrious, Simon Kingsley, and I enjoy being a part of that."

Simon watched her atop her horse, moving gracefully with the beast. The sun glinted in her brown eyes, making them look richer and deeper in a way that Simon found entrancing. Mina's eyes may not be as striking as other ladies, but Simon thought himself a lucky man to be allowed to gaze into them for the rest of his life.

"If only I could find such success with the ladies of Bristow," Mina mumbled, the tone quiet enough that Simon was unsure if she meant him to hear it. When he asked her to clarify, the look on her face made it clear she had not, and it took prodding before she admitted the truth of the matter.

"Mrs. Baxter is the leader of society here, and she has taken a strong disliking to me," she said.

"What could she possibly dislike about you?" asked Simon.

Mina gave him an inscrutable look. Not that it was unemotional, rather Simon could not identify the emotions in it.

When she spoke, it was with a faint smile. "Truth be told, it has more to do with you. She was convinced you would offer for her daughter, and I am nothing more than the upstart who stole you away."

Simon snorted. "Miss Charity Baxter? I shudder to think of myself bound to her or any other member of her family."

"Well, it has left me in a difficult bind, for she holds the reins to society and is determined to cut me out," said Mina. "I wouldn't care in most cases, but it has made it difficult to do much charity work in the neighborhood. And I would love to start a literary or musical club, but that seems an impossibility with Mrs. Baxter leading the charge against me."

Simon was not so oblivious that he had not noticed the low volume of callers and well-wishers his bride had received, but he had not realized the extent of Mrs. Baxter's venom. Though, as he thought of it, Simon realized that outside of Lady Lovell, he could not think of a single person who had welcomed Mina into the neighborhood. Neither the snubbing nor his blindness to it sat well with him.

"Then you must try a different tack," he said with more emotion than he'd meant to reveal. Pulling Spartan to a halt, he turned his focus on Mina as she stopped beside him. "Surely, there must be others whom you can reach out to—other ladies too reserved for general society or ones who are overlooked or ostracized by Mrs. Baxter and her band of shrews."

Mina's eyes widened at his description of the ladies, though she did not disagree with it. Gratitude shone in her eyes, and her smile grew. It was an expression that Simon suspected was more often on her lips than not, if given the right circumstances, and Simon found himself wishing he could make it a more common occurrence.

"Do not be cowed by people like that, Mina," he said. "You are worth far more than them."

Chapter 16

Mina's feet hardly touched the ground for the next week. That ride had changed something between them, and she felt the shift in her husband's attentions. Most days she could hardly wait until mealtime or their morning ride when they discussed their past, present, and future together. There were no grand declarations of love or adoration on his side, though Mina's own feelings grew deeper with each interlude. He was not a perfect man (there was no such thing, after all), but he was perfect for her. The more she got to know him, the more she felt their marriage metamorphosing into what she had dreamt of for so many years.

Even the thought of the impending battle did little to dampen her spirits. Hearing Simon's heartfelt words in her head, Mina felt ready for the coming war. First, to enlist an ally.

The door to the sitting room opened, and Mina put aside her sketchbook, rising to greet Mr. Thorne.

"Mrs. Kingsley," he said with a bow, and she returned it with a short curtsy before sitting and prompting the steward to do so as well.

"No doubt you are curious why I summoned you," she said with a smile to put him at ease.

"As there hasn't been a mistress at Avebury Park since I started on as steward, I have little experience with them, so I am most definitely curious," he said with an echoing smile.

His manner was so relaxed and engaging that Mina felt her lingering nerves fade away. He was around Simon's age, and there was something about Mr. Thorne that reminded Mina of Thea's husband, Frederick, which only made it easier to open up to the stranger.

"I asked you here to inform you of a change in the household staff and to enlist your aid in the endeavor."

A single eyebrow crawled up Mr. Thorne's forehead. "If you didn't before, you have my attention now, madam."

Mina glanced at the door behind Mr. Thorne, double checking that it was indeed shut. It would not do for the servants to overhear and ruin her plans before she implemented them.

"Mrs. Richards is unsuitable for Avebury Park," said Mina, clasping her hands in her lap, "and I am determined to replace her with someone more aligned with what I and Mr. Kingsley desire for our home."

The carefree air about Mr. Thorne evaporated. Mina half expected it to be replaced with anger or denial, but it was calm reflection that greeted her. That comforted Mina, as she did not have the strength for another irrational argument.

"I was unaware that there was a problem in the household staff, other than the usual squabbles," he said.

"Mr. Kingsley has kept your duties focused away from the household itself, so I am not surprised. He hardly seems aware of it himself, other than the general sense of unhappiness that permeates the house."

Mr. Thorne sat patiently as she outlined each of the grievances she had previously presented to Mrs. Richards, though going into more detail than the housekeeper had been willing to hear. Mina knew it was unnecessary to be so thorough. She did not need to explain her decision to anyone other than Simon, but Mina felt no need to be so dictatorial. Besides, if Mr. Thorne understood the details, his cooperation would make her plans run smoother, and his understanding of the full scope of the issue was imperative.

While she spoke, Mina knew she had Mr. Thorne's undivided attention but was unsure of where his thoughts were leading, though she took it as a good sign that he appeared less tense than when she had started.

"Mrs. Richards is a bully of the worst sort," said Mina, feeling the emotion surging with each word as her speech grew to its conclusion. "She makes the staff's lives unbearable, and I shan't stand for it. I have tried to work with her, but she is intractable. I won't have my home be such a pit of despair."

Mina had meant to be calm and direct. It wouldn't do to become overwrought and thus brushed off as an emotional female, but Mina could not stop the growing passion she felt. She detested what Mrs. Richards had done in the Kingsley name, and Mina would not allow it to go on.

"I'm certain that sounds overly sentimental," said Mina, taking a breath to rein in her emotions, "but Mrs. Richards treats the staff little better than slaves. I was made mistress of my father's home when I was thirteen. My mother passed before she had trained me to run an estate, so I had to look to my staff for guidance, and they taught me just how important a partnership between employer and employee is.

"Contrary to Mrs. Richards' belief, I am not interested in allowing them free run of the house. I value discipline and order, but that can be done without browbeating and demeaning those beneath you. To be so harsh only makes them miserable. That misery affects the entire household, master and servant alike. If anything, it encourages the servants to give notice far more often than they would in a better working conditions, which causes constant disruption."

Mina paused for breath, and Mr. Thorne took the opportunity to interject. "Mrs. Kingsley, I do not think you overly sentimental. I think you're prudent and wise. Besides, a little sentimentality never hurt anyone. It's obviously given you a kind and generous heart, which is something that is in high demand

and short supply."

Before Mina had a chance to feel more than a flutter of bashfulness over his glowing evaluation of her character, he asked, "Have you spoken with Mrs. Richards?"

Mina nodded. "Many times, and she simply ignores my directives or runs to Mr. Kingsley."

"And he lets her have her way?"

Mina paused. She did not like that Mr. Thorne's question sounded so accusatory. Certainly, she had felt her fair share of anger over Simon's refusal to support his own wife, but having it aired in public or be said in such a tone felt unfair. Simon was no villain and did not deserve to be painted as such. He was simply oblivious.

"I don't believe he understands what it takes to run a household," said Mina, choosing her words carefully. "Because Mrs. Richards has kept the building standing, he thinks she has done good work and believes her when she claims my changes would cause great upset among the staff. Running the estate keeps him busy enough, I don't wish to trouble him further with the inner workings of the household."

"And you believe Mrs. Richards will trouble him," he said, a dawning of understanding growing in his gaze.

"I know she will," said Mina. "If I terminate her employment, she will simply run to him."

"And he will assume that changing the housekeeper will cause more of an uproar than it's worth," concluded Mr. Thorne, his face relaxing again into a grin.

"You know him well," said Mina, smiling in response.

"I've worked with him for many years," said Mr. Thorne. "There's not many men I value or esteem more than Mr. Kingsley, and I hate to learn that his household is in such a sorry state. Neither of us have paid enough attention to it, and I am very glad you are here to remedy the situation. You have my full support. I will take care of Mrs. Richards, if you wish."

Mina paused. She did wish it. Very much. It would be far easier to allow Mr. Thorne to deal with the staff, but to do so would be cowardly. Mina wanted to be brave. She needed to be.

"I appreciate the offer, Mr. Thorne, but I will handle Mrs. Richards. With Lady Lovell's aid, I have spent the last few weeks searching for a replacement and have found a woman who is perfect for the position, so there will be no vacancy." Mina squeezed her hands, hoping he would accept her next statement. "I was hoping for your aid in distracting Mr. Kingsley while the change happens."

Mr. Thorne broke into laughter, his whole body filling with it. "I can see why you would be so apprehensive about asking me such a thing," he said as he calmed.

Mina blushed, hating that she did so. Every time she hoped she had enough composure to keep her nerves hidden, they inevitably showed through.

"Don't worry, madam," he said. "Your secrets are safe with me. I see the need for discretion, and I fully agree with your assessment of the situation. Though I would never normally go behind Mr. Kingsley's back, it is prudent in the current situation to ask forgiveness rather than permission."

"I'm glad you see it that way," said Mina, the stress flowing out of her.

"I have every confidence that you will have everything situated before he even notices Mrs. Richards is gone," he said.

Mina allowed a sigh of relief and thanked him before they got to work scheduling their coup.

Chapter 17

"**I**s there anything else I can get you, madam?" asked Jennings, standing with perfect butler-like formality.

Mina's hands twisted in her lap, and she released them, relaxing her fingers. It wouldn't do to get worked up before the deed was done. "Is it certain that Mr. Kingsley and Mr. Thorne are out in the east fields?"

"Yes, madam."

"Then send her in," said Mina with a fair amount of strength in her words. She could do this.

Jennings gave her a deferential bow but paused before he left. "I know it is not my place, madam, but on behalf of the entire staff, I wish to thank you for what you are doing."

Mina's eyes widened, and her face paled; she couldn't imagine what terror Mrs. Richards would unleash if she had discovered what was coming and had time to scheme.

"Mr. Thorne told me in the strictest confidence," he said, guessing at her distress. "No one else knows, but I am glad to see a change. It is long overdue."

"Thank you, Jennings." It should not matter so much, but knowing she had another ally in Jennings helped ease her tension.

With another bow, he stepped out of the sitting room, and Mrs. Richards entered a moment later.

"What do you want?" she asked, and any residual fear fled at the unmitigated rudeness. Mina would not allow herself to lose to this tyrant. As the woman had pushed aside all niceties, Mina decided to do the same.

"Mrs. Richards," said Mina, reciting her rehearsed speech, "I appreciate your years of service to Avebury Park, but as it is impossible for the two of us to work together, a change is necessary. We will no longer be needing your services. We will offer you two months wages, but—"

Mrs. Richards let loose a bark of laughter. "No longer be needing my services? You have no authority to sack me. I don't answer to you."

Mina rose to her feet and faced down Mrs. Richards. "I am mistress of Avebury Park, and I have complete authority over what happens in this household."

"I answer only to Mr. Kingsley, not some jumped up pig," she spat.

Hearing those terrible words gave Mina a shock, but they did not have the effect Mrs. Richards had wished. For the good of Simon and the rest of the household, Mina would not retreat.

"You have an hour to get your things packed and out of my home," said Mina, staring down her nose at the small, petty woman.

"Or what? You don't scare me, Miss Hoity-Toity. You are only mistress of Avebury Park because Mr. Kingsley couldn't have the woman he wanted and no one else would take you," she said, her voice hissing like a venomous snake. "And even he—no matter how desperate he was to marry—is unwilling to touch you. Everyone at the Park and in Bristow knows you are his wife in name only."

"How dare you speak that way to Mrs. Kingsley," said Jennings in a near growl before nodding at the footmen. Mina had been so focused on the former housekeeper and deflecting her poison that Mina hadn't noticed them enter. The footmen herded Mrs. Richards out while she threw a tantrum befitting a toddler. Mina heard her voice echoing through the corridors as the footmen threw her bodily from the house.

"I am sorry I eavesdropped, but I thought it prudent. Her things were packed and waiting," said Jennings.

"You anticipated such a scene and the need for a hasty exit?" asked Mina, slowly lowering herself to the armchair, her strength sapped.

"I had hoped for better, but neither you nor Mr. Thorne have witnessed the full power of her fury. I would have told Mr. Kingsley or Mr. Thorne sooner about her behavior, but I was afraid of what she might do," he said, his eyes falling to the floor.

Knowing that she had experienced only a fraction of the pain Mrs. Richards had heaped upon the others made Mina even more grateful that she had followed through, though her heart was weighed down by the shame and pain of Mrs. Richards' words. Such small things from such a small woman should not hurt so, but Mina knew full well that some people have a talent for finding the best target for such weapons.

Mina felt a headache creeping up on her, and she closed her eyes and rubbed at her temple.

"Mrs. Kingsley, if I may..." Jennings' voice was quiet and hesitant, and Mina opened her eyes to see his locked on hers. "I have served a few mistresses in my time, including the previous mistress of Avebury Park." He paused, cleared his throat, but forged ahead. "None of them have had even a speck of your strength of character or goodness. I am beyond grateful that you have come to help us."

The tears that Mina had kept at bay threatened to burst forth. She swallowed and nodded because she had not the ability to express how much his words and the admiration in his eyes meant to her.

Returning to his stoic butler self, Jennings bowed deeply. "I will have the staff keep an eye on Mrs. Richards. With the way things went today, I doubt she will stay in Bristow. No other household will take her after this. But I will make sure she does not disturb you or Mr. Kingsley in the future."

"Thank you, Jennings."

And with that, he left.

Mina leaned back into the chair and allowed the emotional drain to pull the tears from her eyes. The mix of pride in her victory and residual bruises from Mrs. Richards' cruel but apt description of her marriage left Mina unsure if they were happy or sad tears. It did not matter. She would take her moment and then get the new housekeeper of Avebury Park settled.

...

Simon hurried through the corridors, glancing in room after room, but he couldn't find Mina anywhere. They would ride out tomorrow morning as they did every day, but Simon could not wait to show her how the new irrigation system was coming along; with any luck, it would make next year's harvest even more abundant. He had spent most of the day inspecting the work with Thorne, but Mina had been ever present in his thoughts. Simon pictured her excitement about the project and knew that of anyone (save him and Thorne), Mina would appreciate it the most.

Ducking into the western drawing room, Simon found her sitting on an armchair, her head resting in her hand.

"Are you all right, Mina?" he asked, coming to her side.

She jerked and jumped to her feet, surprise and worry pulling at her expression. "Just a touch of a headache. It's been a trying day, but everything has sorted itself out." The words conveyed confidence, but Mina's tone held a touch of trepidation as she watched him. Simon had no idea what she was searching for in his features.

"I can send for a tisane from Cook, if you wish," he said, drawing close and placing a hand on her arm to steady her.

"Thank you, but I think I just need a bit of fresh air."

Simon broke into a smile. "Perfect. I've been anxious to show you what I've been up to today."

"The construction is going well?" she asked.

"I would love to show you," he said, and Mina glanced at the clock on the mantel.

"If I hurry, we should have time," she said before rushing out to change into her riding habit.

...

Simon tried to remember a better day. All in all, it was un-remarkable. Inspecting the estate was a common enough occur-rence, but in the last few weeks, Simon could not deny that things in his life had shifted in a most peculiar and unexpected way. Watching Mina canter beside him as they rode from the east fields, Simon found so many of the mundane aspects of his life far more enjoyable than they'd been previously.

Marriage was a better plan than Simon had anticipated. Having a helpmate was well and good, but having someone at his side who loved the work and appreciated the end result made it far more gratifying.

He glanced at Mina and she smiled back at him before lean-ing over Beau's neck and putting on a burst of speed. Whoop-ing, Simon nudged Spartan to follow, and he sped after her. Neck and neck, they galloped over the hills. Mina turned to-wards him and shouted something, but the wind caught the words. Then Mina's eyes widened, and she reared back, jerking Beau to a halt. Simon's heart stopped when Mina looked as though she were going to tumble from the saddle, but she kept her seat while sputtering and wiping at her face.

"Mina?" Simon called to her, jumping from his horse and running to her side. "Are you all right?"

She paused and looked down at him, her cheeks the color of cherries. "I swallowed a bug."

"A bug?" Simon blinked at her.

"It flew right into my mouth," she said with a shiver, and Simon burst out laughing.

"I thought you were having a fit or something," he said when he could manage a breath. He handed her his handkerchief. "Here I thought I was coming to rescue the damsel like a proper gentleman, and I find my heroic efforts unnecessary."

Mina took the proffered handkerchief. "Do not underestimate your efforts, my handsome knight. Unfortunately, you are saddled with a rather unladylike damsel."

Simon rubbed Beau's neck absentmindedly as he stared up into Mina's eyes that shined with unrestrained pleasure. Seeing her thus, with her lust for life and strength of spirit, it was hard to think of her as anything other than the epitome of what a lady should be.

"And you should not underestimate your ladylike ways, Mina."

The brightness in her eyes softened, and something in Simon's heart tugged at him. The feeling was foreign to him, but in no way unpleasant. Quite the opposite, in fact. Exceptionally pleasant.

"Mr. Kingsley!" A voice called from behind him, snapping the connection. Turning, Simon found Mrs. Thompson waving at them from a curricle with Mr. Thompson looking put out about halting their journey.

Simon got back on his horse and escorted his wife over to the road.

"Are you quite all right?" asked Mrs. Thompson, fluttering a frilly handkerchief in the air at them. "I saw you two stopped there and just had to check."

From the corner of his eye, Simon saw Mina color, though she remained otherwise composed.

"We are fine, Mrs. Thompson. How kind of you to inquire," said Simon.

"Yes, well, that is what neighbors do," she said with a dramatic flail of lace.

Mina's eyebrow arched just a touch. It was faint enough

that Simon was unsure as to whether the Thompsons had noticed it.

"I'm glad you stopped," said Mina, "for I've been meaning to ask if you are planning on attending the musicale we are hosting on Friday. I'm afraid one of the servants must have waylaid your response."

Mrs. Thompson looked at Mina for the first time in the conversation, her smile faltering. "Yes, I am certain it was, but I'm afraid I am otherwise occupied. Perhaps you've not heard, but Mrs. Baxter is hosting a card party that night, and I had already accepted her invitation before I had a chance to respond to yours."

"Of course," said Mina, a hint of humor lurking in the words. "I heard rumor that Mrs. Baxter was planning entertainment for the self-same evening. How fortunate that Bristow will have so many diverting options from which to choose."

"Yes," said Mrs. Thompson, elbowing her husband. He snapped the reins and the curricle moved forward as she said, "It's getting late, and we must be going. How nice to see you, Mr. Kingsley. And Mrs. Kingsley."

Simon narrowed his eyes at the retreating woman; how dare she tack on Mina like a begrudging afterthought.

"I appear to have ruffled her feathers," mumbled Mina. "I should have held my tongue."

Simon glanced at his wife, at a loss as to what she meant.

Mina gave a little shrug and nudged Beau to move. "Mrs. Baxter decided to throw the card party after receiving our invitation to the musicale. Neither she nor any of her circle bothered to respond to the invitation. Of course, I'd known it was unlikely that they would accept, but I couldn't help but prod Mrs. Thompson and let her know I knew."

Mina may have looked peaceful about the situation, but Simon seethed with anger. "How dare they treat you like that. That is beyond the pale. To be so petty and vindictive. It is ridiculous!"

Mina gave him a warm look as they headed back to the

house. "Don't trouble yourself over them. Things are better than they've been, but I doubt I will ever win them over. I took your advice and found some like-minded ladies who enjoy the occasional social function but dislike the endless teas and morning calls. They suit me better than Mrs. Baxter and her toadies. It took some scouring and a lot of help from Lady Lovell, but I find myself quite contented with Bristow society. Even with Mrs. Baxter stirring up trouble from time to time."

Simon wanted to let loose a few choice words best unsaid around ladies. Mina may be resigned to such treatment, but Simon would not stand for it. "Regardless of what they say, Bristow is better because you are here. I, for one, am more than grateful that you are."

There was a pause before Mina spoke, her words tinged with self-deprecating humor. "So, you are not sorry you are saddled with me?"

Simon pulled his horse to a stop so he could give her his full attention. "Saddled? Far from it, Mina. I am blessed to have you in my life."

Chapter 18

S imon marched up the entryway stairs, his hands clasped behind him, his mind wandering. If someone had told him five months ago that his life would be fundamentally enhanced, he would not have believed a word of it. The odd bumps and bruises of the world aside, Simon had been contented with his life. He recognized many of the blessings and opportunities he had in his position and felt grateful for every one of them.

But now...

Now he realized how much his life had been lacking. Taking the stairs up to the second floor, Simon reveled in his home. Something in the air was different. He couldn't put his finger on it. Much of it ran as before, though with minor changes here and there that did not account for the severely improved atmosphere. The house was so inviting that Simon loathed leaving and anticipated returning. He'd never thought his home oppressive, but feeling the stark difference between what it was now and what it had been only a short time before, Simon realized Avebury Park had been wanting.

Passing the library, Simon caught sight of Mina arranging a large vase of flowers while giving instructions to one of the maids. She held a lily in her hand, twirling the bloom by the stem while she examined her work. With a quick slice, Mina took off the end of the stalk and slid it in among the others. Mina had been making good use of their conservatory and gardens, filling every space with flowers and growing things until the entire house smelled of perpetual spring.

Watching her, Simon felt a surge of warmth for the lady who was at the heart of his contentment. Mina didn't just lighten his burden; she made it more enjoyable to bear it. Part of him wanted to step into the room and spend hours talking with her. Discussing housekeeping had never interested Simon. Until Mina. He couldn't think of another person in the world with whom he could spend hours discussing topics that mattered so little to him, but it had nothing to do with the details of her duties and more about the woman herself. Simon wondered if that was how Mina felt about discussing irrigation systems.

And that thought brought a great grin to Simon's face.

Things would be nearly perfect, if it weren't for the lingering memory in Simon's heart. Continuing on his path, he paced the halls, scarcely aware of where his feet led him as Mina's words replayed in his head.

"So, you're not sorry you are saddled with me?"

It had been a week, yet still her question plagued him. Mina had spoken with a touch of humor, but Simon sensed something deeper buried beneath. Uncertainty. Sadness.

He hadn't realized he was in his study until he sat down in the chair, the door firmly closed behind him. Leaning into the wingback armchair, Simon propped his elbow on the chair's arm and rested his chin heavily in his hand.

Things were infinitely better than before. Simon would never deny that. It was clear to everyone at Avebury Park that Mina was a welcome—no, necessary—addition. The things she did for their tenants and Bristow. For him. She served so many, working to increase their happiness simply because it increased her own. Mina could be counted as nothing but a blessing, and he despaired that she did not understand that.

Of their own accord, his fingers pulled open the desk drawer and retrieved Susannah's delicate glove, remembering the day she'd given it to him. Susannah often preferred walking in lieu of a drive because it afforded her the chance to mingle, and that day had been no different. They strolled, arm-in-arm through Hyde Park, and she flitted from person to person with an elegance that entranced Simon. Her beauty put all of nature to shame that day. Simon could still picture the twinkle in her eye when she had 'dropped' the glove on the ground for him; to give it outright would have been too forward, but the look in her eye had clearly bestowed the treasure. Simon had held it so many times that the leather had grown softer, and he could imagine Susannah's hand in it, clasped to his.

Turning his eyes to the window, Simon saw that the weather outside had turned rough and hoped it would disperse before his morning ride tomorrow. He paused at that thought and wondered if the squall could deter Mina; the drizzles that morning hadn't. They'd returned home wet and muddy, but Mina's smile was as brilliant as ever.

Simon found himself grinning at the memory, but then his eyes settled back on the glove clutched in his hand.

Mina. Susannah. To compare the two ladies was unfair. Mina could never hope to match Susannah's beauty. Though in all fairness, there was something about Mina that was quite pretty. Attractive, even. The way she held herself. The smiles and emotions that toyed with her face and shone in her eyes. She had a natural grace that made Simon wonder why more men had not sought her hand. To say nothing of her giving spirit and tenacious goodness.

Simon admired the lady greatly. Respected and valued her opinion when given. Simon could say unequivocally that his life was better with her in it. But holding that glove in his hand, he knew he would never love her the way he loved Susannah. What he felt for Susannah was a consuming passion that struck him the moment he had first seen her. No one before or since had ever inspired such strong emotions in him.

That said, Susannah was married, and so was he. They had chosen different paths. Parallel journeys that would never meet. Mina may not be the love of his life, but she had proven herself to be a perfect companion, and Simon cherished her.

It was unfair of him to hold onto the past. No doubt, Mina sensed it and that was what forced her to question Simon happiness in their marriage. It was unfair of him to mistreat his wife so. It was time to leave the past in the past. Accept that love was no longer a possibility, but happiness and friendship were, and from what Simon had experienced so far in their marriage, he knew there'd be an abundance of both. He would not risk that for the fancies of the past.

It was time to destroy the glove and get rid of the thing that only served as a memory of what he'd lost. Time to move on. But a knock on the door had Simon hiding the glove back into the drawer before the visitor entered.

Thorne strode in, handing a stack of papers over to Simon. "I've finished with the books and plan to have the last of the rents collected tomorrow." He paused, watching Simon with a shrewd eye that Simon knew from experience saw and understood too much.

"You look very contented," Thorne said, taking the empty seat on the other side of the desk. "It's a good look on you."

The grin on Simon's face grew. "Things are going very well. The estate is turning a good profit, the household is settled and running well, Mrs. Kingsley is finding her way in Bristow society. I couldn't ask for more."

Thorne nodded. "Yes, Mrs. Witmore has done a fine job of shaping up the staff. I'm certain that under Mrs. Kingsley's guidance, the household has never run better."

"Mrs. Witmore?" asked Simon.

Thorne's eyebrow rose in an irritating fashion that meant he understood something Simon was overlooking. If it weren't for the fact that the man was so good at his job, so engaging to work with, and so impossible to replace, Simon would have fired him for that saucy appendage long ago.

"The housekeeper," said Thorne.

"What?" Simon sat back in his chair. His mind seized. Mina had gone behind his back and fired Mrs. Richards, a woman who had worked for their family since Simon was in leading strings. He had no particular emotional attachment to the woman, but it seemed a petty thing to do to someone who had worked for the Kingsleys for so long. "What of Mrs. Richards?"

"Sacked. And rightfully so." The eyebrow had fallen back into place, but Thorne's voice held a note of defiance as though begging Simon to disagree.

"It seems you are more aware of what is going on in my household than I am, sir," said Simon. "Please, illuminate me."

And Thorne did, sparing no detail including his thinly veiled displeasure at Simon's part in the fiasco. To hear it stated so plainly in all the sordid detail made Simon feel as though he had failed as a gentleman and husband. He had forced Mina into a horrible position, yet she'd forged ahead and resolved the situation without Simon even being aware that such a massive change had taken place. It was miraculous. Mina was miraculous.

Awe and esteem filled him for the woman who had saddled herself with such a blind and dimwitted husband. Though those feelings were quickly replaced with rage when Thorne recounted what Jennings had told him about Mrs. Richards' foul words to Mina.

"She said that?" Simon growled, nearly blind with fury. "She said that to my wife? Where is she?"

Thorne smiled, though it held no mirth and had an unnatural severity to it. "Jennings had her packed and tossed out before I had the chance to deal with her. However, she kicked up a fuss in town. I spoke with her, and she left Bristow with her tail between her legs."

A surge of jealousy surprised Simon; it came from nowhere, but he couldn't deny that he wished he'd had the chance to put that spiteful woman in her place. Simon couldn't imagine Mina facing that alone. Hearing the tale filled him with such admiration. His wife had formed a veritable bloodless coup in the household with grace, dignity, and strength.

How he wished he could make up for his part in it. He needed to apologize. Make amends. Beg on his knees for her to forgive him. Do or buy something to make up for it. Even as the thought entered his mind, the solution presented himself.

"I need your help, Thorne," said Simon. "It's time for me to do some sneaking around Mrs. Kingsley's back."

Chapter 19

Mina's quill fought to keep pace with the words flowing from her mind, but it was a hopeless cause. There was so much to tell Graham. Correction. There was so much good to tell Graham. Things were progressing beautifully in her life, and Mina was finding it difficult to keep from bouncing from place to place. Sacking Mrs. Richards had been arduous, but in the six weeks since, the entire atmosphere of Avebury Park had lightened.

And something had changed in Simon. He'd become so attentive over the last few weeks. There was a closeness between them that gave Mina such hope. They were a proper partnership. They spent nearly every moment together. Morning rides, walks in the garden, picnics, and evenings of music and reading. It was a miracle she was able to get through her work with Simon taking so much of her time. And then, every once in a while, she swore she saw something in his eyes that brought with it dreams of a true family growing between them. Of course, Mina would never mention the full extent of her fantasies to her dear brother.

Mina's elation made the quill speed across the paper. Her

handwriting was a hopeless mess, though Graham would forgive her and guess it to be a good sign. There was only one moment that made her pause.

> *As to your inquiries about Ambrose, I'm afraid I
> don't have much to tell.*

Thoughts of her youngest brother often troubled Mina. The
lad (though he hated that she still thought of him as such) was
directionless. A ship with full sails and no rudder.

> *Nicholas and Louisa-Margaretta are keeping an
> eye on him, or as much of an eye as they can spare
> with the bundle of joy they are anticipating in the
> spring. Nicholas is not concerned, but I cannot help
> but worry over the company he keeps and the ways in
> which he chooses to waste his time...*

Voices in the hall drew Mina's attention. She dismissed it
at first, returning to her letter, but it sounded as though callers
had arrived, which puzzled Mina to no end; today was not her
day to entertain. Not that she ever received many visitors.

Standing, Mina left the library and strode down the hall towards the noise when a maid hopped into her path.

"Ma'am," she squeaked, "I thought you were in your sitting
room."

"The library has better light this time of year, but that is
neither here nor there," said Mina. "Has someone arrived?"

"Mrs. Witmore was asking for you, ma'am," said Molly with
a tremble and a quick glance over her shoulder towards the
mysterious sounds.

"What about?" asked Mina, her eyes narrowing at Molly's
twitchy movements.

"I'm unsure, ma'am, but it'd be best if you go investigate. I
believe she is in the laundry," she said, pointing in the opposite

direction Mina had been heading.

"I will be there directly," said Mina, "but first—" She stepped forward, towards the commotion coming from the entrance, but Molly would not budge.

"Ma'am! I think it's best if you go now," she said, cutting through the bluntness of her words with a quick curtsy.

"Molly, you have done your best to distract me," said Mina, "but I believe it's time to give up this farce. Mrs. Witmore didn't ask for me, did she?"

Molly shook her head, her face paling.

"Don't trouble yourself," said Mina, patting the trembling girl on the shoulder. "You did your best."

And with that, Mina swept past the maid and within a few steps, she stood at the top of the stairs. Staring down into the entrance, Mina saw that the household was in an uproar. Footmen and maids were being ordered about by Mrs. Witmore and Jennings as they brought in a mountain of luggage. In the middle of the hubbub stood Thea and her family. Mina's heart stopped for a moment before she rushed down the stairs and threw herself into her dear friend's arms.

"What are you doing here?" Mina gasped, clinging to Thea for a moment before sweeping each of Thea's beloved children into an embrace.

"It was supposed to be a surprise," said Simon.

Holding Baby Clarinda in her arms, Mina spun to see him standing beside Thea's husband. Simon's mouth curled up in a rueful grin.

"I tried to keep her away, sir," said Molly, standing on the stairs.

"Mina was bound to find out long before I intended," said Simon. "She is too aware of everything happening in this household. I'm astonished I was able to keep it hidden for so long."

Happy tears threatened to fall from Mina's beaming eyes. Simon had done this for her.

"Auntie Mina," said Seth, tugging at her skirts, "look what I can do!"

The five-year-old pulled his ears wide, crossing his eyes.

"I do better!" shouted his younger brother, Levi, before mimicking the face.

At that moment, Clarinda decided she was done with the silliness and her little features screwed into a look of utter despair a scant moment before letting loose a full-lung wail.

"Someone did not get much of a nap," said Thea, relieving Mina of the baby.

"We have rooms ready for you, if you care to clean up and rest," said Simon.

Mina watched in wonder as her husband guided the group. Apparently, he had everything prepared without her suspecting a thing. Mina was dumbfounded and touched that he had gone to such great lengths to surprise her.

As they herded the Voss family through the house, Simon drew next to Mina and whispered, "Surprise!"

Mina pulled him to a stop, though the Voss children ran ahead with their parents hurrying to catch them.

"Simon, this is the nicest surprise I could've asked for," said Mina. She was embarrassed that she could not keep the tears at bay, but Simon looked so pleased that it brought a whole new level of sweetness to the moment. An impulse grabbed her, and before Mina allowed herself to rethink it, she leaned forward and kissed him on the cheek. Her own burned hot, and she knew she looked like a silly young miss, but she couldn't help but blush at her forwardness. And her first kiss.

When she pulled back, she found Simon's face nearly as red. Though there was a touch of shock in his eyes, Mina sensed it was not out of displeasure. Their eyes locked, and Mina felt that connection that flared between them at fleeting moments. The world around them evaporated, leaving the two of them alone in the hallway. If she leaned forward just a few inches, their lips would touch, though Mina knew she did not have the courage to do so.

Her heart begged for Simon to. Her soul ached for it. A sign. A hint of possibility between them.

Simon cleared his throat and dropped his gaze. "I'm glad it has made you happy, Mina. You deserve it."

Though part of her felt defeated at the sad outcome of the moment, Mina reminded herself to have patience. She saw it in his eyes. Hope and the promise of something greater mingled together in the bond still lingering between them. Mina may want more, but for now, those possibilities were enough.

With a deferential bow, Simon offered her his arm. Mina took it, and Simon drew her close beside him as they followed after Thea's family.

...

"It's been so wonderful having you here, Thea," said Mina, walking arm and arm with her friend through the fairgrounds. The Bristow Harvest Festival was in full swing around them, and the Voss children ran here and there, gaping at the stalls of merchandise and games. Acrobats and jugglers attracted their attention, and several of the children scurried towards the performers.

"I only wish you could stay longer," admitted Mina. "I know it's difficult for Frederick to be gone at this time of year, but I cannot help but be a little selfish and wish I could persuade you all to stay forever."

Thea laughed and nudged Mina with her shoulder while bouncing her baby with her free arm. "You would tire of me soon enough. Besides, it looks as though things are progressing quite nicely for you." Thea gave Mina a significant look.

A smile broke across Mina's face as it often did when broaching the topic of her husband.

"Despite my determination to find fault with the man, I like your Simon," said Thea. "And I think you have built yourself a wonderful life here."

"It has not been easy, but I do love it," said Mina. "And I feel in my heart that it will only get better. Someday soon my

Simon will look at me the way your Frederick looks at you."

With a grin, Thea glanced over her shoulder at the two men in question striding several paces behind them. Her eyes met her husband's, and Frederick gave her a wink as flirtatious as any swain.

"I do believe we are the subject of gossip," said Frederick, an ever-present smile in his tone as he winked at his wife.

Over the fortnight the Voss family had been visiting, Simon had witnessed such displays between Thea and Frederick, and each blatant sign of devotion gave Simon a jolt of surprise. The Vosses often acted like a courting couple, though something ran deeper than the light flirtation found in the London ballrooms. A relationship built upon years of admiration and love.

A twinge of jealousy pricked him, and Simon found himself wishing such things were possible for him.

Frederick called out to his two sons who were in scrapes far more often than not before tossing a question at Simon. "How are things with you and Mina?"

Simon nearly tripped over his own feet. From anyone else, the query would have been impudent, but Frederick had such an air of openness and joviality that it was impossible to take offense.

"Things are better than I could've expected, given the circumstances of our marriage," said Simon.

Frederick sent him a pointed look that spoke more than words.

"We are friends. Good friends," said Simon, feeling as though his valet had tied his cravat too tight.

The look in Frederick's eye turned mischievous, and Simon tried to swallow past the piece of linen strangling his neck. Mina's own brother had not questioned him this much when they'd negotiated the marriage settlements.

"We have a better marriage than most," said Simon, feeling the truth of those words.

"That's not a bad start," said Frederick, casting his eyes towards his eldest, Penny, and calling for her to avoid a mud puddle she was determined to slog through. "Though I think you sell yourself short. I have seen the looks you two share."

"Looks?" asked Simon. He and Mina were close. Even closer than he'd hoped for from a marriage of convenience, but Frederick's tone made it sound as though they were lovesick puppies. "I admire and depend on her greatly, but ours is no love match."

"For now," said Frederick with a chuckle. "Not all love starts off as a roaring flame. Many are more like embers, which take time to build but end up being all the warmer for it."

Simon was definitely being strangled and found himself wishing for the insipid talk of gambling and horses that most gentlemen engaged in.

Frederick grinned. "And now, I have made you uncomfortable. I would ask your forgiveness but as I'm very nearly an elder brother of Mina's, I refuse. She deserves happiness in this life."

Simon could not agree more with that, though he knew the passion Frederick spoke of would never factor into their marriage. Mina wasn't unattractive and had features that were quite pleasing, but Simon could never imagine feeling the all-consuming ardor he felt at a mere glance from Susannah. His feelings for Mina were a pale comparison, and friendship was no substitute for desire.

Luckily, a blast from a fire breather drew Frederick's attention and the conversation dropped. It wouldn't do for Simon to confess to Mina's pseudo-brother that her husband had no such notions for his bride. Admiration, yes. Romance, no.

"Mama!" cried Penny, rushing to Thea's side with a flyer waving in her hand. "Did you see this? There is to be a festival dance tonight. May I go?"

Thea tweaked her daughter's cheek. "You know full well you are too young. You've quite a few years before you'll be terrorizing the ballroom."

Carrying his youngest son and thus smearing a healthy dose of muck across his tan trousers, Frederick joined the ladies. "A dance, you say? Perhaps my lady love will honor me with a set or two."

"Perhaps," said Thea, smiling up at her husband. "What do you say, Mina? It's been too long since we have attended one together."

Simon joined the party and glanced at Mina, expecting a polite refusal, but Mina's smile matched the others' and they launched into plans for hiring one of the village women to watch the children.

"But you don't care for dancing," said Simon, and at that, the conversation died an immediate and painful death. A flash of scarlet stole across Mina's face, while disappointment and irritation filled the Vosses'.

"Mina adores dancing," said Frederick.

At that, Mina's face went from bashful to mortified, and Simon wanted to rip his blasted cravat from his throat. One of the children broke the spell holding their party, and the parents went to deal with some familial crisis.

Standing beside Mina, Simon sought out her eyes, though she studiously avoided his.

"Why didn't you say that you enjoy it so much?" he asked in a low voice.

"As I spend most of the dance by myself, I didn't see the point of dragging you where you did not wish to go," she said in equally hushed tones.

Simon racked his brain to remember that fiasco of an assembly in the first weeks of their marriage. He'd spent most of the dance in the card room, but every time Simon had seen Mina, she'd been surrounded by ladies. Surely, she had danced at least one set. But now that he thought of it, Simon couldn't recall her standing for a single set at any ball or assembly since he had first noticed her at the Hartley's townhouse.

And that was when Simon remembered the hopeful expectation on her face when he'd approached her at the assembly.

The moment when things had gone so sour that evening.

"I am a fool," said Simon, realizing what he had done.

"Only occasionally," said Mina, a small smile curving her lips. "But what exactly are you referring to?"

"You wanted me to ask you to dance. At that assembly," he said. "But I only asked if we could leave."

"That was months ago, Simon," said Mina, gripping his arm. "We hardly knew each other."

"I apologize that I was too blind to see," he said, laying his free hand over hers.

Mina did not speak, but the look in her eyes held such warmth that he felt her acceptance and forgiveness to his core.

Chapter 20

The carriage bobbed along the streets of Bristow, and Mina ran a hand down the front of her gown. The harvest ball was a less formal affair than those in London so Mina was not wearing her best dress, but still, she had spent an inordinate amount of time on her coiffure and toilette. Mina was unsure what to expect of the evening. With Thea and Frederick in attendance, it wouldn't fail to be enjoyable, but with a shy glance at Simon beside her, Mina hoped for something more.

Looking over at her friend, Mina saw a hint of the same in Thea's eyes. Perhaps tonight would be different. Better.

"Are you nervous?" Simon whispered in her ear.

Turning to look at him, she found his face scant inches from hers. "I usually find myself at odds before events like this."

In a move that was growing familiar, Simon shifted his arm so Mina could lace hers through. It drew them closer until Mina felt him shoulder to knee.

"The Mina Kingsley I know would never be afraid of a little dance," he said with a smile, his breath tickling her cheeks.

Mina's heart stopped at that. Simon thought her brave.

That was a word Mina never would've chosen to describe herself. Anxiety and nerves seemed an integral part of her makeup, yet here was the man she loved describing her as the exact opposite.

"You have faced down worse and stood victorious, Mina. You rid the household of a poisonous influence all on your own, despite Mrs. Richards' ferocity," he said.

Mina's eyes widened at the thought that he'd discovered her subterfuge, but she saw nothing but admiration in Simon's expression. Regardless of his previous actions and words, he approved of what she had done with the housekeeper.

"It's easier to stand up for others than it is for oneself," she said.

"I don't believe that to be true for most people," said Simon. "Especially when your lackwit husband sided against you. I, for one, have not had the courage to apologize aloud for how I behaved. I am truly sorry. What you have done in our household is nothing short of miraculous. I should have trusted you."

Mina could not answer with words, so she squeezed his arm. From the corner of her eye, she saw Thea and Frederick looking thoroughly pleased, and Mina felt her cheeks burn as her heart gave a happy flutter.

...

Leading Mina into the assembly rooms, Simon's spirits rose. Her glee was utterly contagious, and the joy radiating from her filled him body and soul. The strength of her smile lit up her face, and she glowed with such vitality and life. If it weren't for the prospect of what was coming, Simon would find himself quite swept up in it. But as they gathered beside the dance floor, he deflated.

Dancing.

If it weren't for that, it would be an undeniably entertaining evening. The Vosses were lively company, and Simon enjoyed

time with his wife. But dancing. Really. One of the many benefits of being an old married man was that he was no longer
forced to dance. As a bachelor, it was a necessity of courting,
and Simon had anticipated never having to do so ever again.
Dancing with one's own wife is gauche, after all.

For Mina, Simon was willing to gird his loins and do his bit
to make the evening fun for her, but the thought of prancing
about in front of everyone was enough to make him want to run
the entire way back to Avebury Park until he was carefully hidden in his bedchamber. Thank the heavens, he only had to suffer through one set. One would raise eyebrows as is.

This was for Mina. Simon kept repeating this to himself and
forced a smile on his face. He'd done enough damage at their
first assembly; he would not make Mina regret coming to this
one. At least the dancing had not yet begun, so he had a stay of
execution. But in short order, the musicians began to play.

On the other side of the room, he saw the vicar standing
with his wife. It wasn't a fib to say he needed to speak with the
Mr. Caldwell. He did. His tenant, Mr. Daniels, was struggling to
make do after his wife's sudden passing. Mina was handling
most of the charitable needs, but Simon hoped the vicar could
help in other fashions. However, that discussion could have
waited until a more opportune moment, but Simon grasped
onto that desperate excuse and made a hasty retreat from his
group. Simon would not shirk his duty to his wife, but it was a
relief to be able to put it off for just a few moments more.

Latching onto Mr. Caldwell, Simon chatted with the man
while Mrs. Caldwell wandered off to her lady friends. He'd not
meant to monopolize the vicar's time, but once they began
speaking, their conversation took up most of the first set.
Though he tried to ignore it, his mind kept wandering back to
Mina, who sat by herself as Thea and Frederick danced.

This was a truly terrible idea. Simon could not keep his
mind on either his wife or the vicar. His thoughts were so divided that he was doing a disservice to both, but knowing what

awaited him if he joined Mina made him hesitant. If it were anything but dancing, Simon would be thrilled to keep her company. As is, he wished it were enough for him to have accompanied her here.

Simon's eyes strayed to the card room when Frederick Voss's hand clapped down on Simon's shoulder.

"I hate to interrupt," said Frederick, "but we are wanted elsewhere."

Simon hadn't noticed that the second set had begun. Surely time hadn't passed that quickly. Giving his apologies to Mr. Caldwell and a promise to continue the conversation in a more appropriate time and place, Simon allowed himself to be led towards the dance floor.

"Don't look so gloomy, Simon," said Frederick. "It is only dancing. Surely, you have done it on enough occasions."

"Yes, and I plan on asking Mina for a set tonight."

"One set?" asked Frederick, pulling Simon to a halt. Turning to give Simon his full attention, Frederick stared at him. "Please tell me you are not serious."

"Of course," said Simon. It surprised him that Frederick thought more was necessary. Husbands do not dance with their wives. "Otherwise, I would be living in her pocket."

"Simon," Frederick said with a sad chuckle that made Simon think of Thorne's self-righteous eyebrow, "with the right wife, there is no better place in the world than her pocket." Frederick gave Simon a long, hard look. It was the sort one would expect from an older brother measuring up a younger sibling. "Dancing is likely the last thing you wish to do."

As Frederick had made the statement with the confidence of one who already knows the truth of the matter, Simon felt no need to confirm it.

"I am the same way," said Frederick. "Never cared to dance when I was single, and I still hate the idea of standing up with anyone else. But it is different with Thea because she enjoys it so thoroughly. Making her happy makes me happy, and I look forward to every opportunity to join her as her dance partner.

Think about that, Simon."

Frederick gave him another clap of the shoulder and walked back to his wife, leaving Simon to struggle with own internal turmoil. If he had to be honest, his animosity towards dancing stemmed from his broken heart. Dancing had been one of the few moments where Simon was allowed Susannah's full attention, just the two of them. The other couples did not matter. On that floor, it was them and only them. He still remembered the feel of her hand in his as they moved through the steps. Even seeing couples dancing brought a stab of regret.

This would never do. Simon wanted to kick himself for trudging through this pain once again. He could not keep doing this to himself or to Mina. That path was gone. Susannah was gone. Pining for her was only making him miserable. It was time to let go of the past and embrace his present and future with Mina.

He'd hurt his wife too much to keep wallowing. Simon knew his broken heart could not beat the same for Mina as it had for Susannah, but that did not mean he couldn't build a good life with his wife. Simon never promised Mina romance, but laying aside his own dislikes to cater to her might make up for that missing aspect of their marriage.

In a few quick steps, Simon joined their group and stood before Mina. Her toes tapped along with the music, and Simon held out his hand to her. Mina looked at it and then up at him as though unsure what it meant.

"Will you do me the honor?" he asked.

Never in the history of spoken language had six words meant so much. Mina's eyes widened, her face lighting with such unbridled delight that Simon felt it flow through him. She looked at him as if he were the greatest hero, and in his heart, Simon made a vow that he would strive to earn such admiration.

Followed by the Vosses, Simon led Mina to the floor. The music picked up, and they joined the dancing throng.

Mina was lightness and joy personified, and Simon could

hardly keep his eyes off her. Her gusto for each dance gave her a presence that could not be denied; she whooped and laughed in the raucous country dances and slid calmly through the staid quadrilles and minuets. Though the other dancers around them changed, Simon stood firm beside his wife, leading her through each set. Her energy could not be contained, and he felt himself strengthened by it.

It was just as Frederick had said. Mina's joy brought Simon joy, and in that moment, he thought he would gladly spend the rest of his life attending such gatherings if Mina were at his side.

Between sets, Frederick and Simon played the gallant gentlemen and fetched the ladies drinks. The moment they were out of hearing, Frederick gave Simon a waggle of his eyebrows.

"How is that pocket feeling?" he asked with a dimpled smile.

Glancing over his shoulder at his smiling bride, Simon did not have the words for it but let his own grin say it all.

...

Simon held Mina's hand as she descended the carriage, her energy was fading fast after the long evening. Thea and Frederick made a discreet exit, disappearing into the house before he or Mina had a chance to say goodnight, though judging by the sleepy expression on Mina's face, Simon doubted she noticed.

Holding out his arm to her, Mina's eyes widened in puzzlement, her eyebrows arching.

"It is only proper for a gentleman to escort a lady home," he explained.

"We are home," Mina replied, though she took his arm.

"Not completely," he said, leading her into the house.

"You are being a goose, but thank you. It's been a most wonderful evening. One of the best of my life." Her tone held such earnestness, and Simon's heart expanded, pushing at the confines of his chest. "I have never danced so much in my life.

Usually, I am lucky to get one set."

Mina said it with such a casual air, not putting much thought into the statement, but the words struck Simon. It was a shame that Mina adored dancing, yet had so little opportunity, and Simon burned with pride that he'd been able to give her such a special evening.

"In all honesty," said Simon, dipping conspiratorially to her, "I quite enjoyed myself, though I am surprised to admit that about a ball."

As they climbed the stairs to the second floor, it occurred to him that if he had to list out his best days, nearly every one would include Mina. They strolled in silence all the way to their adjoining chambers, Mina lost in the memory of the evening and Simon deep in thought at that revelation.

Arriving at her bedchamber door, Mina released his arm and stepped away.

"Mina..." Simon began but faltered.

She paused, turning to watch him.

Allowing a moment to gather his thoughts, Simon forged ahead. "I have never told you how much it means to me that you agreed to marry me. I have thought a lot about what you said about my being saddled with you, and I know I haven't done a proper job of telling you just how grateful I am to have you as my wife."

"Simon, I said that in jest," said Mina.

"I don't believe so," he said, grabbing her hands in his. "I think it came from a place of truth, though you tried to hide it."

Mina's eyes fell to the floor, and Simon waited until she met his gaze again.

"I have made some terrible missteps, and you have paid the price," he said. "In these five months, you have become my greatest ally, partner, and dearest friend. You have breathed life not just into the estate but me as well, and too often without my support or acknowledgment."

Sometime in that speech, Simon's hand reached for Mina's cheek. It had been an unconscious thought, but running his thumb along her skin felt natural. Mina stilled, her eyes connecting with his. A wave of emotion rush through him, mysterious and new, but Simon couldn't understand what it was or what it meant.

His Mina. It was a simple pair of words, yet they encapsulated a wealth of meaning. His wife. His Mina.

"Thank you, Mina," he said, the words scarcely louder than a whisper. Lifting her hand, he pressed a kiss to her knuckles, his eyes closing as he held it for a moment before releasing her. With a bow, he turned and walked into his chambers.

Chapter 21

Mina rolled, tugging the bedsheets with her. It was nearly time to get up, and she'd managed only a few brief moments of slumber. Every time she'd nodded off, thoughts of that kiss entered her mind. It was not the type of kiss she desired, but the look in Simon's eyes made Mina's heart so light she wondered if she could fly through the air like a bird. He felt something for her, though she doubted he understood that it was more than friendship.

Touching her lips to the place where he had kissed her hand, Mina found herself impatient to start the day. To see Simon. Throwing off the covers, Mina walked to the window and drew back the curtains before searching her dresser for the absolute perfect outfit.

"Morning, ma'am," said Jenny as she entered. "Mr. Kingsley said you'd probably be abed a touch longer."

"I'm too restless to sleep," she said, casting a glance over her shoulder at her lady's maid to find the woman carrying a most magnificent bouquet of flowers.

"What is that?" asked Mina.

A grin grew on Jenny's face as she crossed the room to hand them to her mistress. Pristine white lilies made up the focal point, but they were surrounded by an array of purple anemones and lobelia. Mina drew in a breath, reveling in the blossoms' scents. Opening the accompanying note, Mina read, *Thank you for a most wonderful evening. — Simon.*

It was a simple note, but the words etched themselves into her heart.

"Help me dress," said Mina, beckoning to her maid. "Quickly."

...

Simon ran a brush along his horse's neck as he whistled a tune. Both Spartan and Beau were saddled and waiting, though Simon did not expect Mina to arrive for fair bit. When his spies had informed him she was awake, he hadn't been able to contain his eagerness and started preparations for their morning ride so they could leave the moment she appeared. Groomsmen milled about, mucking the stalls and feeding the horses, but Simon hardly noticed them, the stale scent of the stable, or anything else. Simon's mind was full of his wife.

Did she like the bouquet? Knowing Mina, she did, but Simon felt a frisson of uncertainty. His wife had him unsettled. Something between them was changing; a subtle shift that Simon wished he understood.

Simon craved order and continuity. It was part of his very makeup, and that aspect of himself worried about how this transformation might ruin the goodness they'd found together. And yet, there was a wondrous excitement wrapped up in that fear; a thrill that made Simon welcome this emotional dishevelment and wonder what would have happened if he'd truly kissed Mina last night.

In that perplexing moment, he'd let the opportunity slip by. They had stood together at her chamber door, embraced in the shadows, and gazing into each other's eyes, yet it never even entered his mind to give her a proper kiss. Simon had never thought of Mina as kissable. But lying in his bed, listening to the clock tick, Simon found himself considering it. And imagining it. And casting his thoughts back to the time Mina had kissed him.

It was a small thing. A buss on his cheek. A sign of gratitude. But Simon had blushed like a schoolgirl. In the moment, he'd thought it nothing more than a byproduct of living with Mina; her ease of blushing was rubbing off on him. But now, Simon wondered if there was something more lurking beneath that reddening of his cheeks.

Simon didn't know what to make of his wife. Though he called Mina a friend, what he felt for her was unlike any of his other friendships. Certainly, Simon would never have spent an hour agonizing over what flowers to give to Finch or fretted over Finch's reaction to a gift.

And yet, what Simon felt for Mina was not what he felt for Susannah.

Just thinking of that lady caused a sour turn of his stomach. His feelings towards Susannah remained, but even such fleeting thoughts of her made Simon wretched. Clinging to memories of Susannah was unfair to Mina. That was the past.

"Simon!" Mina's voice called to him, and he turned to find her hurrying towards him in a most undignified and purely Mina way. She clutched the edges of her skirt in one hand and her bonnet in the other. Feet from him, her boots slipped in a bit of mud, and she pitched to the side, but Simon leapt forward and steadied her.

"My apologies. I appear to be quite clumsy this morning," she said with her usual hint of self-mockery.

"No, dear. Just in a hurry," Simon replied. He wanted to ask her about the flowers, but the words stuck in his throat and his tongue tied in knots. "Though I cannot reason why you would be so excited to see your good for nothing husband." There, he said something.

Mina stepped closer until he felt the warmth of her. A hint of lilies hung in the air around her, and Simon breathed it in.

Never had their scent been so alluring. Mina dropped the hem of her riding habit and placed that hand on his chest. Her fingers trembled, and he stilled under her touch and looked down at it, wondering what about it made him feel so rattled.

"Thank you for the flowers," she said, her voice soft. "They..." But her words trailed off, swallowed up in her emotions.

"Then you liked them?" His own voice dropped to match hers, and he found himself moving closer.

"Lilies are my favorite," she said.

"I guessed so. Almost every arrangement in the house has them." A lock of her hair hung loose, tumbling down her shoulder, and his fingers grazed it. At first glance, her hair was a plain brown, but in the morning light, he saw touches of red shining in it.

"Simon," she whispered.

Gazing into her eyes, Simon saw tears gathering, and panic stabbed at him. They were such little things, but as one slid down her cheek, he felt as though his heart would break. Brushing it away, he struggled to say anything that would stop them from falling.

"Mina, please," he said, faltering to find the words. "I am sorry...I did not mean..." Though he had no idea what he was apologizing for.

She shook her head, her breath hitching. "No, these are happy tears. It's silly to get emotional over something so small, but it means so much to me..." Her voice caught, and Simon brushed away more tears.

Her eyes were full of her heart, and those feelings enveloped Simon, wrapping around him like a thick quilt on a cold winter day. Giving in to the urge prodding him, he leaned in and pressed his lips to hers. He'd dreamt of this moment many times in the last few hours, and yet this kiss far exceeded any of his simple imaginations. It felt natural, as if he belonged in this moment with her.

Like he was home.

Mina slid her arms around him, and Simon did the same, pulling her tight to him. The moment stretched on as they embraced. Nothing else mattered but being here with his Mina. There were no worries or issues, just the two of them bound together in a perfect point in time.

Gently, it ended, and Simon regretfully pulled away and Mina looked as disappointed as he felt. His hand slid up her neck and rested at her cheek, and Mina leaned into it, a hint of shyness in her eyes. His thumb brushed her flushed lips, and he felt himself leaning into her again.

Spartan whinnied, nudging Simon's shoulder and bumping him into Mina; he was more than willing to ignore the beast, but Beau joined in. Simon glared at the horses with a resigned sigh.

"They are certainly impatient this morning," Mina said, a chuckle coloring her words.

She slid her hands back to Simon's chest and smoothed his waistcoat. It was a simple movement, but it held an intimacy that warmed Simon. His eyes fell to Mina's lips again, but Beau nickered. Simon released her, and his arms felt painfully empty.

Guiding Mina to the mounting block, Simon helped her onto Beau's saddle as he always did. Mina was a skilled horsewoman and required no such assistance, but Simon always enjoyed giving her a bit of gentlemanly attention, even if it was only a hand up and down from her horse. But this time, there was nothing cursory about his aid. No simple steadying hand. Simon lingered, holding her longer than necessary with no other reason than a desire to do so.

Simon's eyes never left his wife as he mounted Spartan, and they headed out into the countryside. Riotous thoughts and feelings overwhelmed Simon as he attempted to decipher what it all meant. He could not categorize what his heart was telling him, but when Mina sent him a demure smile with gleaming eyes Simon realized he relished the opportunity to puzzle it all out.

Chapter 22

This morning's sedate ride had to be the most proficient demonstration of horsemanship in Mina's life, though no one watching would realize it. Beau and Spartan ambled along, but it was a miracle Mina kept her seat while her mind and heart were so utterly occupied with other things. Or one very specific thing.

That kiss.

Mina's mind was a cacophony of questions and speculations, hopes and fears, all while her heart swelled with the euphoria of the moment. None of her dreams had come close to the reality of kissing Simon, and Mina knew she was not the only one affected. Simon's eyes followed her, and Mina's scarcely left his; the looks they shared warmed her through, chasing away the nip of the fall air.

The ride stretched on longer than usual, and Mina smiled to herself that neither of them were eager to return to the house where their duties would force them apart until luncheon. It was not in either of their natures to put off their responsibilities indefinitely, but there was no need to hurry them along, either.

When it was absolutely necessary that they return—and not

a second sooner—they made their way back to the stables. Pulling Beau to a halt beside the mounting block, Mina shifted in the saddle but stopped herself before she alighted. She was not about to pass up the opportunity to lure Simon closer in the name of gentlemanly decorum. They both knew it was unnecessary, but the look in Simon's eyes said he appreciated it as much as she.

Hand in his, Mina stepped onto the block and down the stairs. It was a simple, easy movement, but her mind was so full of Simon that she wobbled on the final step. His arms came around her before she stumbled, his hands falling to her waist. Mina gripped his forearms and flushed a deep crimson.

They stood together, his fingers brushing her hips. Heavens above, Mina wanted to steal another kiss. They were so close that the tiniest of movements would close the distance. Embracing the infinitesimal bit of courage she had, Mina tilted towards Simon.

But a groom stepped forward to take the reins, and Mina's face caught fire at being caught in such a compromising position. Simon looked not the least bit ashamed but glanced over at the young man, giving the groom a grim glare at the interruption. Mina bit her lips but could not hold back the smile.

She stepped away, but Simon caught her hand and threaded it through his arm. She let out a silent sigh, allowing the gesture to pull them flush with one another, and rested her hands on his forearm. Mina stopped breathing altogether when Simon's free hand joined hers, and they strolled, arm-in-arm and hand-in-hand towards the house.

A fall deluge had soaked the countryside for a full two days, but the skies had cleared during the night and the sun was out in full force. The weather had stripped the trees of their leaves, and the groundskeeper and his men were corralling the golden foliage as it skittered across the gardens and lawn. It had reached that moment in the season when the fall beauty was all but gone, yet before the winter snows covered it in a thick blanket of white. Normally, it was Mina's least favorite time of year, but in this instance, she had a hard time believing there was a more glorious day. Casting a glance at Simon, she caught him peeking at her. Yes, a beautiful day, indeed.

Crossing to the front of the main house, they discovered several carriages lined up at the front door, causing Mina to pause.

"Simon?" Mina nudged him and turned his attention to it. "Are you expecting visitors?"

"No," Simon replied. He stared at the carriages for a moment, and then Mina watched every bit of warmth and delight evaporate from his features. "But I recognize the carriages. One of those belongs to my mother, and if I had to hazard a guess, the others belong to my sisters."

Mina heart dropped to her toes. Simon's family. There were many reasons Mina was not overly thrilled at the idea of them showing up unannounced, but first and foremost was the fact that she was entirely unpresentable.

"I cannot go in there, Simon," she said, pulling against him when he tried to lead her forward. "I must go in the back way—"

"You are not going to slip in the back like a servant," he said, the look in his eyes brooking no refusal.

"I look a fright!" Mina pulled the riding bonnet from her head, knowing the brim had bits of muck and straw still stuck to it. During their embrace, the last thing on her mind had been her bonnet, and it had fallen straight into the mud.

"You look lovely," he insisted. "And your appearance should be the last of your worries when it comes to them. I doubt this will be a merry party and judging by the amount of luggage the footmen are unloading, it will be of some duration." His voice sounded as bleak as Mina's spirits.

In any normal situation, Mina would not be overly sensitive about her appearance, but this was her first time meeting her in-laws. Her hem was caked in at least six inches of mud, and her bonnet was unsalvageable. To say nothing of her hair. In her hurry to meet Simon, Mina had urged Jenny to do only the bare necessity with her coiffure, and most of her tresses had tumbled free of their pins. And then there were the flecks of mud peppering her from head to toe; while the bits of grime on Simon made him look rugged, Mina was certain they were not so flattering on her.

Simon stepped in front of her and grasped Mina's hands. "You look like a wild woodland faerie who has been enjoying a morning ride with her husband. They may be my family, but you have nothing to prove to them. They couldn't even be bothered to attend our wedding, for goodness sakes."

"We hardly gave them any notice," said Mina.

"Thea managed it, and they could have, too," he retorted, his gaze never faltering. "If they dislike my woodland faerie, then they can go impose themselves on someone else."

The words were grand enough, but the feeling Simon infused into them gave the statement a weight that sunk straight into Mina's heart. He wasn't saying what he thought she needed to hear; Simon believed it. Mina still thought him wrong about her appearance and would rather be given the opportunity to clean up, but with the glint of approval in Simon's eye, Mina found herself unable to fight him.

Moving to his side, Mina took his arm again, and he drew her tight against him.

"Woodland faerie, indeed!" She harrumphed at his nonsense, though a smile tickled her lips.

Her residual fears had Mina gripping Simon's arm, holding on for dear life as they crossed to the front door, and then he leaned over to whisper into her ear, "I shan't allow you to be fed to the wolves, my dear."

My dear. Those two words were a commonplace endearment—Imogene punctuated every sentence with them—but coming from Simon, they left her heart feeling like a bread pudding straight from the oven.

And with that, Mina held her head high with the elegance of a mud-streaked duchess and climbed the front stairs. The entrance buzzed with people; Mrs. Witmore and Jennings directed footmen and maids hither and thither, while several couples and children accosted Simon. Swarmed as they were, Mina's hand clenched Simon's arm, and he squeezed it back.

"Mother," he said with a bow that seemed too formal for family. "Mina, may I present Mrs. John Kingsley?"

Mina had tried for a properly deferential air, but at his introduction, her eyes shot to Simon and he sent her a brief wink. For him to word the introduction thusly placed Mina firmly on higher footing than his own mother. Mina did not know enough about the lady to have any expectations concerning the coming visit, but his words made it clear to everyone precisely where Mina stood in his estimation. Judging by the narrowing of his mother's eyes, Mina knew it was not lost Mrs. Kingsley.

Her eyes traveled Mina, stopping at every blemish and imperfection. It was enough to make Mina wish for a hasty retreat, but holding firm to Simon, Mina stiffened her metaphorical spine.

"Madam," said Mina with a proper curtsey.

Mrs. Kingsley's responding bob was barely perceptible. It was Simon's turn to tense, and Mina to give him a reassuring squeeze of the arm.

Continuing with the introductions, Simon turned Mina to his elder sister and her husband, "Mr. and Mrs. Norman Andrews."

Emmeline Andrews ushered her children forward. "Show your manners," she prompted.

The three children looked more impeccable than any children ever should and calmly walked to their mother's side. The two elder daughters gave possibly the most perfect curtseys Mina had ever witnessed, and the youngest (a boy no more than three years of age) gave a bow befitting the most elegant of gentlemen.

"And you must excuse my eldest three," said Emmeline. "They were most anxious to meet their new aunt, but I'm afraid Kenneth is at school, and Joanna and Lucinda's studies could not be interrupted. They have only a few short years before they are to be presented, and it is imperative that they continue their lessons with their dancing instructor and governess if they are to be a success."

Then came Priscilla Ramsbury, the youngest of the Kingsley family.

"Where are Walter and the boys?" asked Simon.

Priscilla waved the question away. "Walter is off with friends at one of their estates for hunting or some such thing, and Roger and Thomas are both at school."

Mina hid her shock. Though they'd never formally met, Mina knew of Priscilla, who'd been one of the most sought-after debutantes of her Season. If memory served, Priscilla had married quickly, but it couldn't have been more than eight years ago. Meaning, her eldest was six or seven, at the very most. Though it was not unheard of to send a child away to school that young, it was not a common occurrence; Mina could not imagine sending away any of her brothers at that young an age.

"But you overlooked Benedict," Mrs. Kingsley said to Simon. Her eyes narrowed and lips pursed, as though issuing a challenge.

A man moved to stand beside Mrs. Kingsley, and she slid her arm through with an intimate air that made it clear that he was no mere acquaintance, which was an uncomfortable discovery on many levels. Mrs. Kingsley was a regal woman firmly in what many call her 'mature' years. Not as old as Imogene, but clearly deserving of the title of grandmother, and the man at her side was a child in comparison.

Mina knew that was an unfair assessment. He was full grown though at least a couple years younger than Priscilla. He was of thin build and with features so flawless that he looked beautiful rather than handsome. Mina knew men like him often made women swoon, but he was too feminine for her tastes. She preferred Simon's misaligned nose to Benedict's delicate one.

Simon halted when he spied Benedict, and his eyes fell to the proprietary way Mrs. Kingsley stroked her fingers against the man's forearm. Though Simon's face showed no outward sign of distress, Mina felt his inner battle, but decorum won out, and he made the introductions between Mina and Mr. Benedict Swinton.

"I was terribly distraught that we were unable to make the wedding," said Emmeline, "but we came as soon as we were able."

"That was over five months ago," said Simon.

Emmeline had a stiff air to her. Far more than the rigidity of her spine, Mina felt as though Emmeline Andrews was the type who never smiled unless at a polite interlude during a properly correct conversation. And never with one's full mouth. Just a delicate upturn of the lips.

"We sent you a letter of congratulations, but we've all had so many obligations that it was impossible to come sooner," she said with a tone of genteel reproof, as though affronted that he thought her so gauche as to overlook such a social nicety.

The letter Emmeline referred to had been all that was proper between two passing acquaintances but held none of the familial sentiment Mina had been expecting. The letter of congratulations from Mina's rough and tumble seafaring brother had expressed more warmth and sentiment than Mrs. Emmeline Andrews'. Mina already had a strong sense of Emmeline's personality and was not looking forward to spending more time with her. Or Mrs. Kingsley, who continued to watch Mina with a pinched expression as though Mina were covered in manure and not mud.

"We have brought a surprise," said Priscilla, smiling at Simon in a way that reminded Mina of a snake about to feast on a poor mouse. Mina had only spent a few moments among the Kingsley family, and she was already ready for their visit to be over.

"I am certain that you all are enough of a surprise," said Simon. His tone conveyed much of what Mina was feeling in that moment, and she held tighter to Simon's arm, hoping it strengthened him as it did her. She did not understand the dynamics of this family, but she knew it was distressing her husband.

All thoughts of Simon's emotional well-being vanished when the group parted, and Mina saw another couple approach. Her blood chilled as the lady drew closer, gliding with a grace that Mina knew she could never match. The lady smiled with impeccable coyness as she batted her eyes at Mina's husband, bringing Mina's worst nightmare into vicious reality.

Every bit of Simon's being seized up as Susannah floated towards him. Her bright blue eyes trapped his in her gaze while a demure smile crossed her lips.

"It is good to see you, Mr. Kingsley," she said, her voice like golden honey.

Priscilla joined arms with Susannah, beaming at the lady. "My dear friend, Susannah, moved into our neighborhood, and I was so astonished to discover that you two were acquaintances. When Mama and I decided to come for a visit, I knew I must invite her to join us. Is this not delightful?"

"She practically dragged us here." Susannah dropped her gaze, glancing up at Simon through her lashes. "I do hope we aren't an imposition."

At that, Simon noticed Susannah's husband standing beside the ladies.

"Mrs. Ramsbury assured us it would be too diverting to pass up," said Mr. Richard Banfield.

Diverting was not the word Simon would have chosen, but his voice failed him, leaving Simon decidedly mute.

"Perhaps it would be best if we showed you to your rooms," said Mina.

Simon flinched. Though she still held his arm, he had all but forgotten she was standing there. Staring at the woman he loved while holding the arm of the woman with whom he'd shared an intimate moment not long ago was not a comfortable situation to be in.

Releasing Simon's arm, Mina approached the housekeeper and spoke a few whispered words before turning back to the group. "We do have rooms ready for you, if you care to refresh yourself."

"Yes," said Emmeline with a quick glance at Mina. "I am sure we could all use a moment to refresh ourselves."

A hint of a blush stole across Mina's cheeks, though she kept her composure. In any other situation, Simon would have been proud of her backbone, but Susannah's eyes bore into his, and it was hard for him to think of anything else but the clear blue perfection of them. Despite himself, Simon felt a swelling of desire, and his mind called up fantasies he'd tried hard to bury. She was a siren's call destined to drive him mad.

Mina did not look at him, and he was far too glad for it. Susannah's pull on him was as strong as it had ever been. It was a craving that Simon felt uncertain he could overcome. With a monumental internal struggle, he fought it back, desperate to keep those feelings locked in a hidden part of his mind, never to disturb him or his wife again.

But as Mina ushered the other guests towards their rooms, Susannah came up next to him, taking his arm as they mounted the steps, and Simon panicked at the overwhelming jolt of feeling her touch gave him.

Chapter 23

Mina forced herself to focus on the task at hand. They had the space to house Simon's family and the Vosses, but it took a fair bit of maneuvering to get everything in place. Under Mrs. Witmore's command, the household staff were handling the upset far better than Mina. Forcing a placid look on her face, she fought back the tears threatening to make an even bigger fool of herself than she already had. Seeing that woman on Simon's arm was nearly enough to crush her, but Mina refused to give up so easily.

When all was settled, including the various children and their staff in the nursery, Mina hurried to her bedchamber and decided Jenny deserved a massive pay increase. Having anticipated her mistress's dire need, the woman stood ready with a bowl of warm water in one hand, hairpins in the other, and a freshly pressed gown laid out on the bed. Mina was a gudgeon for insisting on taking extra care with her toilette. She wished the opinions of the party did not matter to her, but with the enemy circling, Mina knew she needed to prime whatever weapons she had. However puny.

Mina hadn't even begun to think about all the work a last-minute house party was going to bring. Entertainment and meals would need arranging. Mina's schedule would need clearing in order to play hostess. But those were worries for later.

And she refused to wonder where Simon was. The possibilities were too terrifying.

A knock at the door, and Mrs. Witmore entered, carrying a bundle of nerves with her.

"Madam, you must come quickly," she said, hurrying over to the vanity as Jenny placed the last few pins in Mina's hair. "Mrs. Kingsley—the other Mrs. Kingsley—is upset, and she will not listen to reason."

Following Mrs. Witmore through the house, Mina sensed this was what her life was going to be for the next few weeks. Uncertainty, alarm, and a heaping portion of discomfort. It had not been a full hour since their arrival and Mina already wished her in-laws to the other side of the country. Them and that trollop.

Mina heard her mother-in-law's voice coming from down the hall, and a perverse part of her wanted to lecture Mrs. Kingsley on proper decorum, for her tone and volume were anything but genteel.

"It must be taken down immediately! I will not have it there!"

"Yes, ma'am, but Mrs. Kingsley put it there—" said a maid with a tremulous tone.

"I am Mrs. Kingsley," she said, and Mina heard something crash, as though the lady had thrown her reticule. "And I order you to take it down."

Turning the corner, Mina found the youngest member of staff shivering under the frosty glare of Mrs. Kingsley. In any other situation, Mina probably would have found herself trembling alongside the girl, but seeing the poor child being berated by someone who should know better gave Mina the courage to stand strong.

"What is going on here?" asked Mina, hiding the fury in her voice.

"This girl disobeyed me when I ordered this be taken down immediately." Mrs. Kingsley pointed to a painting on the wall. To the casual observer, it might seem a strange request, but as the subject of the portrait was none other than Mrs. Kingsley's late husband, Mina suspected there was a terrible history there.

"I will not allow that man to be displayed as though he is befitting such an honor," Mrs. Kingsley said, her eyes stabbing the canvas.

Being hung in a side corridor in an inconsequential part of the house did not seem like much of an honor, though Mina was not about to point that out to the lady; its location was an immaterial issue.

"Where is the housekeeper?" asked Mrs. Kingsley. "I demand to speak with her."

Mrs. Witmore opened her mouth, but Mrs. Kingsley spoke over her. "Not you! You are not the housekeeper. The other woman."

Mina watched Mrs. Kingsley sputter, attempting to remember Mrs. Richards' name, and Mina found herself thinking it was a good thing the former housekeeper was not present to hear her former mistress struggling to recall her name. For all Mrs. Richards' spouting off about her former mistress, the former housekeeper had made no lasting impression on Mrs. Kingsley.

"Mrs. Richards is no longer employed at Avebury Park," said Mina. "And even if she were, I am mistress of this household and it is my right to hang any painting I see fit. I apologize if that upsets you, but I will not remove the portrait of Simon's father."

She had spoken carefully, striving to maintain a respectful tone, but seeing Mrs. Kingsley's darkening expression, Mina realized it had done no good.

"Do you know what that man put me through?" she asked, marching over to Mina. "I will not abide that painting being hung in my home."

Mina felt her resolve shake under Mrs. Kingsley's glare, but Simon's words of support resurfaced from her memories. No matter what Mrs. Kingsley thought or felt, Simon liked seeing Mina stand up for herself. Mina was mistress of this house. This was her home, and she would not be browbeaten in it.

The two women held a silent battle, their eyes locked until Mrs. Kingsley broke and stormed down the hall.

Mina let out the breath she'd been holding and felt like collapsing onto the floor. In her mind, she knew she should seek out Thea and verify that her true guests were still comfortable and that the interlopers were not causing them problems, but Mina was desperate to see Simon. So much had changed in the last few hours, and Mina felt drained. She did not know what was going on in his head or what this situation meant for the two of them, but she longed to feel his arms around her again.

"I'm sorry for bothering you, madam," said Mrs. Witmore. "I tried to deal with it myself, but she would not listen."

"Don't trouble yourself," said Mina. "I would not want you to face down that dragon alone. Please let me know if there are any more issues."

"Yes, madam."

Mina heard Mrs. Witmore leave, but her eyes were locked on her father-in-law's portrait, and she found herself wondering what had happened to the Kingsley family that had torn them so apart.

...

After the overwhelming bustle and movement in the rest of the house, the conservatory was blessedly silent. Mina stepped inside, brushing past the greenery growing around her, and sought out the secret nook. One section of the wall had a recess with plants carefully placed in front of it to block a bench from casual view. It was a perfect hiding place.

Though obscured, Mina saw Simon sitting there, his fore-head scrunched in a desperate manner. It had been a good long time since Mina had seen such troubled looks on his face. Though not uncommon when they were first married, they had been absent for several weeks, and it hurt to see that worry return. Mina wanted to run her fingers over the furrow and smooth away the heavy cares dragging him down.

Instead, she satisfied herself with squeezing onto the bench beside him.

"Jennings mentioned you had gone into hiding," she teased. "He suggested we send out a search party, and I was about ready to send a footman to the Nelsons to see if we could borrow their hunting dogs to sniff you out."

Simon's lips pulled into a smile, but it was a forlorn version of his usual one.

"He mentioned you had an altercation with Mr. Swinton," she said. Mina did not want to discuss Mrs. Kingsley's paramour, but it was a good starting point. What she wanted to ask him about what the one thing she couldn't bear to; Mina didn't know if she would ever be ready to broach the subject of Susannah.

"I should have thrown him from the house," said Simon. "Should've thrown them both out." There was a hint of a growl in his tone, but mostly, he sounded lost. It reminded her so much of her brothers after their mother had passed; little boys trying so hard to be brave when all they wanted to do was cry. Just thinking of it brought a prickle of tears to Mina's eyes.

"Father would have," he added in a tone so soft Mina was sure he hadn't meant her to hear it.

Their topsy-turvy relationship aside, Mina could not watch him hurt without giving some comfort. Reaching over, Mina wrapped an arm around his shoulder. His eyes stared off into the distance at some past pain, and he leaned into her.

"Flaunting her latest lover in her husband's home," Simon muttered. "She has no shame."

Mina took a breath, steeling herself to ask the question. "What happened to your parents? I had a bit of an altercation with your mother about your father's portrait. Her reaction seemed..." Mina paused, searching for the word before adding, "unnaturally angry."

Simon gave a huff. "That is one way to describe the fiasco that was my parents' marriage." He sighed, rubbing at his face and scrubbing at his hair.

"They were a love match," he said. "A love match despite the fact that both their parents had arranged marriages for them. They eloped and caused a massive scandal. A lot of society shut their doors to them, and it hurt my mother to have her beloved soirees and teas and balls denied her. Eventually, that hurt turned into resentment for my father.

"And he was just as bad. He married a young miss and assumed the demure face she showed in public was genuine. My father never cared to be crossed or disobeyed, and it was a blow to find out his wife was a domineering woman who wanted different things in life."

Mina's arm slid down from his shoulder, and she rubbed his back while Simon continued in a toneless voice.

"My childhood was a constant cycle of my mother leaving to seek out something better than a socially ostracized life in the middle of the countryside. Father would hunt her down and order her to leave her latest lover. She'd refuse, and he'd cut off her pin money. She'd live on her friends' charity for a bit, but when that was gone, she'd be forced home to play the part of doting wife and mother until she amassed the money necessary to leave again."

Simon paused, his jaw tensing as he gathered his thoughts. When he spoke again, it was in a whisper. "She often told me she wished she'd never fallen in love with Father because it had done nothing but poison her life." Simon took a breath. "I was never sure if she meant she regretted me and my sisters, too."

At that, Mina wrapped both arms around Simon, clinging to him as though holding the broken pieces of his soul together.

There were no words to heal his hurt. No simple phrases could fix the heartache his parents' selfishness had caused, no matter how Mina wished it otherwise.

"It's difficult to believe that even after that, you chose to get married," said Mina.

Simon shifted, turning his head to look at her with a whisper of a true smile. "That was easy enough once I found someone the exact opposite of my mother."

Mina huffed. "Having done battle with her, I will take that as a compliment."

Simon's hand moved to rest on Mina's knee. Though she was acutely aware it was there, Mina suspected it'd been an unconscious movement. She tried not to read meaning into it, even if her heart beat faster.

"In all seriousness," he said, his smile dropping again, "I am not entirely certain why I thought it was the right path for me. My sisters are not pattern cards for happiness. Emmeline and Norman married for love, and now Norman is more hostage than husband, completely at the mercy of my sister's never-ending need for perfection."

His voice grew angrier with each sentence. "And Priscilla is in even worse shape. Her husband adored her, and after only a short time together, he can hardly stand to be in the same county as her. She takes no joy from him or their children."

They sat silent, Mina holding her sad, broken husband. It was no wonder he had such a poor understanding of love. He'd only ever seen twisted, blackened forms of it. Mina felt overwhelmed at the thought of teaching him what pure, selfless love was in the face of such despair. She wanted to shout at him that what those people had felt was not love. Lust and passion were not the same as genuine love.

"But I'm not being entirely honest," he said. "I know why I chose to marry, despite all those examples of how terrible it can be."

Simon sighed, his gaze dropping to the ground. "I had one example of a good marriage. They were more than two people

bound together by ceremony. They had a relationship that seemed like it had been plucked from the storybooks. It wasn't just that they doted on each other. They were two halves that fit together to make a better whole. They were partners in every sense of the word, and it was clear to anyone with eyes that they had a deep and abiding love.

"Seeing Sir Gilbert and Lady Lovell showed me what was possible," he said. "A loving marriage and a happy family. They proved to me that it could be done, and that it was worth searching for. They gave me hope."

Having never met Sir Gilbert, Mina knew little of the man except that his wife still cherished him though death had separated them for many years. It didn't surprise her that Simon had sought after a similar love for so many years; Mina often felt a twinge of envy when Imogene spoke of her husband.

"I spent years searching for that kind of love, and then I found everything I had dreamt of. For a brief moment, that life was before me, only to evaporate and disappear forever when—" Simon stopped short, glancing at Mina as though he'd forgotten who he'd been speaking to, but the damage was already done. Mina didn't need him to finish his thought for her to know full well what he'd been about to say. His unspoken words hung in the air between them like a pestilential vapor.

"I apologize," he said, shifting away to break contact with Mina. It was a small thing, but it cut her to the core. "I don't mean to hurt you," he added, but it wasn't his words that hurt. It was watching their camaraderie evaporate before her eyes as Simon locked himself away from her.

"I made it clear I was not expecting love in this marriage and never indicated I was trying to find it," Simon said, standing. He stepped away from the bench, putting frigid distance between them. "This is all coming out wrong. I don't want you to think..."

Simon swallowed, and his eyes caught hers for a moment before falling away. "I wholeheartedly believe what I've said before. You are a blessing in my life, I value our friendship, and I am grateful that you are my wife, but do not raise your hopes, Mina. I have no heart to give you."

With those final words, he left Mina alone, taking her heart with him.

Chapter 24

Mina lay on her bed. She would prefer getting into it, but no amount of sleep could ease her weary soul. She stared sightlessly at the far wall, her eyes sore and puffy. Her role as hostess insisted she attend to her guests, but Mina could not face them. Whenever she thought the tears were done, something would spring to mind and release a whole new torrent.

Things had been going so well. It was impossible to believe that only a few hours had passed since she and Simon had shared that sublime kiss together. It was all gone now.

New tears rolled across the bridge of her nose and fell onto the pillow. The most divine morning of her life, and Simon discarded it after a single look at Susannah. Mina knew—absolutely knew—he had felt something significant during their embrace. She had seen it in his eyes and felt it in his touch. Simon had felt an inkling of love, only to repudiate it mere hours later.

The door opened.

"I wish to be alone," said Mina.

Footsteps came across the room, and Thea climbed onto the bed to lay face-to-face with Mina.

"Dearest?" asked Thea, grasping Mina's hand.

That was all it took for a new flood of tears to pour out. Sobs wracked Mina, making speech impossible. Tears wetted the pillow as Mina recounted all that had happened between trembling breaths.

"Things were going so well," Mina cried, "and now they are ruined!" She knew she was spiraling down a deep pit of despair, but she had no desire to crawl out of it. She let the misery of it wash over her, and welcomed its heartbreaking embrace.

"I feel like a child again, hoping that if I were good enough then my family would be happy again," said Mina. It was something she had not admitted aloud, but the truth of her feelings came spilling out into the open. "Trying to fill the impossible hole left behind by my mother. Wanting to make others happy when all they wanted was someone else."

Mina shook beneath a sob, her vision blurring.

"Oh, dearest," said Thea with a watery smile. "Please, do not give up. Simon was raised believing that love is the same as attraction. He doesn't understand what love truly is, and what he feels for that woman is fleeting compared to what he feels for you."

"I wish I could believe that."

"Mina," Thea said with an authority that forced Mina to pay attention, "even in the scant weeks I've been here, I have seen his feelings for you grow. There is no doubt in my mind that he loves you, and that you two belong together. He just does not recognize it for what it is. Simon thinks it is friendship or admiration, but he does not realize that those form the base of the deepest love there is. As much as I want to give him a good kick in the shins for how he has hurt you, I do not want you to give up on something that makes you so happy."

"Until now," grumbled Mina.

Thea gave a low chuckle and a half smile. "Until now. But there is still hope. Men don't always have the soundest judgment. Remember when Frederick broke things off with me? Papa convinced him that it was imperative for my future happiness to be with a man who could buy me new frocks every week."

"And rather than tell you in person," said Mina, "he made it known by escorting Sally Jenkins to the Solstice Festival." Mina did not know whether to laugh or cry at the memory. Yesterday, Frederick's combined idiocy and audacity would've had Mina in stitches, but that was because Thea's story ended well; it was difficult to find the humor in it while still gripped in the heartbreak of unrequited love.

"Sally Jenkins!" said Thea with dramatic exclamation. "The girl who had more beauty than brains and showed up wearing that monstrosity of a bonnet."

"It smacked Frederick in the face every time she turned her head." At that, Mina did grin. Frederick had spent the evening picking feathers out of his teeth.

"And when he finally came to his senses and spoke to me directly, it resolved itself to everyone's happiness."

"Except your papa's."

Thea huffed. "Yes, it took him longer to come around, but he did, and he loves Frederick as much as any father-in-law. But dearest, it was you who helped me through those terrible days. You talked me through the heartache and helped me to not give up on the greatest blessing in my life." Tears filled Thea's eyes, and she brushed them aside. "I will not let you give up so easily. Even if I do wish to club Simon over the head."

"I thought you wanted to kick in the shins."

"That, too," she replied. "I may want for this all to end up happy, but I would like to see him suffer a bit first."

They lay together, Mina's heartbreak easing until the clock chimed that it was time to dress for dinner. She didn't have the strength to face it. Not with those people in her home. But she also knew she could not lie around moping until they left.

A knock at the door signaled Jenny's arrival.

"Thank you, Thea," said Mina, giving her friend's hand a squeeze as they climbed off the bed.

"I am not leaving yet," said Thea, gathering Mina and Jenny to the vanity. "If you have to do battle with those trolls, then I intend to make sure you are properly arrayed for a victory."

"There is not time enough to bring about the impossible," said Mina. She had meant for a light-hearted tone, but residual heartache tinged her words with a bitterness that made Mina wince.

Thea faced Mina, her hands on her hips. "I will not allow you to speak about my dear friend in such a manner. Besides, one does not dress to impress others. One dresses for oneself. There is no impressing the ladies infesting your house, but with the proper preparations, it will help *you* feel ready for battle."

"But you need to dress—" began Mina.

Waving an impatient hand, Thea approached Mina's closet. "I am not in the enemy's sights and would be just as happy to attend dinner dressed as I am. It's been years since I have bothered with such things, and I do not miss such formality."

Sorting through the gowns, Thea pulled out the exact one that Mina would have chosen for herself. Moments later, she was seated before the vanity, and Thea and Jenny began their work.

...

The ladies and gentlemen sat around the massive table, the wood surface reflecting the candlelight around them. Cook and the rest of the kitchen staff had outdone themselves by assembling the last-minute feast filling the table; the food was not the finest, but it was delicious and well prepared, and Mina wished she could enjoy it. With any other dining companions, it would have been a lovely meal, but this was interminable. A fitting end to such a baffling day.

With the exception of Thea, the rest of the ladies were attired as though attending some prestigious event in the upper echelons of London society rather than a quiet country dinner.

They were pinched and primped to the point where every movement must have been uncomfortable. Mrs. Kingsley's neck was encased in gems that were more gaudy than gorgeous, and Mina had to wonder why the lady felt it necessary to display such overblown finery.

Mina's own appearance paled in comparison, but it did not matter as she was pleased with Thea and Jenny's ministrations. Thea had managed some twist of Mina's hair that made a few ringlets cascade in a most becoming way. How she had gotten it to curl so perfectly in the first place was a miracle. That, combined with wearing one of her favorite frocks that was a deep shade of midnight blue, which complemented her brown eyes, Mina felt decidedly confident. She may not be as regal as the other ladies, but that was not the point.

Staring across the table at Simon's handsome figure would have been a delightful sight if not for Susannah's nearness. It wasn't until the time had arrived to proceed into the dining room that Mina was informed of Mr. Richard Banfield's elevated birthright. With uneven numbers and most of the company being family, Mina had planned on using an informal seating arrangement, but according to her in-laws, it would not do for the grandson of a baron to be treated in such a shoddy fashion, leaving Mina to escort the baron's grandson and Simon to the baron's grandson's wife.

Even still, it would have been marginally better if Mina had been afforded the pleasure of Thea or Frederick seated on her other side, but the rest of the party had arranged themselves in a way that left the Vosses shoved towards the unenviable middle of the table. If either Thea or Frederick cared about such social slights, Mina would have been offended on their behalf. Instead, she was left to mourn that as hostess she was forced to sit at the end of the table, sandwiched between Mr. Banfield and Priscilla, both of whom proved to be as irritating as Mina's first impression warned her they'd be.

"Mina," said Priscilla, taking a bite of roast goose, "I've been meaning to ask you who your modiste is. The cut of your gown is so flattering for your figure."

"It is a Madame Notley creation," said Mina without elabo-
rating further. Under normal circumstances, Mina would not be
so tight lipped with a dinner companion, but she had no interest
in indulging Priscilla's taste for shrewish conversation. Mina
would not ignore her sister-in-law, but neither did she have to
invite trouble by being talkative.

"I am not familiar with her," said Priscilla. When Mina did
not reply, Priscilla asked, "Where is her shop? In London? Bond
Street, perhaps?"

"No," said Mina, skewering a turnip on her fork. "It is a local shop in Bristow."

"Oh," she said with a smile calculated to appear genuine,
but Mina saw the falseness beneath it. "Living economically is
a prudent approach, especially when one does not travel in the
highest circles of society where one's dress is far more important than out here in such rural places."

Prudence warned Mina to remain quiet. It was not as if
Mina cared for this woman and her opinions. She was simply
another of those unhappy creatures whose only joy came from
tearing apart those around them. But Mina was tired of her
backhanded compliments and subtle put-downs. "Both Simon
and I believe it is important to give patronage to the local shops
when possible. Besides, I prefer wearing simple country styles,
especially when it aids Bristow's economy."

Mr. Banfield interjected with some inane and semi-witty
remark that caused several others to titter with polite laughter,
but Mina ignored it, focusing on her food instead. Thea caught
her eye and gave Mina a commiserating look while Frederick
made a face that was such a perfect mimic of Mrs. Kingsley's
sour expression that Mina choked on a bite of potato and had
to take a sip of her drink to keep from having a coughing fit.
Emmeline noticed the display and looked positively affronted
at such boorish behavior.

As he had throughout the meal, Mr. Banfield leaned forward to see around Mina and make some flirtatious comment

to Priscilla. He was not so rude as to ignore Mina's existence in its entirety, but she wished she could switch seats with her sister-in-law to avoid being in the middle of their insipid banter. Priscilla was a prime example of how glaring flaws in one's personality could be overlooked with enough beauty, for she had little else to recommend herself, unless Mr. Banfield valued caustic conversation flavored with a scant dash of intelligence. Mina knew that was an unkind assessment, but no one else could hear her thoughts, so she felt only a fleeting hint of guilt for it.

"When I was mistress of Avebury Park," began Mrs. Kingsley, and Mina stifled a groan at what she knew was coming, "we had the most elaborate dinner parties with the most exquisite menus."

Mrs. Kingsley had better tact than Priscilla. Her words sounded as though she were simply reminiscing but still conveyed her utter disgust for Mina's simple country fare. With the exception of Thea, whose eyes narrowed at the lady, and Priscilla, who was too like her mother to miss the veiled insult, no one else discovered the barb hidden in the innocuous words.

"I'm certain they were magnificent, just like yourself," said Mr. Swinton, taking hold of Mrs. Kingsley's hand and kissing her knuckles with a look that made Mina want a bath. Mrs. Kingsley patted his cheek with a look as brazen as a lady of the night soliciting a client.

Mina regretted having so many courses. Perhaps tomorrow she would offer only a main course. With no sides. That would make dinner a quick affair.

"I have a question, Mr. Swinton," said Frederick.

Mina knew that tone. It usually meant he was about to cause trouble. In any other formal dinner, Mina would beg him to stop. In this one, she wanted nothing more than to encourage it. Frederick was not a cruel man, but he did enjoy bringing discomfort to the deserving.

"Yes, Mr. Voss?" he replied, after releasing Mrs. Kingsley's gaze with a lovelorn sigh that would do credit to Covent Gardens. In a way, his performance made Mina pity the man. He had no pride.

"I could swear I have met you before, sir. What school did you attend?"

Mina didn't know where Frederick was headed with this line of questioning, but as he had been tutored by his vicar, she knew the two men could not have met at any formal school.

"Harrow," said Mr. Swinton.

"And when did you graduate?"

"Three years ago."

"Then that makes you one and twenty?" Frederick picked up his glass, taking a drink with a thoughtful look. Mina suspected she knew what Frederick was getting at, and judging by the look on Mrs. Kingsley's face, she did, too. Though Mr. Swinton was blissfully unaware.

"Yes," said Mr. Swinton. "I had planned on Oxford afterwards, but there was a financial hiccup in my family."

"The weather has been quite nice for this time of year," blurted Mrs. Kingsley.

"That must have been difficult for you," said Frederick, ignoring the interruption. "But as I am three and thirty, I am far too *old* to have met you there." He put such a strong emphasis on 'old' that Mina lifted her napkin to cover her laugh while Thea hid hers behind her glass, and Mina feared Thea's shaking hand would spill the drink.

"Yes, I'm closer to Simon's age than yours," Frederick added, maintaining a perfectly serious face. "But it's wonderful that you found a way to occupy your time until your fortunes turn. My family also had a financial hiccup and I was forced into a life of trade, too, but I chose to sell farm supplies instead."

Emmeline gasped, but Mr. Swinton stared at Frederick like a poor, confused puppy. Neither Mrs. Kingsley nor her daughters appreciated the joke and stared at Frederick, who pretended to be ignorant of his intended *faux pas*.

"But I'm not in trade," said Mr. Swinton.

"Of course not," said Frederick, taking a bite and looking far too sweet and innocent for what he'd just implied. "It was a slip of the tongue."

Mr. Swinton smiled and nodded before turning a sultry look on Mrs. Kingsley that only served to fluster her further.

Glancing to Simon, Mina caught his attention. His eyes danced with mirth, and his lips twitched, though he remained composed. Together, they shared a secret laugh, and then something softened in Simon's eyes, the moment shifting for a brief instance.

Susannah tapped Simon on the forearm, and the moment was gone as soon as Simon turned his attention to his dinner companion.

Chapter 25

D inner finally finished, but the evening was far from over. The ladies had left the dining room as a group, but the moment they were in the sitting room, the two factions separated to their respective sides. Mina and Thea sat with their heads together in the corner, enjoying a brief respite before the gentlemen joined them. Thea repressed a giggle as she recounted again the various things Frederick had said during dinner, leaving Mina quite jealous at having been stuck beside her far less entertaining guests.

At that moment, the man in question slipped into the room and snuck to Thea's side.

"With the exception of Simon, those men are a total bore," said Frederick. "I was able to sneak out, but I'm not certain you ladies are faring any better." He nodded towards the great divide.

"Mina," he said, raising his voice to be clearly heard by both parties, "have I told you about the time I was mucking out the stalls—"

Emmeline gasped again as her fan flapped at full strength, while Thea pulled out a handkerchief and pretended her giggle was a sneeze.

"Oh, don't you worry, Mrs. Andrews, it was high quality muck. My manure is considered the finest in the county," said Frederick, who had never mucked out stalls in his life. Though the mere fact that he was 'in trade' was not much of a step up in the eyes of those judgmental ladies.

"Frederick," hissed Thea, as though she felt obligated to keep him in check, though the reproof lacked sincerity.

"Do you wish me to stop?" he whispered, and Thea replied with a grin that said she did not.

"If you do, sir, I will move you into the bedchamber next to Mrs. Kingsley," said Mina.

But the other ladies were spared from whatever scandalous story Frederick was about to fabricate when the other gentlemen joined the party. Not that the additions would stop Frederick if he put his mind to making a jest of things, but the shift in attentions interrupted him.

Mina caught Simon's attention, and he moved to join her and her companions. Her soul swelled to see him seeking her out. Then Susannah flashed a brilliant smile at Simon, and like a raven with shiny bit of metal, Simon veered towards the trollop. Mina deflated.

"Fool," muttered Frederick.

Thea gave Mina's hand a squeeze before murmuring to her husband, "And so were you, dear heart."

His face fell, but Thea nudged him with her shoulder, and he wrapped an arm around her and planted a kiss on her cheek.

Mina forced a smile. If she acted as though nothing were amiss, perhaps it would be true.

"Yes, we must have some entertainment," said Susannah, tapping Simon playfully on the arm, and Mina wanted to break every one of Susannah's perfectly shaped fingers.

"Mina," Simon said while motioning for her to join him, and she stood to play the role of hostess.

Head up and shoulders straight, Mina addressed the group. "As the Vosses are leaving us shortly, I had planned on an evening of music for the entire family. Thea plays the pianoforte beautifully, and her daughter, Penny, has a lovely singing voice."

"You mean to include the children, too?" asked Emmeline with wide eyes, tapping her fan against her palm.

Mina refused to let herself become discomposed. "I realize it is a tad unusual to include the children in evening entertainments, but with so many here tonight, it would be great fun for all of us."

"That sounds brilliant," said Simon.

Susannah giggled, and even that which would be cloying on any other woman had the perfect ring of mirth. "I never took you for a music aficionado," she said, grinning up at him.

"I wouldn't say that," he replied, giving her a chagrined smile, "but Mina plays and sings magnificently, and under her guidance, I have learned to appreciate it. She put together a musicale a while ago that was a major success."

"Then I would love to hear her perform," said Susannah, gliding over to Mina and taking her arm, "but I have to say that I am certain the children must be exhausted. It has been a long day for them, and I would hate to see the poor dears worn to a thread."

"And neither I nor Priscilla are musical," added Mrs. Kingsley.

"And my voice is not strong enough to sing tonight," added Emmeline.

"So, I fear there aren't enough performers," finished Mrs. Kingsley.

"We would be forced to cut the evening short or I, Mrs. Voss, and Mina would have to do several numbers. I would hate for Mina's voice to get worn out," said Susannah, looking crushed, while placing a comforting hand on Mina's forearm. Mina wanted to wrench herself from Susannah's grasp; it took all her dignity to keep from fulfilling that childish impulse. Though Mina couldn't decide which she hated more at that moment: Susannah's touch or that the lady was using Mina's Christian name without permission. Both actions conveyed a false familiarity that Mina found grating.

"Perhaps we could do something different. Cards, for example," said Susannah with a smile as though that commonplace evening activity were a wonderful and unique idea.

Following Susannah's lead, the other ladies gushed about how it was the perfect thing, creating an excitement that swept the gentlemen into their plans. Releasing Mina, Susannah rang for the servants to bring in tables and effectively wrested away Mina's role as hostess.

Everything Susannah said had such an artless air that Mina did not know how to do battle with such an adversary. Calling out Susannah's feigned goodness as manipulative and false would only paint Mina as petty.

Thea took Mina's arm, giving it a squeeze of support.

Emmeline's husband begged off, hiding behind a newspaper, but the others grouped together and before either Mina or Thea realized what was happening, they were pressed into playing whist, while Frederick was cornered by Mr. Swinton for a few rounds of piquet. Overwhelmed with the upending of all her plans, Mina was unable to stop herself from being paired with Priscilla, of all people, and assigned to a table with Simon and his partner, Susannah.

As the cards flew, Mina endured torture after torture as Susannah flirted and fawned over Simon. If it were not so unbearably painful, Mina would've been impressed with her skill. It came easy to the woman, like an extension of who she was, flowing out of her like the breath in her lungs. And Mina had no arts or wiles. No entrancing eyes to bat.

But more than Susannah's behavior, Simon drove the dagger into Mina's heart. He met each of Susannah's teasing comments and charming smiles with one of his own, and with each, Mina felt more and more like a frumpy, dumpy spinster. She had Simon's ring on her finger and his name on her wedding certificate, but it was all for naught as he cooed and courted Susannah.

All those little moments Mina had shared with her husband

felt juvenile and small. Tiny moments of possibility compared to the larger than life reality that was Susannah Banfield.

"I must offer my supreme apologies," Simon whispered into Mina's ear.

She turned, their faces right close together. A smile was on Simon's lips, and Mina felt a flickering of hope: he had realized his mistake and was apologizing for his behavior.

"I had no idea Priscilla was such an abominable player," he said in hushed tones. "I'm certain you would have won if not for your atrocious partner."

Mina couldn't breathe. She could not do this. She could not pretend anymore. Not with him so oblivious.

"Mina, are you all right?" asked Simon, his hand reaching for hers. "May I get you a drink? Or do you need some air?"

Mina shook her head. Things were clearly not all right.

"Mr. Kingsley..."

Mina closed her eyes against the sound of Susannah's voice. She took a breath and opened them again to find Simon's head pulled close to Susannah's, her hand on his as she asked something that Mina could only assume was of the utmost importance to require such an interruption.

Mina did not care about propriety. There was nothing left for her to give to this evening. Hostess in name only, no one but Thea and Frederick cared if she were here. Mina's presence did not matter.

"I hate to be so rude," said Mina, begging silent forgiveness for the lie, "but I feel peaked, and I desperately need to lie down."

Mina stood, and the gentlemen jumped to their feet. Mrs. Kingsley and Priscilla looked triumphant, sharing a conspiratorial smile that Mina knew she would stew about tomorrow when she had her wits about her. Mina expected similar elation on Emmeline's face but found only disgust. No doubt, it was in response to Mina's vulgarity, but the shoulds and should nots of society that Emmeline clung to mattered little to Mina in that moment.

Simon took her elbow and led her to the exit, and Mina sent Thea a silent assurance that all was well. Another lie.

"Let me help you to your chambers," he said, the picture of solicitousness.

"You wish to?" she asked, stopping just outside the doorway to hold his gaze.

"Of course, Mina," he said, his brow furrowing with that worried frown of his.

But Mina's next words were cut short by Susannah's voice calling to Mina's husband.

"Mr. Kingsley, you cannot think to abandon your guests," she teased.

"One moment," he said, glancing over his shoulder at her before returning his gaze to Mina.

"Perhaps Frederick can escort you," he said. "It would be rude for both of us to leave."

"I do not need an escort," she mumbled and turned, hurrying out the door. She hated that a corner of her heart hoped Simon would come running after her because Mina knew it would not happen. She listened for his footsteps all the way through the halls and to her chambers, but there was only her solitary steps and hitching breaths.

Chapter 26

M ina rubbed a finger at her temple as she read over the menus for the day. Mrs. Witmore was rattling off the complaints she'd received from various guests, looking as downtrodden as Mina felt. She was tired of conflict. Tired of every minor issue being compounded into a disagreement. After a fortnight of their constant drain on her spirit, Mina was losing the will to fight.

Mrs. Kingsley and Priscilla were bent on showing their superiority over Mina by turning every issue into a battle for supremacy. Emmeline's harping was easier to bear; no one measured up to her expectations for proper decorum, thus it was impossible for Mina to take Emmeline's constant fault finding to heart. Even still, being bombarded with disappointment and disapproval was exhausting.

And then there was Susannah.

Every time Mina turned around, Susannah was there, demanding Simon's attention. It had taken two days filled with her constantly calling for 'Mr. Kingsley!' before Mina realized what was at the heart of it. Whenever Simon's attention strayed towards Mina, Susannah surfaced with some question or need that required his immediate consideration.

Mina had known women like Susannah before. The fishers. Mina's father had adored fishing but hated the taste of fish; he'd spend hours using rod and reel to pull his prey from their homes only to throw them back the moment they were caught. Mina had witnessed many a lady who treated gentlemen in the same manner. Ladies who twisted a good man's affection around their finger, only to toss him aside the moment she lost interest in the game. In countless ballrooms, dining rooms, card rooms, and any other room where the social elite gathered, those fishers cooed and teased, giving their prey just enough encouragement to believe they had a chance to win the fair lady, only to be rejected at the fisher's prerogative. And Susannah was among the worst of those kinds; Simon was a toy she had tossed away yet did not want anyone else to play with.

If it hadn't been for the fact that Susannah's schemes were destroying her peace and happiness, Mina might have felt sorry for the woman. To be so desperate for attention that she couldn't allow a former admirer to find happiness in the arms of another was something to pity.

Mina reined in her thoughts, pulling them away from that woman; it was bad enough Susannah commandeered every other waking moment. And it was bad enough watching her husband dote on the woman every time she beckoned.

Menus. The list of dislikes was lengthy, and Mina was left wondering if she cared enough to keep fighting or if she should just give in. A spark of pettiness wanted to assert her position and force the menus she desired. Of course, a proper hostess would be aware of her guests' tastes and plan accordingly, but as they hadn't been invited in the first place, Mina did not feel particularly hospitable. To say nothing of their lack of manners that made them undeserving of consideration.

Mina sighed. She didn't have it in her to put up a struggle. Thea and her lovely family had departed just days after the Upheaval, leaving her without allies and surrounded by people who at best ignored her and at worst despised her.

Menus. Mina jerked away from such morose thoughts.

They weren't helping.

"Make the changes," said Mina. "Give them whatever they want. I don't care." Her throat tightened, and she gave up speaking, dismissing Mrs. Witmore with a wave.

The housekeeper took the menus from Mina, hesitating as she watched her mistress with sympathetic eyes.

"Madam, if I may be so bold as to say..." Mrs. Witmore caught herself for a moment before forging on. "Do not let them break you. They cannot stay forever, and then things will be good again. You'll see."

Mina smiled at the woman as she curtseyed and left, feeling a tender warmth settle in her heart. So, perhaps she had some allies left. Mina appreciated Mrs. Witmore's optimistic view, but she was afraid that once the invaders left, there might be nothing to revive between Simon and her.

And as if summoned by her very fears, the man in question entered the sitting room, his hands clasped behind his back.

"Mina," he greeted her, though the furrowed look deepened as he drew closer. "You look pale. Are you quite all right?"

"I am well," she replied. It was true enough. Other than persistently fitful nights, her body was healthy.

"I've been worried," he said. "You've seemed so melancholy since Thea and Frederick left."

Mina wished she could look at his face and say she did not love him. She wished her heart no longer yearned for those beautiful moments they'd shared together that flirted at the possibility of what they could become. This situation would be so much easier if she felt only friendship for her husband; then watching him with that woman day in and out would not be such a burden.

"I missed our ride this morning," said Mina, her listless spirit draining her words until they were as gray and lifeless as she felt. In the three and a half months since starting that habit, they had forgone their morning ride only once when the weather had been severely uncooperative. Even still, they'd spent that time together in Simon's study instead. But this gloriously clear morning Mina had arrived at the stables to find Spartan and his master missing.

Simon's eyes dimmed, and his face fell. Bringing his hands forward, he revealed a bouquet of amaryllis blossoms.

"We have run out of lilies," he said with frown. "It appears I need to keep a larger supply of them in the conservatory."

Mina took the bouquet, running her fingers over the petals, her heart breaking from the strain of keeping up with Simon's moods. Inattentive one moment and doting the next. If he stuck with one, it would be so much easier to move past this torment. But the kindness softened her heart, leaving it all the more bruised when his affection returned to Susannah.

"I apologize," he said, sitting on the sofa beside her. "It was unintentional. Truly. I had planned on our ride, but Mrs. Banfield asked me for a tour the estate. I thought I could take her on a short one and be back in time, but the morning got away from us. Can you forgive me?"

"It doesn't matter, Simon," she said, her eyes tracing the various colors across the petals. "I'm certain it was far more enjoyable riding out with Mrs. Banfield."

There was no answer, and Mina knew he must be thinking of a politic thing to say without offending his wife or lying. But an earnest 'no' drew her eyes away from the flowers and to Simon's face.

"It wasn't," he said, and Mina saw the truth in his eyes. "I missed you, deeply. It's been bad enough that I get so little time with you while our guests are here. Our morning ride is one of the only moments we have to spend together alone. I spent the entire time thinking about you and how you were waiting for me. More than anything, I wanted you there with me."

Mina couldn't withstand much more of this. Every time she was scant moments away from falling apart, he did something or said something to piece her back together. Hearing those heartfelt words patched up the cracks in her heart, giving Mina the hope that she could bear things a little longer. Simon still cared for her. At some point, Susannah would leave, and Mina could rebuild and then ensure that Susannah Banfield never stepped foot in Avebury Park again.

"Do you forgive me?" Simon asked, resting his hand on her knee.

A cruel part of her wanted to withhold the words Simon wanted to hear. A quick apology could not atone for everything Mina had suffered, but for now, she just wanted to enjoy a moment when they were not at odds with each other.

Mina nodded, and Simon smiled, his hand giving her knee a squeeze.

"I know it's been difficult," he said. "My family is not easy to be around in the best of circumstances, but they have given their word that the entire party is leaving in a fortnight."

A fortnight. The end of this torture was in sight, and that alone gave Mina a modicum of strength. A fortnight. Those two words were like a prayer. Mina may be faltering, but she could hold on for another two short weeks.

"It seems as though Bristow is not socially stimulating enough for them," he said with a roll of his eyes.

"That's odd, since they spend most afternoons calling on every person of notice in the area," said Mina, allowing a conspiratorial smile to curve her lips. "It appears that your mother is quite taken with Mrs. Baxter and her daughter. I have been told many times how gracious she and her circle are and how they were welcomed with open arms."

Simon snorted. "We could lock them all away together so they shall never bother us again."

Mina sighed, allowing her head to rest against Simon's shoulder. "That would be heavenly."

The door to the sitting room inched open, and Mina looked to find no one there. Tiny footsteps snuck around the back of the couch, and Simon sent a questioning glance to Mina just as they saw a flash of a brown braid peeking from the corner.

"It seems we have a visitor," Mina whispered, and Simon's eyebrow raised.

Sliding to her feet, Mina snuck around one side of the couch while Simon circled around to the other. Mina lunged at the invader, and Eloise Andrews jumped with a shriek. Throwing her hands over her mouth, she laughed, her grin peeking from between her fingers.

"I think someone snuck away from her nursemaid again," said Mina.

"Can you come and play now?" asked Eloise, her blue eyes wide and pleading. "You promised."

"Yes, I did," Mina replied. "What do you think, Simon? Are you up for some playtime? Or do you have work to do?"

He glanced at the clock before turning back to Mina and Eloise. "I'm sure Mr. Thorne can manage without me for a little bit."

"Yay, Uncle Simon!" she said, rushing to hug his waist.

Grabbing Mina's and Simon's hands, Eloise marched them to the nursery.

Simon sent Mina another questioning glance, and she smiled back at him.

"The children have grown restless away from all their usual toys," she explained. "They brought some, but not enough to keep them entertained, and our nursery is not well stocked. So, I go up and play with them for a bit most afternoons."

When they arrived, they were greeted with a chorus of "Aunt Mina!" and a rush of hugs. Little Hugh tugged on her skirts, and Mina scooped him up, kissing his sweet, soft neck.

"Who is this rascal?" asked Simon. "I know I don't get to see my nieces and nephews nearly as often as I wish to, but I think I would recognize them."

Mina shifted the boy, switching him to her left arm. "He is the Banfields' oldest, Hugh. Allan is their other boy, over there," she said with a nod to the nurse holding the squirming baby.

"The Banfields'?" Simon stilled, staring at the child in Mina's arms.

Mina searched his face but could not read anything in it.

"I had no idea their boys were here," he said.

Noah and Patience grabbed his hands, commandeering Simon to build a block castle, and Eloise handed Mina some paper. Mina forced her attention away from her confusing spouse and towards the child begging for attention. Following Eloise to a tiny table with tiny chairs she could never fit on, Mina knelt down beside the girl. With her free hand and while juggling Hugh, who thought it was great fun to grab the pencils in Mina's hand, she sketched out dozens of fanciful creatures for the dear girl to color.

Chapter 27

Never had Simon been so grateful to be alone. He walked the corridor, his hands clasped behind his back and his mind stuck on his problems. Before his mother and her horde had arrived, thoughts of the estate had preoccupied him, but now it was an unending struggle between his wife and Susannah—Mrs. Banfield. He must think of her that way. He was not free to take such liberties, and if he ever hoped to gain control of this situation, he had to be strong. Firm. In a sennight, they would be gone, and Simon would do everything in his power to ensure that his path never crossed Mrs. Banfield's in the future.

The only blessing in this situation was that Mina hadn't noticed his struggle. Her duties as hostess kept her too focused on taking care of their guests to have discovered his feelings for Mrs. Banfield. That aside, fending off the barbs and underhanded attacks from his family took enough of her attention. Simon hated that Mina had to deal with such things, but it was better than her unearthing his romantic past with Mrs. Banfield.

Clearly, Mina harbored hopes for their marriage that Simon knew would never come to fruition. It was painful enough that he'd been so forceful during their discussion about love and marriage in the conservatory; Simon would not hurt Mina further by allowing her to discover the reason behind their loveless marriage.

Mina was strong. She could handle Simon's family. Simon had seen her outmaneuver Mrs. Baxter and all the vitriol Bristow society had to offer. But in his heart, Simon sensed that discovering his history with Susannah might be more than Mina could bear.

Simon wanted to curse. He wanted to let loose a string of words that would make their guests run for their carriages. Marriage was supposed to make his life simpler. A marriage of convenience. The thought made him want to laugh. At present, there was nothing convenient about his life.

Not that it was Mina's fault. Nor his marriage. Both had made him very happy.

And Susannah bore no blame. Though Simon could blame her for visiting, it wasn't her fault that his heart was so firmly attached to her.

Simon halted. He supposed the closest thing to a scapegoat was Priscilla for bringing Susannah in the first place. Simon was certain Priscilla knew enough about what had transpired between him and the young Miss Susannah Weston to have known better than to bring her into Simon's home. Things had been going so well before they had arrived.

Continuing his march, Simon longed for a bit of peace.

And Mina.

Simon saw her on a regular basis, but there were too many interruptions. Any time he managed to find some time alone with his wife, someone pulled him away. And regardless of Mina's forgiveness, Simon was ashamed about their missed ride. In the few days since, he'd made sure not to repeat the offense, but it was getting difficult to put off Susannah's—Mrs. Banfield's—requests to see more of the estate.

Eventually, the lady had agreed to do so in the afternoon to allow him to keep his appointment with his wife, but that compromise had left him with an inkling of guilt. Simon wondered why. It was not as though he were forbidden from riding with anyone else, but it still felt wrong. Enough so that Simon had sent a note to Mrs. Banfield to beg off. And then he had spent the next few hours studiously avoiding all his guests.

A maid curtsied as he passed, and Simon gave an absent nod.

And then there was the ill-fated ride itself. The fact that he enjoyed Mina's conversation and company was no surprise, but that he enjoyed it more than Susannah's was. Simon had spoken the absolute truth to Mina. He had missed her during the ride. He'd been given the opportunity to spend time with the woman he loved, yet throughout it, Simon found himself wishing for Mina instead.

In fact, the more time he spent with Susannah, the less Simon sought her out. The opposite was true with Mina. Simon may not know much about love, but it seemed as though he should desire the company of the woman he loved first and foremost.

Simon wished he understood it. If he could just put this confusing jumble of emotions into words, perhaps he could. There was no questioning his feelings for Susannah, but Simon could not grasp what it was he felt for Mina. It was more than mere friendship. Far more.

He stopped and blinked at the empty hallway. Simon had no idea where he had been going. His study? That was the most logical conclusion. Though the work on the estate was slowing with the onset of winter, there was still much to be done. Not at this moment, but Simon would find something to keep himself busy. He'd gotten very good at busywork as of late. It was easier than facing Mina and Susannah.

He was such a coward.

This would all be over soon. In one week, life would return to what it was, and Simon's rocky path would smooth out again.

Picking up his pace, Simon consciously made his way to his

sanctuary. And stopped. To his left, the library door stood open, and he saw Susannah standing in front of the broad window, looking out at the gardens. He should walk past. Ignore it. Ignore her. Keep walking. Hide in his study until she was gone from his life.

But Susannah's shoulders were stooped, and she had such an air of unhappiness about her. Simon could not leave her in such distress. It was ungentlemanly and inhospitable. Though he looked forward to her departure, Simon was still her host and needed to see to his duties.

Drawing up beside her, Simon saw tears dripping down her cheeks. Catching sight of him, Susannah flinched, her delicate brow twisting in agony. Reaching into his pocket, Simon offered her his handkerchief.

"What's the matter?" he asked.

Susannah dabbed at the tears and opened her mouth to speak, but her face crumpled, and she sobbed into the square of linen. Taking her by the elbow, Simon led her to the sofa, and sat beside her. Reaching for his hand, Susannah clutched it, while wiping at the tears with her other.

"Oh, Simon—" she said, her cheeks heating at that. "I mean, Mr. Kingsley. I will be better in a moment."

"What can I do for you?" he asked.

"There's nothing to be done," she said. "But thank you for kindness, sir."

"Please tell me what is troubling you," he said.

Susannah's chin wrinkled, fresh tears glimmering in her eyes, and she looked down at their clasped hands. "I cannot say. Not to you, Mr. Kingsley."

"Then may I fetch someone?" he offered. "Your husband? Or one of the ladies?"

"No," she said, rising to her feet and stepping away. "Not them. I don't want the ladies to see me in such a state. And my husband..." Her words died as a fresh bout of tears shook her.

Simon stood to join her and came to her side. "Susannah, please. Tell me what's wrong."

Her tear-soaked eyes met his the moment Simon said her Christian name. He knew he should not have done so, but in such a moment, formality seemed unimportant.

"Oh, Simon," she said, looking down at the space between them. "What ails me is something that cannot be fixed. Unless you have a way of turning back time."

Susannah brushed a finger across his waistcoat; the feeling was little more than a flutter, but Simon felt it through his entire being. She stepped away, returning to the sofa, but Simon was glued to his spot.

"I thought marrying Richard was the right decision," she said. "My parents raised me to believe that a marriage of prestige and consequence was of utmost importance. But as the years pass, I find his social standing means less and less to me."

Simon did not want to hear this. He knew he should leave, but he was rooted, unable to tear his eyes from Susannah as she bore her soul to him. She stared at his handkerchief in her hand, her fingers running along his monogram.

"The greatest regret of my life is that I didn't break off my engagement the moment you proposed," she said, as though the words were ripped from her soul.

Simon had no response. The silence stretched between them, and he tried to swallow, but his throat wouldn't work. The sunshine from the window glinted off her golden head, reminding him of that fateful day. His angel.

"We made our choices," Simon said. "It's best to move forward and not dwell on the past." He had told himself that same thing many times. It hadn't resolved the issue, but wallowing in regrets was not the path to happiness.

Susannah looked up from Simon's handkerchief and whispered. "Are you happy with her?"

"Yes," he replied without hesitation. Before this upset in their lives, Simon had been very happy with Mina. In truth, he would be again once their guests were gone. Once this particular guest was gone.

A rueful smile crossed her lips. "I am glad of that, dear Simon, even if it does make me envious. You deserve happiness."

"You do, too," said Simon. The look in her eyes drew him to her side, pulling him towards her as if he had no control over his feet. Simon sat beside her, Susannah's leg brushing his. He knew he shouldn't be so close. He didn't want to, but Susannah had placed a spell over him.

"Do you love her?" she asked, fresh tears gathering at her eyelashes.

Simon wished he could answer as before. An unequivocal affirmation. He loved his wife. He did not regret his past. He did not feel Susannah's loss. But to admit any of those things was unfair to him, Susannah, and Mina.

"Perhaps it will grow in time," she said, laying her hand on his forearm. "Perhaps you and she will have a better future than Richard and I."

Staring at her hand on his arm, Simon felt weighed down. A drowning man. He should have never stepped into the library. Yet another regret to add to his list.

"My heart is already lost," he said. "I do not have another."

Simon didn't know what possessed him to say such a thing, and he wished the words recalled the moment they left his lips, but the hopelessness he felt wrenched them from him. Susannah's eyes darted to him, catching his in a gaze filled with such misery and pity that Simon's heart twisted in his chest.

"Oh, Simon!" she cried. Shooting to her feet, Susannah ran from the room.

Simon's soul collapsed, and he slumped forward, catching his head in his hands, praying for this torture to end.

...

Mina walked the halls in search of her husband. For the first time in the three long weeks since their guests had arrived, Mina felt giddy; the feeling filled her as she clutched the paper in her hands. Picturing Simon's face when she presented it to him made her feet move faster, her eyes scouring for the missing man.

It was true that Simon and Mr. Thorne had compiled a list of necessary repairs to be made during the renovations of the tenants' cottages that spring, but Mina suspected they hadn't thought to consult the men's wives. Those cottages were the women's domain, and they understood far better than their husbands about the smaller details of it. The men would know the larger issues, such as the leaking roofs and cracked walls, but they wouldn't necessarily notice the windows letting in drafts or the cupboards doors that were falling off their hinges. With a bit of time, Mina had compiled it all and was anxious to show Simon.

Passing the library, Mina heard Simon's voice and turned to join him. But then Susannah's melodic words struck Mina's ears, chilling her heart and freezing her steps. 'Eavesdropping brings nothing but pain,' her mother had liked to say, but Mina could not have moved if she wished to. Susannah's tears and her perfectly crafted declaration played Simon as elegantly as a piano virtuoso, hitting each key with precision. Mina felt the falseness in every word, yet Simon was blind to the theatrics. The carefully executed verbal crescendos. And then the finale.

"My heart is already lost," he said. "I do not have another."

With a dramatic cry, Susannah fled the room while clutching Simon's handkerchief to her chest. The moment she crossed the threshold, the woman's composure returned as if that scene had not happened. She spared only a passing glance for Mina. It held no gloating or malice. It was an empty dismissal that perfectly conveyed just how little Susannah thought of Simon's wife.

Mina watched her rival glide down the hall, the woman's body moving with absolute grace and dignity. Stepping to the library entrance, Mina watched her husband mourn that woman, tying himself in knots over her.

Of their own accord, Mina's feet moved, drawing her away

from the library and to Simon's study. She sat on his chair, placing the list of repairs on his desk, her mind blank. Her eyes fell to the drawer—the one she had not dared open since the first time she'd been in this room alone. Now, her hand reached for it and found Susannah's glove still sitting there.

Staring at that little piece of leather and thread, Mina realized she was done waiting for Simon to come to his senses.

It wasn't due to the words she'd overheard. Simon had said many of those same things to Mina directly. She knew he believed his heart belonged to that woman. Mina knew that his head was so mixed up about what love was that he could not see the truth. Mina knew and understood it all; nothing Susannah or Simon had said was a revelation.

No, it wasn't the words. It was Simon's folly. His weakness. The fact that he was in that library in the first place. Mina knew he was an honorable man and had given his vow of fidelity, but there were only so many times one could play with fire before one got burned.

And though unintentional, Simon had been unfaithful in so many ways. Over and over, he threw himself into these private situations with Susannah. They may have been a result of Susannah's manipulations, but it was as though Simon were not even trying. He had chosen to enter that library. To sit beside her. To hold her hand. To give his handkerchief. To use her Christian name and speak of things too private to discuss with someone who should be only a passing acquaintance. He was unwilling to let go of Susannah Banfield and unwilling to show Mina the respect she deserved as his wife, friend, and companion.

Mina was done being the consolation prize. Done being the person with whom Simon was willing to settle. Done with waiting for those people to leave so things could return to the way they were. Mina was tired of begging Simon to love her.

She was done with Simon Kingsley and this farce of a marriage.

Chapter 28

There was not another soul in the hallways as Simon left the library. He was grateful for every silent step as he put distance between himself and the site of that awful scene. Susannah's words played in his head, a never-ending loop of despair. She was miserable, and it hurt Simon to his core.

Making his way to his study, Simon stepped inside and went to his desk, halting when he saw the lower drawer sitting open. Shaking his head at his own absent mindedness, which seemed to be getting worse as of late, he sat down and reached to close it. Simon noticed Susannah's glove resting there, and he picked it up. He had meant to get rid of the thing a dozen times before, but every time he went to drop it in the fireplace, he'd been unable to do so.

But things were different now. They were changing. Watching Susannah's heart shatter made Simon realize just how damaging wallowing in his feelings for her could be. Her present was fixed yet her choices of the past still clung to her, destroying whatever chance for happiness she had in the future. Past, present, and future were all intertwined, and Simon was desperate to avoid getting tangled in it.

Standing, he walked to the fireplace and tossed the glove into the flames before he allowed himself a second thought. His life with Mina was a good one. Not the one he had wanted, but it was good. If he didn't let Susannah go, his marriage would become a thing filled with sorrow and bitterness. Simon felt liberated as the flames ate away Susannah's token of love. In one week, their guests would be gone, and Simon would never see Susannah Banfield again. Life would move on.

It was time to let go of his past, embrace his present, and build his better future. Start a proper family with Mina. Simon felt a smile tug at the corner of his lips at the memory of their time in the nursery with his nieces and nephew. That smile grew as the image shifted into a vision of that self-same scene but with *their* children. Their family.

Turning his back to the fire, Simon found a list sitting atop his desk. He read it once and then again. There was no note explaining it, but Simon recognized Mina's handwriting. Studying it, he realized what it was. He and Mr. Thorne had already compiled a list of repairs to be made in the tenants' homes, but he would put a pony on it that Mina had made a list of her own. Judging by the types of things noted, Simon guessed she had spoken with the tenants' wives.

His wife. His Mina. Tenderness swelled in his heart, spreading his smile. Though things had been so difficult of late, Mina was still working hard for their future. She was a miraculous woman.

Glancing at the clock sitting on the bookshelf beside him, Simon was startled to find that he had lost most of the afternoon stewing in the library. There wasn't much time before he'd need to dress for dinner, but he wanted to see Mina. Needed to. That afternoon had been a revelation, and though he would never tell her the whole of it, Simon was anxious to speak to her about their future.

In quick succession, Simon checked all her favorite places in the house but found no sign of his wife. Or any other person, for that matter. He supposed the guests were not back from their social calls, and the staff must be busy with their work.

"Molly!" Simon called, seeing a maid hurrying along with a bucket of water. "Have you seen my wife?"

Molly's eyes fell to the ground, and she shifted from foot to foot. "No, sir. Not in a while."

Simon nodded and continued the search. Mina was likely off visiting with someone about the village school and her plans to improve it. Simon wracked his brain to remember whether she had mentioned any such appointment. But his memory proved useless, so he started towards her chambers. Perhaps she was seeking a little solitude from his mother and sisters.

Approaching her door, Simon found it open. Mrs. Witmore was directing several maids as they stripped every bit of Mina from the room and packed it into trunks.

"What's going on here?" he asked, stepping inside.

Mrs. Witmore turned to face him, wearing a mask of neutrality, though it could not hide the fire blazing in her eyes. "We are packing, sir."

"What for? Where is Mrs. Kingsley?"

"She took a couple portmanteaus and left not ten minutes ago."

"Left?" The word shocked Simon. Something must have happened. Perhaps her brothers or the Vosses needed her help. Simon could easily see Mina rushing off to them, but not without telling her husband. "Did she say where she was going?"

"No," came the brief reply.

"Did she say why?"

"No."

"Did she say anything?" Simon fought to keep the frustration from his voice. Whatever Mina was up to, Mrs. Witmore did not deserve his temper, but her supremely unhelpful answers were stoking his emotions.

"She and her lady's maid packed a couple of portmanteaus and gave me instructions to pack the rest of her things."

"All of them?" Simon could not fathom any scenario where such a thing would be necessary.

"Yes."

Simon jogged to the stables. Mrs. Witmore was no help, but since Mina had left only ten minutes before, he should be able to catch her and get some explanation for this insanity.

...

Spartan tore down the road, tearing up the distance between Simon and the carriage cresting the next hill. The wind whipped his hat off his head, and he let it go, his eyes riveted to his goal. Fear, worry, confusion all ripped at him, urging him to move faster. None of this made any sense, and he knew something must be terribly wrong for Mina to behave in such a bizarre fashion.

Overtaking the carriage, he called for the coachman to stop and pulled Spartan to a halt beside it. Hopping from the saddle, he threw open the carriage door and saw Mina and her maid inside. Simon froze at the look on her face. It held no emotion, no spirit. An empty shell sat before him.

"What do you want, Simon?" Mina asked, her voice as hollow as her expression.

Her question shook Simon from his shock. "What do I want? My wife decamped without a word. What do you think I want?"

"Susanna Banfield," she replied. "That is what you want, so go and get her. With me no longer standing in your way, I'm certain you two will be quite happy together."

Fury swept through Simon, burning out all other thoughts and emotions. "How could you possibly think I would do that?" His voice rose with each word. He could not keep it in check. "After everything you know about my family, how could you think I would ever behave in such a manner? How could you think so little of me to expect me to carry on as my mother does?"

Mina's eyes snapped to his, the empty gaze replaced with a fire of her own. She stepped out of the coach, shoving past Simon. "I have spent the last three weeks watching you trip over yourself for that woman, and you think I have no reason to doubt you?"

"That is doing it much too brown," he scoffed. "I was playing host to my guest. Nothing more."

"Do not start lying now, Simon Kingsley," Mina said through gritted teeth. "I have two eyes and two ears, and I am tired of being treated as second-rate by my husband. I shan't do it anymore."

A twinge of guilt played in the back of Simon's mind, but it was overridden by a surge of self-righteous rage. "You knew what you were marrying into. I never promised you my heart, and I cannot help that it loves another. Regardless, I would never stray. I would never treat you with such contempt or ridicule."

"But you do," she said, the emotion growing in her voice. "I am your wife, but any time that woman is even near you, it's as if I do not exist. I've spent my life being overlooked or mocked by society, but I never thought my own husband would do that to me.

"Can't you see what she is, Simon?" Mina shouted. "She is manipulating you, leading you on and making you think she cares for you when all she cares for is herself! Everything in her life is about her status and her wants and her needs. Even her children are nothing more than an accessory. And you blindly run to her side whenever she calls."

"Leave Susannah out of this," he spat.

"You were the one who brought her into our marriage." Mina looked more furious than Simon could ever remember her being, but it only fed into his own temper. "Can you even tell me why you think you love her?"

Simon scoffed. "You expect me to answer that? To tell you why I love her?"

"No," she replied. "I'm hoping you answer that question for yourself."

"I am not discussing Susannah with you," he growled and stopped. Simon took a breath, allowing it to give him a modicum of control. Mina glared at him, but he saw the pain behind it.

"Please come home," he said, his tone less calm and more biting than he'd wanted. "In a few days, she will be gone, and this will be over. Things will get back to normal."

The ferocity drained from Mina, her whole body wilting as if she did not have the strength to keep upright. Her eyes held his, her heart and soul gone from them. "Don't you understand, Simon? I do not want this anymore."

Simon stilled, his eyes widening. He could not believe she was saying this.

"I married you because I thought we could build a happy life together. I thought..." A flash of heartache stole across her face, and her breath hitched. "I thought you would grow to love me as I love you. That with time, you would see me and understand what we have together. But I shan't stand around begging you to do so. Not anymore."

Simon opened his mouth, but Mina kept speaking. "The problem is that I do not respect you anymore. You cannot see what an incredible thing we have between us. You allow yourself to be blinded by coy smiles and flirtatious comments and refuse to see that you are far happier with your frumpy wife than a woman who only pays attention to you if there is no one better around. You may be willing to live with a relationship like that, but I am not. You may have thought this sad, unwanted spinster would put up with it, but even I have too much self-respect for that."

They stood, staring at each other for several quiet moments. Simon couldn't believe Mina thought that about him. He thought she understood him, and she clearly did not.

"If you think so little of me, then perhaps it's best you leave," he said.

Lifeless and void, Mina's eyes held his. If it were not for the tear running down her cheek, Simon would've thought her a corpse. Then she stepped into the carriage and drove away.

Chapter 29

Simon slammed his chamber door, ripping off his jacket and flinging it onto the chair. Mina did not respect him. She had said that to his face. He had done nothing wrong. He had been solicitous and kind to a houseguest, and Mina no longer respected him for that. What tripe!

He dropped onto the bed but rose back up again. Simon was too enraged to sit still. He prowled the floor, desperate to expel this angry energy, but to leave his chambers meant facing the others, and he was in no fit state for that. In other circumstances, Simon would have jumped on Spartan and spent the next few hours taking his frustrations out in a bruising ride, but Mina had spoiled that for him. Any time he even thought of the stables, it dredged up memories of her.

His eyes caught sight of a vase of flowers sitting on the side table, and Simon cursed. He couldn't be rid of her even in his own chambers. Snatching the vase, he launched it out the door, and it crashed to the floor, scattering water, flowers, and bits of porcelain across the hall. Let the servants deal with the mess, and let him be free of reminders of his faithless wife.

Slamming the door shut again, Simon paced while his every thought led back to Mina. She thought so little of him. Thought him so dishonorable and false that he would defile his marriage and Susannah's. Mina thought him an immoral rake.

For all her accusations that Simon did not know Susannah's true nature, Mina obviously did not know his.

...

Simon's fingers drummed the dining room table as he stared at his plate of food. Or rather, scowled at it. He knew he should eat but found himself unable to do so. He wanted to be alone, but after spending the evening locked in his room, he could not neglect his guests any further. A quick appearance at breakfast, and then he would be free to disappear again.

The others dined on eggs, ham, tomatoes, and an array of fine foods while Simon's usual breakfast of sweet rolls and tea sat before him. A pot of Mina's favorite blackberry jelly sat beside it, and Simon felt an urge to hurl it across the dining room.

"It is unfortunate that our hostess has abandoned us," said Emmeline, delicately dabbing at the corner of her mouth where there was not a speck of food or mess to clean up. No bit of sauce or crumb would dare such an affront to Emmeline Andrews. "But it is nice to have our numbers rounded out. It was far too uncouth to have such an awkward arrangement at meals."

Simon gave his sister a venomous look and caught sight of his mother sharing a secret smile with Susannah. He tried to brush it aside, but with Mina's accusations plaguing his thoughts, it was none too easy.

"I, for one, will never forgive that woman for treating you so shoddily," said Priscilla.

Simon's glare flew to his other sister. "What do you know about it? Have the servants been talking?" If they were spreading rumors about Mina, he would sack the lot of them. His anger with her aside, she did not deserve to be the object of gossip among her own staff.

"No one said a word, but it's clear as day, Simon. She

packed her things and left," Priscilla replied, taking a sip of tea. "What other way can that be interpreted other than she left you? And after all you have done for her. It's abominable."

"Done for her?" The words shocked Simon. The way his sister spoke, it was if Mina were nothing more than muck beneath his boots.

"And for her to bring such shame and scandal to the family. We've been through enough already," added Emmeline, taking a sip from her teacup while leveling a cold eye on her mother.

Simon opened his mouth to give his sisters a proper set down, but Susannah spoke first.

"Ladies," she said with a sigh, "what has happened is terrible, but there is no reason for us to add to the hubbub with our speculations and gossip."

If only Mina could hear that. After all her indictments against Susanna's character, it was she who defended Mina. Simon felt flush with validation.

"After all," Susannah continued, "it's sad that the poor lady did not feel adequate to the job of running an estate such as Avebury Park, but she never did have much of a talent for dealing with society. It must have been difficult to be thrust into such a position. I only hope she finds her proper place."

That gave Simon pause, and the vindication in his heart cooled. The delivery sounded sincerely kind, but something in the words gave Simon an uneasy feeling that there was an underlying meaning. The conversation around him continued in much the same vein, and throughout it, Susannah's comments were always polite but each held that tiny speck of something beyond his grasp. Something sharp. Compared to her companions, she was sweetness personified, but the more Simon paid attention, the more bite her words held.

"With her figure, it was a miracle anyone was willing to marry her," said Priscilla with a mirthless giggle.

"Enough!" Simon barked, slamming his hand against the table. He could not listen anymore. Standing, he took his leave.

...

Simon hid in the formal sitting room. In normal circumstances, it was too public a place to hide, but with the guests off to socialize over tea and cakes, it was private enough at the present. He could not sit in his chambers anymore. The air was stifling, though it was not much better here. Or in any of the other half dozen rooms in which he had attempted to find some solace. As this was Mina's least favorite room, it held the fewest memories of her, making it his choice by default.

Leaning his head against the headrest, Simon closed his eyes and rubbed the bridge of his nose where it ran a little crooked. With time, life would even out. He would go back to the way things were before Mina. Mrs. Witmore would run the household, and Mr. Thorne could handle some of Mina's other duties. Simon had managed before Mina, and he would manage after her.

Perhaps.

Even with the bitterness of her betrayal, it was difficult to picture returning to his life before her. His anger fell to the back recesses of his mind as memories of their months together surfaced, the joy of those precious weeks overshadowing the hurt of the last day. Simon could not think of another time when he had been so happy, and there would be no way to recapture that on his own.

The fire stoked again when he thought back on his family's venomous words about Mina. Simon was plenty furious with her, but the way they had spoken hurt him as if he'd been the target of their attack. They dismissed Mina as useless and unwanted, which could not be further from the truth. Even as he wanted to curse her name, Simon could not deny that she'd been a blessing and a boon in his life.

It made no sense that he should feel that way. Simon seethed at the thought of her abandonment, but in the next moment, he missed her. Needed her. And so his heart bounced back and forth, tearing apart his sanity.

Simon still could not fathom what Priscilla had meant about Mina's figure. She may be far plumper than the pinnacle of fashion, but the memory of her pulled up against him, his arms encircling her generous curves left little to be desired. Very little, in fact. Just the thought of it made him want to grab her up in an embrace. True, Priscilla could not know that, but even looking at a distance, Simon didn't see what it was that Priscilla found so objectionable. Mina was uniquely pretty. Eye catching, even.

And then she threw everything away. Turned her back on her husband, her estate, and ran off because she was jealous. Simon could not help his heart. He had been honest from the start. He'd never lied to Mina or plied her with false adoration. Simon wished he could have handed her his heart and loved her as she apparently loved him, but there was no undoing what he felt for Susannah.

Yet, why did he love her? Mina's question badgered him. Quantifying love seemed an impossibility, but he kept coming back to it. Susannah was kind. Or Simon had thought so. Seeing the hints of something dark beneath that sweet facade made him doubt it.

But love was more than that. The things Simon felt for Susannah were too strong to be anything else but love. Just thinking of Susannah stoked a fire that burned through him, making him crave her like an alcoholic in search of a bottle of whiskey. It could be nothing else but love.

Besides, it was not as if love made sense. Love was illogical. Everyone knows that one falls in love; one does not choose it.

Simon heard the door creak, and he opened his eyes to find Eloise standing before him, a puzzled look on her face.

"Are you unwell, Uncle Simon?" she asked.

Very, but the things that ailed him were not for Eloise to know. "I'm fine. Just a touch tired. What can I do for you?"

"I'm looking for Aunt Mina," she said, her hands locked behind her as she rocked forward on her toes. "I colored all the drawings she gave me." Holding out her arm, Eloise displayed her art. She drew closer, climbing up onto his lap to show him. A smear of jelly from her hand caught his jacket, but Simon's valet had proved proficient at removing such stains after his last encounter with the children. Not that it mattered; her cuddles were worth being dunked in a fountain of jelly.

Simon spent a moment admiring the drawings as Eloise pointed out a few additions she had made to Mina's original sketches. Apparently, the castle desperately needed a dragon flying above it, and Eloise had put her own crude rendering next to Mina's pristine picture.

It was a silly little thing. A nothing sort of thing, but it carried with it the memory of watching Mina draw it. Laughing and playing with the children. At such a happy thought, Simon should have felt better, but it weighed down his heart, until it felt as though it were made of lead.

Mina had left him, leaving him a lonely man in a lonely estate.

"Can she play?" asked Eloise, turning back to her original question.

Simon's voice caught, and he swallowed down the emotion. "No. She left." It was the first time he'd said the words aloud, and they were like a vice on his soul.

Eloise's face crumpled, looking rather like Simon felt.

"Mr. Kingsley?"

Eloise jumped from Simon's lap, and he stood to greet Susannah.

"There you are," she said. "I have been thinking of a way to cheer you up, and I thought a ride would be the just the thing. The weather is perfect, and there is still much of the estate I've yet to see. I've been most anxious to view it in its entirety."

That was one of the last things Simon wanted to do. In his present state, he couldn't stand the torture. Riding the estate was their passion—his and Mina's—and to do so with anyone else would be a poor replica of it.

Susannah smiled at him. Without Mina calling attention to

it, Simon would never have noticed the coy flavor in that expression. It felt unseemly to believe Susannah could be so false,
but the more he watched her, the more he noticed those little
things. Compared to Mina's open, artless nature, Susannah's
seemed more calculating. But he was just being overly analyti-
cal. Mina had gotten in his head. That was all.

"What do you think, Mr. Kingsley?" asked Susannah with a
slight flutter of eyelashes. She actually batted her eyes at him.
The realization struck Simon so forcefully that he did not hear
a single word more the woman said.

Eloise came up beside Susannah and tugged on her skirt
with her clean hand. "Madam?"

"Don't touch my dress with that sticky hand," Susannah
said, brushing her skirts away.

"I wasn't going to," said Eloise, holding the offending appendage at a safe distance.

"Well, you still should not grab my dress like that," insisted
Susannah, her voice softening a touch. "I would hate for it to
wrinkle."

"Sorry, madam," Eloise whispered, stepping closer to Simon to lean against his leg, her eyes slightly wet while she carefully kept the jellied hand far away from his trousers.

A forgotten memory came to Simon's mind, and he heard
his mother's voice as clear as if she were standing next to him
speaking those self-safe words when he had greeted her one afternoon with smears of mud on his hands. Simon was sure he
had looked as crushed as Eloise did; he had certainly felt it.

And that brought with it the image of Mina kneeling on the
floor with the children, playing with them in a way none of their
own parents ever did. Including Susannah.

Seeing her child in Mina's arms had shocked Simon, and
not because of the situation between Susannah and Mina. He'd
had no idea that the Banfield children were among the party.
Never once had he seen or heard them. Standing in the nursery,
he had excused it as his own fault for not noticing. What mother
did not mention her children? But now, watching her lecture a

child about a tiny mess that had not happened, Simon could not think of a single time when Susannah had. Simon often forgot she even had children because they were so nonexistent in her life.

And if Simon needed any confirmation about how little Susannah valued her own offspring, Simon only had to look at the way Eloise addressed her. Madam. Not Mrs. Banfield. If Susannah ever spent any time with the children, Eloise would have been introduced and would address Susannah accordingly. Yet the girl did not seem to know Susannah's name.

Simon felt as though he were looking at a stranger, and it terrified him. The fantasies in his mind were crumbling, and Simon did not know what to do about it. He needed time away from Susannah and her batting eyelashes to clear his head and think.

Taking Eloise's hand, Simon led her out of the sitting room.

"Where are you going?" Susannah asked.

"To entertain some children," he said without sparing a backwards glance.

Chapter 30

S imon dismissed his valet, preferring solitude to the servant's none too careful ministrations and displeased
looks. Just another person who sided with Mina. Mr.
Thorne had been curt and spent most of the day giving Simon
the most severe glares. Dinner looked perfectly cooked, but Simon had not eaten a single bite as it consisted exclusively of
dishes he found distasteful. Other than his guests, there was not
a single person at Avebury Park who liked Simon at the moment.

And that rankled him.

Simon was willing to own that Mina had been right to question Susannah's personality, but everyone acted as though he
had pushed his wife out the door. It was she who had left him.
She decamped, not Simon. If Mina had been willing to stick it
out, things would have gotten better.

And then there were her indictments of Simon's character.
Even if his eyes were opening to Susannah's carefully crafted
persona, it did not excuse what Mina had said about him. Simon
was a good and faithful husband. He treated his wife with respect, yet Mina practically accused him of seducing Susannah
and carrying on an illicit affair under their own roof. Perhaps

he had been more cordial than necessary at times, but the idea that Mina thought him such a cad was unforgivable.

Life had been turned upside down and inside out. Simon didn't know how he felt about any of the women in his life. With all the unwanted revelations about Mina and Susannah, Simon had no idea where he stood on any front. Life would be easier without women in it.

But even as he thought it, he knew it was untrue. Up until three weeks ago, one special woman had made his life far easier and happier than he ever could have imagined. In some ways, it was even better than what he'd hoped to find with Susannah. Mina enlivened his days in a way Susannah never had, and it made Simon wonder which of the two ladies he'd rather spend his life with. While he preferred not delving into that quagmire, the question hovered in his thoughts. If circumstances were different and their marriages had never happened, who would he rather have at his side?

What he felt for Susannah—had felt? Simon wasn't sure what his feelings were at present—was strong and intoxicating. Alluring.

What he felt for Mina...

Simon thought back on his time with her, untangling the mess of emotion pestering him. What he felt for her was different. Strong, too. But different...

It was...everything.

Simon's breath caught. Everything. Mina was everything.

Looking back on his life before her, Simon saw it was a dark, sad, and lonely thing. He'd found purpose in his role as master of Avebury Park, but he hadn't been happy. Not truly. And then Mina entered his life and filled it with brightness and cheer. She turned his house into a home, and not because of the way she organized the household but because she was in it. She made even mundane things pleasurable just by being a part of it.

Mina even made dancing enjoyable. Dancing, for goodness

sakes! Before her, Simon viewed it as a tool of courtship, nothing else. Something he tolerated in order to spend time with a lady. Even with Susannah, the dance itself hadn't be pleasant, but the opportunity to be close to her was. But Simon had adored escorting Mina around the dance floor. Adored making her happy.

Simon's mind churned, sifting through those realizations as he reflected on all the ways Mina made his life better. And then all thought came to a halt as a great bolt of lightning struck his brain.

Mina was his other half.

Hands touched his back, and Simon jumped. Whirling, he found Susannah standing before him, his bedchamber door sealing the two of them inside, alone. Stepping forward, Susannah ran her hands up his chest, smiling at him with such lewdness that it reminded him eerily of his mother's behavior towards her paramours. Simon stepped back, but Susannah moved with him. His legs hit his bed, and he fell backwards with her landing atop him, their bodies pressed together.

"What are you doing?" he asked, his voice coming out in a juvenile squeak.

Susannah smiled and ran her hands along his chest, stirring up emotions that were best not felt for anyone other than his wife. Gently but quickly, Simon pushed Susannah aside and stood, taking a breath and turning his mind away from the voluptuous woman on his bed.

"There's no need to be shy, dear Simon," she said with a laugh, sliding off the bed and slinking towards him. "I've given Richard his heir and spare, so we are free to..." her voice dipped into a purr, "further our acquaintance."

Eyes he'd thought so brilliant and beautiful were filled with an invitation that left no question as to Susannah's intentions. This was no crying woman mourning the loss of the love Simon had thought they both felt. This was a calculating harlot, for Simon could not think of another way to describe a woman propositioning a married man while her own husband was just a few rooms over. It was revolting.

Susannah reached for him, and before Simon could stop it, she pressed her lips to his. Any confusion or doubts about his feelings for the woman fled, leaving him with an overpowering nausea. In all the times Simon had pictured kissing Susannah, he'd never foreseen that outcome, but there was no warmth left in his heart for this woman who rubbed up against him, forcing her attention on him like a desperate light-skirt.

A veil lifted, clearing Simon's vision to see the world in new levels of vivid clarity. Everything about Susannah was a lie, and Simon was a fool for caring about such a selfish creature. Every one of Mina's accusations against her were proving true, and Simon felt like the worst sort of bounder for holding Susannah up as some paragon when Mina had more quality, goodness, and spirit in her little finger than Susannah had in her whole being.

Simon forced the woman away, wiping at his mouth as though it would somehow erase the foul taste.

"Go back to your husband, Mrs. Banfield," he said, putting distance between them.

Her brow wrinkled, a coquettish smile twisting her lips. Simon could not fathom how he ever thought such a vile creature gorgeous. It was as though her features rearranged themselves into a completely different woman. Looking at her, Simon saw no beauty or attraction. Not even a morsel of his passion was left. Seeing the truth of who she was had erased it all.

"My husband has been warming Priscilla's bed for a while," she said, "and he is welcome to her. I married him for his status, but now I desire more than a cold marriage bed."

Mrs. Banfield stepped towards him again, but Simon held out a hand, stumbling in his haste to back away from her.

"I would never break my marriage vows. Not with you or anyone," he said.

The woman crossed her arms, a huff of a laugh on her lips. "What marriage vows? As you have not graced your wife's bed, I see no marriage to speak of."

Shock drained the color from Simon's face, but a flush of anger quickly chased it away. "Who told you that?" he demanded.

"Everyone in the neighborhood knows you have no desire for Mina. How could you?"

A groan escaped him, and Simon covered his face, wanting to disappear into oblivion. For Mina's name to be bandied about in such a manner was heartbreaking. For it to happen because of his own actions was unpardonable. Simon's heart wrenched at the thought of her being fodder for the town gossips. He knew enough of the world to know all blame would be laid at Mina's doorstep. She'd be viewed as the culprit, not Simon's fickle heart.

Hands brushed his arms, and Simon reared back. "Do not touch me, madam."

"Simon, why are you acting like this?" Pure, unfeigned confusion was written on her face; it seemed the only true thing about her.

"I have not given you leave to use my Christian name, Mrs. Banfield," he said, crossing to the chair to retrieve his suit jacket. He couldn't stand being so undressed in front of her.

"You cannot be serious," she said to his back. "You have made it all too clear you would welcome this."

Simon gaped, his head jerking around to stare at Mrs. Banfield. "Whether my wife is here or on the other side of the world, it makes no difference. I am a man of honor, and I do not break my vows, and to think that you would do so under the same roof as your husband and children is abhorrent."

Her face burned red, her whole body shaking as Mrs. Banfield threw an accusatory finger at Simon. "You have flirted with me at every opportunity. You have sought me out time and again. You have done so openly and in front of your precious wife. You have made it abundantly clear that you would welcome this. It was you who threw your bedchamber door wide open for me the moment I stepped into your home. So, do not dare to call me and my actions abhorrent, Simon Kingsley."

He couldn't breathe. His strength drained from him, and his legs couldn't hold him upright anymore. Sinking onto the nearest piece of furniture, Simon thought back to his actions, but it all became a jumbled mess in his head. Though he had not thought his behavior so unscrupulous, Mrs. Banfield's words confirmed every one of Mina's indictments. Any defense Simon may have mounted collapsed under the weight of Mrs. Banfield's recriminations.

In all his life and all his disappointments and trials, Simon had never been one to cry, but he felt tears gathering in his eyes. He'd been such a fool, and that foolishness had hurt the one person in the world who did not deserve it.

And then Mrs. Banfield dealt him the killing blow. "Most assume we've already entered into an arrangement. Even Mina knows it to be true and ran from the house."

"Do not speak of her!" Simon shouted as he shot to his feet, all too pleased to have an outlet for the anger he wished to unleash upon himself. "You do not have the right. She is more than you could ever hope to be, and I will not have her name tainted by your filthy lips. I want you and your family out of our home at first light. You are no longer welcome here."

Without another word, Simon stormed away, wishing he could summon the very fires of hell to engulf him; there was no punishment devised of men that was suitable for what he had done. That look of abject despair and hopelessness on Mina's face when he had cast her aside would haunt him to his dying days.

Breaking into a jog, Simon ran for the front door. Shouting to Jennings for his horse and overcoat, Simon set the household in a dither as they scurried to do his bidding.

"What a state you are in, Simon," said his mother as she entered the foyer. "Whatever is the matter?

Simon gritted his teeth. He had not the time nor inclination to deal with her.

"Where are you headed?" she asked.

Simon took his overcoat and gloves from Jennings. "I'm going to find my wife and beg her forgiveness."

A flash of a smile crossed Jennings' face, though it disappeared in a trice. Turning to the footmen, Jennings threw himself into readying things far faster than he had been moving before.

His mother scoffed. "Why would you do that now that she is gone?"

Simon rounded on his mother, but the woman was oblivious to his thunderous scowl. The look of confusion and disbelief on her face matched Mrs. Banfield's so perfectly that Simon felt another wave of nausea sweep through him. They were two peas in a rotting pod.

"Simon, why would you want that ungainly cow when you have a beauty like Susannah on your arm?" she asked.

All movement in the hall stopped, silence descending as every gaze turned to his mother. With that amount of outrage pointed her direction, it was a wonder she did not burst into flames.

"Stop!" Simon hissed through gritted teeth. "I will not hear another word of your poison. From the moment you stepped into our house, you treated Mina with nothing but disdain. She gave you hospitality and kindness, and you tore her down in every possible manner."

And he had not done any better. Simon's fury turned inward, stirring up his shame until he felt swallowed up in it. Though unintentional, Simon knew the wounds he'd inflicted on Mina were far worse.

"The Banfields are banned from Avebury Park," he said, coming to a decision that was three weeks too late. "So are you and your ilk. Until you can treat my wife with proper respect, you are not welcome in my life."

His mother drew an affronted hand to her chest. So false. So practiced. So manipulative. But Simon saw through it now.

"You would bar your own mother from her own home?" she said with a gasp.

"You never cared about being a part of my life before now. I am simply returning the favor." Simon had no more time to waste discussing the past. He turned away from his mother, who gaped like a carp, and Jennings had the door open before Simon reached it.

"Have them all out at first light," he ordered. "Toss them out on their ear, if needs be."

Jennings beamed and bowed in acknowledgement. "The carriage dropped Mrs. Kingsley at Lady Lovell's, sir."

Simon gave him a nod and jogged down the front steps and straight to the stables, hollering for his horse.

...

Simon stood just inside Lady Lovell's front door. He'd not been expecting a warm reception, but he'd been standing there for over an hour, his hat in his hands and his overcoat still on. If it weren't for the fact that the skies had opened their floodgates and thoroughly drenched him, Simon suspected he wouldn't have been allowed even this small liberty. Simon hoped it was a good sign that they did not want him dying of exposure on their doorstep.

Turning his hat in his hands, Simon thought of all the things he might say to Mina. With each, the enormousness of his betrayal weighed him down, crushing his soul. There was nothing he could say or do to make it right. Simon did not know if he even dared ask Mina to forgive him, let alone return home.

There was nothing greater in the world that he wanted, but Simon's shame recognized he was undeserving to even see his wife. But he owed her an apology for his callous behavior and an acknowledgement of his wrongdoing. It could not make up for things, but perhaps it would bring Mina a bit of peace and comfort.

Every minute ticking by only confirmed his unworthiness. Without his anger to cling to, guilt tore him apart, pointing at every misstep, every misdeed. He was not good enough for Mina. That much was clear. There was no redemption for him, but Simon knew he had to do something for his beloved wife. If only he could make her happy again and give her a good future. Even if he could not hope to have her at his side, Simon needed to make sure she was cared for and had everything she desired.

"Mr. Kingsley."

That was the first time he had ever heard his name spoken as if it were an obscenity.

Looking up from his hat, Simon saw Lady Lovell standing at the top of the stairs. The woman moved with slow determination, her cane snapping against the floor like a shot from a pistol. There was nothing of the benevolent grandmother in her face as she stared him down. He wanted to drop his gaze, but he knew he'd earned every bit of her palpable scorn.

"Have you finally come to your senses?" she asked. If Simon did not hate himself so much at that moment, her barb would have hurt, but his self-flagellation was doing a thorough enough job of tormenting him. There was no breaking an already broken man.

Simon wanted to open his mouth and shout to Mina to forgive him and beg her to come home, but he knew she would not. She had lost all respect for him. Those were her words, and Simon knew that was a near impossible thing to rebuild.

"She was right," said Simon. "About everything, and I am ashamed to know that I have caused her so much pain."

Lady Lovell watched and waited.

"I did come here to beg her to return home, but I know..." Simon cleared his throat and paused, searching for the words. "I do not..." He tried again. "Mina deserves to be happy, and I have clearly destroyed her happiness. I came to apologize, admit my fault, and make sure that she is provided for. I don't deserve to ask anything more of her."

Lady Lovell's eyebrows lifted, though her expression remained frosty. "You are a fool, Simon Kingsley. You're so determined not to be your parents that you ran headlong into becoming just like them. So sure you understand what it is to love and be loved that you threw away your life chasing after a mere shadow of it, rather than having the tiniest bit of awareness to realize you had already found it. But love cannot survive in a selfish heart, and your blind quest for your happiness has crushed a dear lady."

Lady Lovell fell silent and watched him, as though expecting Simon to object.

"You are right," he said, refusing to defend himself against a single one of Lady Lovell's claims. Blind and selfish, Simon had more than earned both descriptors.

She narrowed her gaze at him, watching him with calculating eyes.

"She's not here." With that, the lady turned and marched away.

Simon stepped forward, but a footman moved to block him. "Where is she? Please, Lady Lovell, I beg you."

She halted, giving a soft sigh.

"I promise I will not bother her," he pleaded. "I just need to make sure she is well."

Lady Lovell turned to meet his gaze. Her rigid posture softened, and sorrow dimmed her eyes. "No, Mina is not well, and she is not in Bristow. I shan't tell you where she went, but if you cannot figure it out for yourself, then you don't deserve to see her again."

Chapter 31

Simon dropped from Spartan's back, his legs barely holding him upright. Two days of riding. Every time he thought to rest, his need to see Mina pushed him forward. His boots sunk into the mud as he trudged towards the one door in England he did not want to visit. Objectively, the small house looked warm and inviting, but Simon suspected he would find neither during this interlude.

With a bare moment of hesitation, Simon rapped his knuckles against the wood.

The door opened, and a broad woman gave him a broader smile. "May I help you, sir?"

"I'm looking for Mr. or Mrs. Voss," he said.

Before the maid-of-all-work moved, Thea appeared and stepped around the woman, her expression vicious. Swinging her leg with all her might, Thea gave Simon a mighty kick to the shins. She must have been wearing iron slippers because it connected with such force that he felt it through his entire leg. Then the door slammed in his face, barely missing his nose.

"Thea, please," he begged. "Just let me explain."

But silence was the only reply. Turning around, Simon drew his greatcoat around him and plopped down on the front step. Sooner or later, someone would have to speak with him. A few flutters of snow fell from the sky, sprinkling his jacket and hat, and Simon hoped it was sooner.

...

The sun was setting when Simon heard a cheerful whistle coming down the lane. Frederick Voss passed through the front gate and froze when he saw Simon camped on the doorstep. Rising to his feet, he walked to Frederick, but before Simon uttered a single word, a fist struck his face, laying Simon flat on the ground. The easygoing man Simon knew was gone, and an avenging angel stood above him.

"That is for making our wives cry," said Frederick.

Simon grabbed his jaw and touched the tender spot. Getting to his feet, he flexed his mouth. "How did I make Thea cry?"

"By making Mina cry. They come as a matching set. If one cries, so does the other." Frederick stepped around Simon, heading for the front door. "Mina isn't here, so don't bother asking for her," he said without giving Simon a backwards glance. "We received a letter from her saying she was alive and well, though it was so tear soaked Thea could barely make out the words."

Simon dropped his head. Just the thought of Mina suffering brought tears to his own eyes. Scrubbing at his face, Simon sniffed and rubbed at his nose. When finished, he found Frederick watching him, but Simon couldn't hold his friend's gaze.

"I didn't come here expecting to find Mina. I know she would go to Rosewood Cottage, but I don't know where in Herefordshire it is. If I have to scour the entire county, I will, but I was hoping you would help me. I need to tell her she was right and apologize. I need to know she is safe and provided for. I will not impose upon her any further than that."

It was silent for a long time before Simon finally met Frederick's eye again. The man looked grave, giving him a long, hard evaluation, and Simon knew he'd never measure up. After a moment, Frederick motioned for Simon to follow. They didn't go inside the house but around to the garden where a bench was sheltered from the weather.

"Why should I tell you where Mina is?" asked Frederick. "Anyone with eyes could see that trollop was leading you a merry dance. You went from adoring your wife to chasing after a bit of petticoat in the blink of an eye. You broke Mina's heart and tossed her aside. So, why should I help you?"

Grateful that Frederick had opted to talk rather than run him through, Simon told him all. From the first moment he met Mrs. Banfield to the present, Simon held nothing back. Even the details he wished to never divulge, he shared. Having spent the last two days with nothing to occupy his time but his own guilty thoughts, Simon had done plenty of pondering and had plenty to say. The sun set, and the stars filled the sky as he spoke. Lamps inside the house shone through the windows and onto the garden, giving the two men the barest of light.

"Mrs. Banfield entranced me from the moment I saw her," he said, shuddering at the memory he'd once held so dear. "I don't even know how to describe what I felt when I was near her. It was intoxicating. I thought it was love, but it's clear I have no idea what that word even means. It makes me sick that I harbored such feelings for her for so long."

For years, even the thought of that woman would have been enough to stoke a blaze of emotions, but speaking of her now dredged up no feelings in him. No pleasant ones, at any rate. The hideousness of her character made it impossible to view her with anything but disgust, snuffing out any of the warmth he'd previously felt.

"And Mina?" asked Frederick, staring at the soggy ground as he gouged it with the heel of his boot. If it weren't for the fact that Frederick had landed him a facer, Simon might have thought he was uninterested in the conversation, but his throbbing jaw reminded him not to underestimate the jovial man.

"Mina." Her name felt sweet on his lips, and Simon allowed

himself a moment to savor it while he stared off at the distance, trying to capture in words the things he'd spent the last several days contemplating.

"When I met Mina, it was different," he said. "We became fast friends. Being with her was so easy and enjoyable. She was interesting. Fascinating, really. I looked forward to seeing her whenever I could. Anticipated the chance to talk with her. And the more I got to know her, the more I felt for her. It was greater than friendship, but since it was so different than my feelings for Mrs. Banfield, I didn't recognize it for what it truly was. I kept clinging to the past, blinding myself to what I'd found in Mina."

Simon wished he could go back and shake sense into his past self. Plant him a facer and make him see the truth. Keep him from making all those horrible mistakes. Simon shifted, his eyes tracing the shapes in the darkness while he embraced the heartache he so justly deserved.

"And what was that?" asked Frederick.

Simon let out a breath, sending tendrils of fog swirling from his mouth. "Happiness. So much more happiness than I'd ever hoped to find in a marriage. Mina makes my world better just by being in it. She is the best person I know. My confidant and friend, and yet so much more than that."

It was difficult to explain something Simon did not entirely understand himself, but the words kept coming true and unwavering from his heart.

"She shines," Simon whispered. Mina's face came into his mind and warmth filled his heart, burning strong and fierce with a depth unlike anything he'd experienced before. "Even covered in mud with her hair falling to pieces and straw sticking this way and that, Mina is gorgeous. More beautiful than the finest of ladies swathed in silk and dripping with diamonds."

It pained him to think that he'd once thought her dowdy. Unattractive. Frumpy was the terrible word Mina had used. Having been so obtuse, Simon couldn't pinpoint when it had changed for him, but the more he embraced his feelings for

Mina, the more he felt their veracity. They filled him. Consumed him. But not in the wantonly destructive manner he'd felt for Mrs. Banfield. No, his feelings for Mina wove themselves into his flesh and his bones, strengthening and building him until he was so much more than he'd been before. More than he could ever be on his own.

Simon paused, feeling for the truth of the words before he spoke them. "She is a part of my soul, and when she left, she took it with her."

Mina was a miracle, and Simon had thrown her away. 'It's best you leave.' Those had been the words he'd cruelly tossed at her. Mina—his strong and loving Mina—stood there in the road, pleading for him to see sense, and he had told her to leave. Clutching to his ridiculous pride, he had turned away the dearest person in his life.

For a man who never cried, Simon was surprised to find more tears filling his eyes. He wiped at them, but it did little good, for more replaced them. Never had anything or anyone in his life mattered so much to him. He would give away Avebury Park in a trice to undo what he'd done to Mina.

Frederick sighed. "Many a person has mistaken attraction for love, only to have it fade away into bitterness. And many others have overlooked the possibility of it when they did not feel burning desire at the offset of the relationship. But real love is so much more than mere lust."

His eyes turned to the window where Thea watched them with an unrelenting glower. "When I first met Thea, I felt all that silly heart-pounding attraction that accompanies courtship. I loved her. Or at least I thought I did. But I came to understand that all that surface emotion is nothing more than a poor imitation of what real love is. What I feel for her now is so much deeper and stronger. It's based on years of selflessness, friendship, and respect. We do have passion in our marriage, too, but it has been fed by that love and not the other way around."

"The flames versus the embers," mumbled Simon, thinking

back to their conversation at the harvest festival. Only a month had passed since that moment, yet everything had changed for Simon. He hadn't understood Frederick's words then, but he felt them to his core now.

Mrs. Banfield was a flame. Hot and bright, but with little substance. Losing her had hurt, but only because he'd fed the fire—stoking it, tending it, refusing to let it die. And with one gust of wind, it was gone, as though it had never been. But Mina was the embers. His feelings for her burned deeper and stronger, bringing with it a wealth of passion and desire that eclipsed what he'd felt before. Without her, Simon barely functioned, and he doubted he would ever recover from her loss.

He loved Mina, and he had ruined it. Destroyed it. Trampled it beneath his boots.

And now more tears were coming.

"Farrow," said Frederick, as he got to his feet and brushed off his trousers.

Simon wiped at his eyes and glanced up at the man. "Farrow?"

"The cottage in is Farrow," he repeated, crossing his arms. "Though you best not let Thea know I told you. She is more in favor of bludgeoning you than helping you."

Simon stared at Frederick, understanding refusing to dawn.

"Go, get Mina," said Frederick, as though explaining something very simple to the greatest simpleton. "And none of this apologizing and crawling back home nonsense. Go fix what you have broken."

"I can't," Simon said, shaking his head. "I've lost her love and respect, and I shan't force my company on her. Mina is self-sacrificing enough that she might put my wish for reconciliation above her own desires, and I will not allow that to happen."

Frederick gave Simon an exasperated look. "Do not go back to being a blockhead again. I almost lost the love of my life because I was in the same position as you and nearly made the same imbecilic decision you seem determined to make. I hurt

Thea, and I convinced myself she was better off without me. I get on my knees and give thanks every day that I came to my senses. I cannot imagine the empty void my life would be if I had given into my fears and refused to trust that Thea could forgive me."

"You said love is based on friendship, selflessness, and respect," Simon argued. "She told me she does not respect me—"

"I know what she told you, but a woman does not mourn that greatly over someone she does not love," said Frederick. "If there were no hope for you, Mina would not have shed a tear."

Frederick held Simon's gaze for several stern seconds before strolling to the house. From his perch, Simon watched through the window as Frederick entered, his wife and children gathering round to welcome him home. It was the exact type of scene Simon had dreamt of for so many years.

Sitting there, alone and desolate, Simon felt like a poor beggar sitting in the cold, scraping by and barely surviving. And that was what his life was. Though full of creature comforts, it was empty of anything of substance. Work. Simon did not want that to be the only thing filling his days. He wanted what Frederick had. With Mina. And if there was any chance he could create that future for them, Simon had to try.

Chapter 32

Mina held her prayer book, watching Mr. Hughes at the pulpit. She should be listening, but Farrow's vicar tended to drone. If the parishioners pushed past the monotonous tone, they'd find his sermons quite enlightening. They were well written and insightful, but the delivery lacked the charisma needed to hold the congregation's attention. At home, Mr. Caldwell was so engaging that it was easy to overlook the lightness of the doctrine taught. But he was at the beginning of his career. No doubt Mr. Caldwell would improve with time, though Mina would not be there to witness it.

Taking in a quiet breath, Mina held it, trying to keep thoughts of home from overwhelming her. It amazed her how they cropped up at the most inopportune times, striking when least expected. Mina let her breath out in a huff. She didn't know who she was trying to lie to; home was constantly on her mind. And now, she was telling lies upon lies. It wasn't home that preoccupied Mina's thoughts. It was Simon.

Mina wondered where he was and what he was doing, though speculation on that front brought stronger pains than she could bear. Try as she might, she was unable to stop herself from picturing Simon and Susannah embracing. She wanted to despise him, but it was impossible to maintain her burning anger under the torrential downpour of sorrow.

Whispers sounded behind her. The villagers had a habit of doing that whenever she was near. Mina knew it was well meant. The arrival of Farrow's newest resident was the most exciting thing to have happened in many months, so Mina couldn't blame them for speculating about her. Besides, even with the abundant tittle-tattle, Farrow felt like a veritable Eden after the maliciousness of Bristow society.

At least she would never have to face those people again. That could be counted as a blessing, even if Mina had been making progress before her life had disintegrated. She wondered if Mrs. Pratt would continue with their plans for the Bristow Ladies' Literary Society. They hadn't done much more than discuss the possibility of such an undertaking, but Mina hoped the lady would forge ahead with it.

The service ended, and Mina hurried from her pew, not stopping until she was free of the church. She hoped the polite smiles she gave the congregants as she passed was enough to keep her from being painted as rude or aloof, but Mina couldn't face the questions about her circumstances. Not yet.

Walking along the country lane, Mina pulled her cloak tighter around her. With her pin money, she had enough to pay for her living expenses, but carriages were a luxury she would do without from now on. It was a small price to pay for her dignity. Regardless of what else she felt about Simon, Mina was proud that she had not wavered. She was through letting others step on her. Simon had said that he loved seeing her stand up for herself, and Mina wondered if he felt the same when she'd done so to him.

Following the bend in the road, Mina caught sight of her home. Rosewood Cottage. Mina still could not understand where the name had come from as there were no roses or woods anywhere near the property; it sat on a little hill, surrounded by rolling grasslands. But the name didn't matter for this was the life Mina had wanted. The quiet country life. The life she'd dreamt of ever since her grandmother had willed the cottage to her.

If only those simple dreams were still enough.

What had once seemed a perfect situation was now a sad shadow of it. Simon had shown Mina a hint of how grand a loving marriage could be and the thrill that came from being wrapped up in the arms of the man she loved. Before he had entered her life, Mina had been contently ignorant of love's addictive power. She had yearned for it but hadn't truly understood what she was missing. Now that her eyes had been opened to the greater possibilities, it was difficult to find the same solace and contentment at Rosewood Cottage that she'd had as a spinster.

Enough. Mina halted, squaring her shoulders and giving herself a good mental shake. Taking a deep breath of the chill air, Mina forced her mind away from such damaging thoughts. She would heal. Her heart would mend. Grieving was necessary, but allowing such misery to fester would only make things worse. She would be happy again. With time. Somehow.

Continuing down the road, Mina distracted herself with thoughts of pleasanter things. Surely, her life would be different than at Avebury Park, but that did not mean she had to be miserable. She would write her brothers, giving them all the support and attention they needed. She would be a doting aunt to Nicholas's future children. And Mina wondered if she might write to little Eloise. Leaving her and those other lonely children had been difficult. Perhaps this afternoon Mina would sketch some more drawings for Eloise to color and send them to her.

Arriving at the front gate, Mina hoped Mrs. Engle had tea ready. She was frozen through and desperately needed the warmth. Mina pushed open the door and called out to the housekeeper as she removed her bonnet and cloak, placing them on the pegs beside the front door.

Mina turned to find her sitting room filled with flowers. Every hothouse blossom in all of Herefordshire must have been there, creating a veritable garden in her little cottage. The scent of it filled her lungs, and her eyes roamed the rainbow of colors. It was breathtaking, and Mina was overwhelmed by the beauty of it.

Until she saw an envelope nestled among a bundle of lilies.

Dearest Mina.

She recognized Simon's handwriting. Mina stared at the letter, a flutter of fear making her hands tremble. She couldn't do this again. She didn't have the strength to let him back into her life. To read his words would be to invite more pain by filling her head with dreams of a happy resolution for Simon and her. The fact that even a flicker of hope came unbidden into her heart at the mere sight of his note terrified Mina.

No doubt Susannah had rejected him once she'd realized her opponent had quit the field, and now Simon wanted to make a go of it again by performing some grand romantic gesture that would convince his wife to come crawling back home. But Mina would not go back to being second best.

And yet, her hand picked up the note and her fingers broke the seal.

A flower for every reason why I love you. — Simon

Love. Mina's chin trembled. He wrote of love.

A hand brushed her arm, and Mina whirled around to find Simon standing there, a look in his eye that Mina was too overwrought to understand.

"Mina," Simon whispered, reaching out for her, but she stepped back and bumped into an end table. Mina glanced around for a way to put distance between them, only to find herself blocked in by flowers and furniture. Simon's face fell, his hands dropping to his side.

Tears filled her eyes, and Mina hated that they were there. She would not do this again. Not again. Her heart twisted at the sight of him. She yearned for his embrace, yet refused to allow herself to welcome Simon and his fickle feelings. Mina couldn't think. This was all too much.

"Mina, please—"

"Love!" she said, holding up the note. Her hand shook, crumpling the edge of it. "You think that telling me what I have been desperate to hear will bring me back? I don't want false words, Simon," she said, tossing the paper away.

"They aren't false, Mina," he said, stepping closer, but Mina stepped back, bumping into the end table again. "Dearest, please."

His tone was agonized, but Mina could not see him through her tears. An arm wrapped around her and a hand came to her face, brushing the droplets from her cheeks.

"Please, don't cry," he whispered.

Being encircled in Simon's arm felt like being home, as though it were meant only for her, but Mina knew it wasn't. Not in Simon's mind. Mina didn't know how to do this again—how to shove him away—but she knew she must. Mina pulled from Simon's grasp, and he released her, stepping back to give her space, though not enough for Mina's peace of mind.

"Please, I cannot do this again," she said. "I am not strong enough for it. Please, just leave me alone."

His hands reached for hers, but Mina flinched away, and he took another step back.

"You were right, Mina," Simon said, a desperate gleam in his eyes.

"What?" Mina whispered. If it had been any other set of words, Mina would have kept pushing until Simon was out the door, but those words utter with total conviction made Mina pause.

"You were right," he repeated. "About me, my behavior, Mrs. Banfield, everything."

Tears filled Simon's eyes, and Mina could hardly breathe at the sight of it as he swiped them away.

"Mina," he said, his hands inching towards her as if testing her reaction. Mina didn't move, and he carefully clasped them. "I cannot tell you how sorry I am." Simon's head drooped, and he took a quick breath before meeting her eyes again. "I treated you so poorly—" his voice hitched, and his head fell again. His thumbs stroked the backs of her hands.

Another pause. Another breath. And then he met her gaze again. "I didn't understand what I felt for Mrs. Banfield. But I know now that it was nothing but a silly obsession based on empty passion—"

Mina stiffened, tugging her hands from Simon. "The absolute last thing I want to hear is how attracted you are to that woman!"

Simon's eyes widened as he frantically shook his head. "No, I didn't mean...I don't...I'm making a muck of this. I did not mean it that way. Please, Mina," he said, his eyes closing and shoulders slumping. When he looked at her again, Simon's gaze was filled with anguish. "I was a fool."

Mina knew that too well. Simon was a fool, but he was also a terrible liar, and when Mina searched his face for any hint of falsehood, she found nothing but his earnest heart opening up to her.

Simon stepped closer and caressed her cheek, his eyes warming at the feel of it. "I was blind. I thought I knew what love was. I thought..." He sighed, shaking his head. "It doesn't matter what I thought, but I know—" His voice cracked again, and Simon cleared his throat. "I love you, Mina."

The emotion in his eyes seized Mina's heart. It held every hope and dream she'd ever harbored, but it was too much to believe. Shaking her head, Mina tried to step away, but Simon pulled her closer, a tinge of desperation settling in his gaze.

"My life is empty without you," he said, "and I cannot let you go without telling you that I love you, and that I despise myself for making you feel less than the miracle you are. You are not second-rate. You are better than I could ever hope for, my beautiful, loving wife."

Tears rolled down Mina's cheeks.

"I know I've hurt you," Simon whispered, "but please, let me try to make it right between us. I cannot live without my other half."

His other half. Mina recognized the reference. Sitting beside him in the conservatory, Simon had opened up to her, sharing his deep yearning for a loving family of his own. All the years of searching for it had been based on witnessing only one successful example of it: the Lovells. He'd described them as two halves that made a better whole. And now, Simon had just called her *his* other half.

There was no calculation in his eyes. It was an earnest declaration, and in that moment, it meant more to Mina than all the other words he had said, for she understood just how much it meant to him. They were two halves of a better whole. The two of them were Simon's ideal.

There was so much Mina wanted to say, though she had no idea where to begin. There was too much in her heart and mind to put into words. Slowly, cautiously, Mina touched Simon's cheek. His eyes closed, and he leaned into her hand, sighing as if that little connection to her was a balm for his heart.

"I love you," whispered Simon, the words sounding like the anxious prayer of a soul in need.

Leaning in, Mina touched her lips to his. Simon flinched, his eyes flying open. He stared at her for a brief second, his eyes wide with shock, but there was an underlying desperation to believe that her gesture meant what he hoped it did. Mina moved to close the distance again, but Simon was quicker, his lips meeting hers as his arms clutched her tight against him.

The feel of it was so much more than any of the other moments they'd shared. Mina melted into him, allowing his love to wash over her. In that kiss, Mina felt the future unfolding before her, one with the type of love that lasted a lifetime and longer, a family of her own, and so many of the glorious things she'd dreamt of.

And most of all, Simon.

Nothing in his life had prepared Simon for this moment.

The power of Mina's touch and kiss drove all thought from his mind. He reveled in the feeling of her tender lips, her face, her hands, and yet it was more than that. The feel of their love flowing through him gave him a power he never knew he had. His heart thumped in time with hers, joining them together. Two souls united.

Simon could not imagine greater bliss, and he could not believe that this was just the beginning for them and their life together.

They broke apart, their breath coming heavy as Simon leaned his forehead against hers. "I hope this means you are coming home."

Mina gave a watery chuckle, her eyes shining with such joy that Simon felt his eyes filling at the sight of it.

"Of course, my love," she whispered.

Just hearing the words gave Simon the first bit of peace he'd felt since the moment she'd left him. Mina's thumb brushed across his cheek, wiping away a tear.

"You must forgive me, dearest." The endearment rolled off Simon's tongue as if it had always been there, and Mina's smile brightened at it. "But it appears you've married yourself a watering pot. I never had a tendency to get emotional before, but in the last few days, it appears the floodgates have opened, and I cannot get them shut."

Mina leaned forward, laying her head on his shoulder, and Simon rested his cheek against it.

"Yes, but you are *my* watering pot," she said.

Simon chuckled and placed a kiss on her head, reveling in the feel of it. "Body and soul, my love. Body and soul."

Exclusive Offer

Join the M.A. Nichols VIP Reader Club at

www.ma-nichols.com

to receive up-to-date information about upcoming
books, freebies, and VIP content!

About the Author

Born and raised in Anchorage, M.A. Nichols is a lifelong Alaskan with a love of the outdoors. As a child she despised reading but through the love and persistence of her mother was taught the error of her ways and has had a deep, abiding relationship with it ever since.

She graduated with a bachelor's degree in landscape management from Brigham Young University and a master's in landscape architecture from Utah State University, neither of which has anything to do with why she became a writer, but is a fun little tidbit none-the-less. And no, she doesn't have any idea what type of plant you should put in that shady spot out by your deck. She's not that kind of landscape architect. Stop asking.

Website   Facebook   Instagram   BookBub

Made in United States
Troutdale, OR
01/14/2024

16934280R00162